DANTE'S CIRCLE REBORN

A DANTE'S CIRCLE COLLECTION

CARRIE ANN RYAN

Dante's Circle Reborn
A Dante's Circle Collection
By: Carrie Ann Ryan

ISBN: 978-1-950443-06-2

DANTE'S CIRCLE REBORN

A DANTE'S CIRCLE COLLECTION

DANTE'S CIRCLE REBORN

NYT Bestselling Author Carrie Ann Ryan returns to her bestselling Dante's Circle series with a collection of four never before published and highly anticipated romances.

FALLEN FOR ALPHAS

Liam and Alec watched their Pack fall from grace and fought with tooth and claw to make it rise from the ashes again for the Alpha. Once from rival families and now true packmates, they've fought their attraction for longer than they should have. Now, as they leave the den in search of a rogue wolf, they'll finally have a chance to entice their wolves—if they can overcome their struggles and survive what lurks in the darkness.

AT LAST SIGHT

Jonah assumed he'd seen everything there was to see throughout his long life. He battled dragons, lions, and anything else that came across his path. Now, it's his job to protect the cubs under his care—something far more dangerous than anyone ever counted on. But when he comes to face to face with Dante's sexy new bartender, everything changes. From his first look into those silver eyes, he was lost. But they're eyes that can kill if the world isn't careful, and some want them for their own.

BLOOD'S FIRST KISS

Calypso's position as a representative on the Conclave for all mermaids is in jeopardy if she can't uncover the true lineage of a mysterious stranger. Especially since his mere presence seems to rock the already shaky foundation of their people.

Micha knows exactly what he is: the one supernatural being that everyone claims cannot exist. And he's been searching eons for his mate. Now that he's found her, all bets are off. But he must keep his past a secret, no matter the consequences.

REAPER'S SONG

He remembers his death. Even remembers parts of his life. But as a newly made reaper, he must do the one thing he knows he cannot: reap his soul mate. No matter that she can see death coming.

AUTHOR'S NOTE

Dante's Circle is the second series I ever wrote, and the second I completed. I honestly had no intention of going back to the world, not because I didn't love it, or because I didn't miss the lightning-struck women. I simply needed to move on to the other stories in my head, and I felt as if the Dante's Circle series had ended where it needed to.

I know Liam and Alec were left dangling a bit, as were Jonah, Caly, and that secret of mine, Torrent. However, the main characters had their HEAs, and I wasn't ready to go back to the worlds.

Five years later, I was moving across the country and realized that I *needed* to write a few more words. I rearranged my schedule and added one more set of romances to the Dante's Circle series.

For the characters, and for you, dear readers.

Each of the four short stories in this collection has glimpses of romance. They lead to HEAs but are *not* full novels. They are shorter than the other romances in the series and are important moments in these characters' lives, but not *all* of their moments. I hope you love meeting new characters and getting glimpses of the ones we've loved in the past.

Will I ever return to the world of Dante's Circle? As always, never say never. After all...I have an idea. I suppose it's up to the characters whether I ever get to write more.

Thank you and happy reading!

FALLEN FOR ALPHAS

CHAPTER 1

When the fist smashed into his jaw, Liam figured he probably deserved it. As this wasn't the first time he'd been punched in the face, he didn't move back at the impact, didn't stumble, didn't even budge from his spot. In fact, his body stayed exactly where it was. His wolf, on the other hand, wanted blood. It scraped along his skin, the ache a familiar burn; its claws ready to attack. He didn't let the wolf have control. He never did.

That's what made him as strong as he was. He wasn't the Alpha of his Pack. However, he was damn well close in terms of dominance.

Of course, he had to *prove* it before he could flatly state it. It wasn't as if any of his Packmates could just let things go and let everyone breathe without bloodshed.

Hence the fist to his jaw.

"You're weak," Michael spat as he shifted from foot to foot, his fists at the ready in front of his face as if they were in a boxing ring and not in the middle of the den. They weren't even in the Pack circle, prepared to do an actual dominance fight that would lead to title recognition. "You don't deserve to be the Beta. Just because you've licked the boots of our Alpha since birth, doesn't mean you can rule."

Liam sighed. He might be best friends with the Alpha, Hunter, but he didn't lick the other man's boots. Not even that one time when he'd been so drunk that he'd actually fallen at Hunter's feet. Of course, Hunter and their other friend, Alec, had fallen right next to him since they'd been just as intoxicated. They'd been young, celebrating a recent mating of one of their other friends, and not on duty for the following twelve hours.

"You don't want to go there," Liam said slowly. His wolf pushed at him. Still, he didn't let his inner beast out, not when Liam could take Michael down in his human form alone. Of course, the other guy didn't know that, or if he did, chose to ignore it. So many people underestimated Liam and would likely continue to do so.

If Liam were to become the Beta of the Pack, he wasn't sure the preconceived notions would change. That was if he even *wanted* to become the Beta. His wolf was taking its time deciding if the position fit him. As for his human half, Liam wasn't sure he wanted the responsibility.

He was a council member and helped rule his Pack's governing body. However, his duties were mostly performed through his family. They had been one of the original five families that had representatives on the council. Being second in command to Hunter would be a giant leap in everything, though it wasn't something he was ready for, let alone something he truly wanted.

Liam ducked under another punch and kicked out, forcing the other wolf to the ground. Michael didn't stay down long, and Liam hadn't put too much force into the kick anyway.

He needed to get his head in the game so he didn't end up with too many bruises after this. He didn't want to deal with Alec's glares because he'd let the fight go on too long and was in his head the whole time.

Liam wasn't sure he wanted to deal with Alec at all.

And because he thought of his friend and didn't have his mind on the battle in front of him, Michael got in another lucky punch. The impact forced Liam back a step this time, and he tasted blood. He pressed his tongue to his teeth, grateful when none felt loose. The only two wolves who had ever almost knocked one out had been Hunter and Alec. He'd be damned if this little pup in front of him would be the third.

The gasp from the crowd surrounding them forced a

growl from Liam's throat, his wolf just that much closer to his skin. He let his claws slide from his fingertips, done with this pointless fight. Did the others around him think he'd lose to this wolf that was nowhere near his dominance level?

Well, he'd show them. He had to.

"Michael, boy, one day, you'll be a wolf worthy of the strength you possess. For now?" Liam shrugged. "Grow up." He slashed, his claws digging into Michael's shoulder. The other wolf cried out, going to his knees. Liam punched the man in the face for the comments he'd made about their Alpha, his friend, and then Michael was down for the count.

Dominance battle won.

However, it wasn't a true dominance battle as they hadn't fought in the circle, nor had it been sanctioned. The others would know where Liam sat in the ranks if they didn't already. The actual choosing of the Beta, fight or not, hadn't happened here.

Given what had happened in the months since their former Alpha, Josiah, had stepped down due to his age and power level, Liam wasn't sure the choice would ever be made. Hunter needed not only a Beta but also a Tracker. He'd been taking his time in choosing because it was his right as Alpha, and he couldn't just pick his two best friends.

It didn't matter that Liam and Alec were the next two

on the dominance scale right under their Alpha. Things were never quite as easy as they should be. Hunter needed to make a decision, but he couldn't even begin to start that process until the necessary dominance fights were complete within the circle itself.

Others had already done their fighting within the sacred stones that had once made their original Alpha's home. Neither Liam nor Alec had stepped foot inside. He wasn't sure why Alec was hesitating, and that only made Liam want to wait that much longer.

That was par for the course for them.

Alec hesitated while Liam waited, and neither of them ended up satisfied in the end.

Liam pushed those thoughts from his mind and rolled his shoulders, wincing as he did. Michael's lucky punch hadn't been Liam's first in recent weeks, and now he could feel the aches and pains from not using his full strength in the match. He needed a hot shower and a beer, and then maybe he'd get over what had happened today. He still couldn't bring himself to think about what a fight like this would mean, and what he would have done if the battle had been sanctioned.

As he turned towards his home, he froze at the sight of Alec standing at the edge of the crowd—close enough to watch, yet far enough away that no one could touch him.

That was Alec in all ways lately.

Alec's jade green eyes darkened when they met Liam's. The other man's jaw tightened, tension evident in even his breathing. A breeze caressed them both, slipping through the dark brown strands of Alec's hair. The other man's biceps bunched as he moved his arm up to push the hair from his eyes. The action caused his scent to catch on the wind, and Liam inhaled.

Mistake.

The heady scent of man and wolf knocked Liam back so hard, he almost ended up right on his ass. He did his best to hold back from growling or letting his wolf come too close to the surface. He couldn't let anyone else find out what exactly went on with him when he was in the presence of his best friend.

It wasn't that he was ashamed of being attracted to another man. As most of the wolves in his Pack were bisexual, Liam wanting Alec bent over in front of him wouldn't be frowned upon.

It was the fact that Alec hadn't shown any signs of *wanting* to be with Liam that killed him a bit inside and kept him from reacting in the way everything inside him wanted him to. And that was something Liam had to learn to deal with, even if part of him broke every time he caught sight of his best friend.

Another scent carried on the breeze, and Liam turned to see his Alpha striding towards them. Hunter had always been a badass wolf, large and scarred from countless dominance fights on his way to becoming their leader. He'd changed in the time he'd spent in the hell realm.

And by hell, Liam meant *literally*.

Hunter had been betrayed by their Pack and had been sent to the hell realm to fight in the Demon Games. Despite being sent there to die, Hunter had thrived instead. However, he'd lost a part of himself along the way. In the end, he'd come out stronger, though more wary of those he had once trusted with his life.

It had been a stroke of luck that he'd met a demon, an angel, and a woman who had once been human during his captivity and had been able to find his freedom. That woman, Jamie, had introduced Hunter to her best friends —six other lightning-struck women, who all eventually became paranormal creatures in their own right. And that was how Hunter had met his mate.

Becca wasn't a wolf. She was a leprechaun, who was not only the Pack's savior, she was also their healer. She'd saved her mate, saved them *all*, and rescued the Pack in the process.

From the look in his Alpha's eyes now, however, Liam didn't think Hunter was coming towards him to stroll down memory lane. It had been a couple of years since Hunter had returned with Becca at his side, and while the other wolf had become more settled, he was no less deadly.

The fact that they were still trying to figure out their hierarchy thanks to politics and wolf dominance trials just reminded Liam of their immortality and the idea that sometimes it wasn't as easy as saying *yes*.

"Another fight?" Hunter growled, his eyes glowing yellow. While most wolves had normal-colored eyes while in human form, Hunter's had become permanently yellow and gold following his time in hell. Liam thought the man's eyes would have turned that color anyway eventually, considering the strength of his wolf.

Liam shrugged, wincing again. "Michael started it. I ended it."

Hunter's nostril's flared. "You're not twelve years old, Liam. For hell's sake, you let that pup play with you before you finally showed your wolf. Are you trying to start more fights? Do you not want to get in the circle and show the others what you are?"

What if I don't know what I am?

The stray thought went away as quickly as it appeared, and he wanted to curse himself once again for allowing the weakness that had plagued him since he'd been a child to return with a vengeance.

"I beat him, didn't I?"

"And you got hurt in the process," Alec snapped as he stormed up. Liam had scented him approaching, of course. He could always tell when Alec was near, wind or no wind.

"I'm fine," he lied. He wasn't okay. However, it wasn't the blood on his mouth or the twinges in his shoulder that mattered at the moment.

"The hell you are," Alec whispered so low that only Hunter and Liam could hear.

Hunter looked between the two of them, his eyes seeing much more than Liam wanted him to see. "Come back to the house, both of you." He held up his hands. "This isn't up for discussion. Liam, let my mate heal you since you can't seem to take care of yourself. Alec, you come too, as I have an assignment for the both of you." He growled low. "Disobey my order, and you won't be happy with the consequences."

Liam tilted his head, studying his friend. Hunter rarely ordered people to do things. His dominance was so immense that others generally intuitively did what they needed to in order to keep the Pack safe and healthy. Yet for Hunter to *order* them just then—something he had never truly done with Liam and Alec...something was up.

He didn't want to risk the wrath of his Alpha and friend, though it grated on his wolf to back down without a fight. Still, he nodded. The fact that his wolf even *wanted* to fight his Alpha, even a little bit, told Liam that he had more issues than he thought.

Out of the corner of his eye, he saw Alec nod as well, and the two of them followed Hunter back to his place. Liam had spent countless evenings at Hunter and Becca's home, begging for dinners and playing with their daughter, Hazel. The domicile was like a second home to him. Yet, tonight, he somehow didn't think it was going to be quite like it always was.

For some reason, he didn't think *anything* was going to be like it had been before.

He hated when his wolf got into his head. Its instincts were far more tuned in to everything around him than his human half most days.

When they got to Hunter's place, Liam couldn't hold back a smile as Hazel ran to them, her wide eyes so like her mother's. She was a tiny ball of Becca with the brown hair of her father. And because the dominant genes in her DNA were all wolf, that was what she shifted into.

There were no hybrids in their world, unlike what some of the books might say in popular fiction—not that the humans knew about the supernatural. The genes that were in greater abundance were the ones that won the war regarding which paranormal creature a child of two different species would be. And unless they lived in backwoods places like the hell realm, the child's home accepted them, no matter what they turned into.

Hundreds of thousands of years ago, each of the realms enjoyed their own form of peace, mating with one another so frequently that, eventually, the paranormal strains within each child were diluted enough that they created a new type of being: humans.

Once, humans knew about their paranormal forbearers and had learned to live alongside them. Eventually, however, humans forgot about the magics and bonds that surrounded them, and the paranormals were forced to remain a secret.

In the past few years, some humans had found out about paranormals. The protection of the hundreds of realms in existence required that they keep their lives shrouded in secrecy.

Hazel, Hunter and Becca's little girl, however, didn't have to worry about the struggles of the realms right then. All she needed to do was grow up into the dominant and hilarious wolf she was turning out to be.

Liam reached down to pick her up, but Alec moved in front of him instead, intercepting the little bundle of joy. Alec didn't normally smile or laugh like he was doing just then. Hazel, like her mother, seemed to be good at pulling any wolf out of their shell.

As soon as Liam straightened, he cursed, his body aching. *That* was why Alec had cut him off. Having the little bundle of strength slamming into him would have hurt like hell. For a moment, he'd forgotten how much pain he was in after the fight. It was one of the reasons they'd been summoned to the Alpha's house to begin with.

Alec held Hazel in his strong arms, not bothering to look behind him.

Hazel, on the other hand, waved. "Hi, Uncle Liam!" She grinned at him, and he fell in love again. Hunter was seriously going to have a ball of trouble on his hands once she was old enough to find a mate. Liam was kind of looking forward to that, even if he would probably end up being one of her overprotective uncles.

"Hi, Hazel darling," he said with a small smile. "I missed your face."

She had a crush on him he knew, though she called herself Alec's best friend. From the day she'd been born, she'd inserted herself into their lives, and he'd been content with it. Hunter and Becca had made a perfect kid, and he was damn jealous.

She blew him a raspberry. "I missed yours more." She kissed Alec's cheek. "Uncle Alec is still my favorite because you forgot Mom's birthday."

Liam held back a wince as Alec let out a rough chuckle. He wasn't going to live that down anytime soon. As soon as he thought that, Becca walked out of the front door, her large belly appearing a little sooner than the rest of her. Hunter growled low and cupped his mate's face before kissing her hard. He kept one hand on her belly and their unborn child, leaving Liam with a sense of longing.

If he was able to mate with the one wolf he wanted to, he'd never see his mate pregnant. Though, honestly, he'd be happy with that. He and Alec could adopt, and they'd raise their children alongside Hunter and Becca's.

Only Alec refused to mate with him, and Liam wasn't sure he'd ever be ready to give himself to someone else like that.

There were reasons things were the way they were, even if they ended up hating each other in the end.

When Hunter pulled away, Becca frowned at Liam. "What have you done to yourself now?" she asked, her hands on her hips.

Hunter let out a growl, but Alec answered. "He got into another unsanctioned fight and let that weasel Michael get in a few good shots. Meaning, Liam's bleeding, and he's still not the Beta."

Liam growled low and deadly. "Alec."

"Not now," Becca said sternly. She might not be a wolf, but her powers as a healer and leprechaun and the Alpha's mate with magic of her own was immense. He wasn't about to mess with her. "Fawkes and Leslie are out back with the twins, Hazel. Why don't you go play with Lavender and Raven and let me heal your uncle Liam? They're in wolf form if you want to change and play as a pup."

Hazel wiggled down from Alec's arms and ran past her parents, stripping off her clothes as she went. Becca rolled her eyes at her daughter's antics and smiled. He wasn't surprised that Fawkes and Leslie were at the Alpha's home. The demon, Fawkes, had lived with Hunter when he'd first left the hell realm. The two of them had a history, and when the demon mated Leslie, they'd helped watch Hazel, preparing for their own future children.

Thankfully, with a trick of fate, the twins had turned wolf and not demon. Though Leslie was a submissive wolf, and Fawkes was a very dominant demon, the kids had ended up shifters and not demons. Liam was grateful for that, considering the sacrifice demons had to make at a certain point during their lives.

Becca cleared her throat, and Liam shook his head, aware that he'd been letting his thoughts wander rather than dealing with what he needed to.

"Get inside and take off your shirt," Becca said.

Liam opened his mouth to say something, and she cut him off.

"And don't make a joke," she snapped. "I'm pissed off at you, and I'll use my magic to kick your ass if you don't sit down and shut up." With that, she stormed back into the house, and Liam followed her, aware that Hunter's gaze rested on him.

Alec glared as well, and Liam had a feeling this talk might kill him.

Slowly.

Once he was in the living room and seated, Becca used her powers to heal him. It wasn't perfect, and it hurt like hell. His shoulder stopped aching, and his mouth quit bleeding. Normally, Hunter would have let him lick his wounds and deal with it. However, the Alpha apparently had a plan for him.

"What is it?" Liam asked, gritting his teeth as Becca finished up. "You wanted me healthy for a reason."

Hunter snorted. "If you would stop getting yourself hurt, it would make things easier. Or maybe if one of you would step up and actually help me lead this Pack, I wouldn't have to pull rank right now."

Liam straightened his shoulders. "Excuse me?"

Hunter flipped him off, and Becca shook her head at the three of them. "You're not excused. I need a Beta and a Tracker in this Pack. We haven't had a Tracker in over a decade, and it's past time. We're long-lived, I get that, and sometimes, Packs go for a century or more before positions are filled. But I'm tired of this. My mate is about to give birth again, and I don't want my children unprotected. I could choose who I want and have that choice made in a ceremonial fight. We know this. And yet, the two people I *know* can stand by my side won't."

Alec glared, and Liam had the grace to feel ashamed. It wasn't that he didn't want to help…it was that he wasn't ready…wasn't sure *what* he wanted.

"I don't know what is going on *between* the two of you. Whatever it is, it's affecting the Pack," Hunter growled.

"Hunter," Becca admonished softly.

Liam and Alec were silent. *Of course,* they were silent. God forbid they actually speak to one another about the tension that had been riding them and undermining their friendship for years.

"It's none of your business."

Alec's low growl surprised Liam, and he turned to his friend at his words. He hadn't expected Alec to say anything, and yet...

And yet Liam had known walking into the house that things were about to change.

"I need a Beta and a Tracker," Hunter repeated. "If I don't choose soon, I'll have to let the sanctioned fights begin, and we'll end up with others at my side. Where will our Pack be then, guys?" He ran a hand over his face, his body weary. "I'm tired. I lived through hell. Literally. And yet you guys are sending me to the brink of hell again."

Hunter met Alec's gaze, then Liam's.

"I know it's technically none of my business as Alpha what goes on between you. However, you're also my best friends, and if you can't figure out how to deal with the...tension...then I don't know what happens next." Hunter paused. "And because I'm not only your friend, I'm also Alpha, I need to protect the Pack as well as both of you. So, I'm sending the two of you away on a mission."

Liam stood quickly. "What the hell?"

Becca gave him a sad look before putting her hand on her mate's knee. "Let him finish, Liam. Please."

He didn't sit. However, he did keep his mouth shut. His wolf pushed at him, needing to fight *something* because it couldn't do anything else.

"There's a rogue wolf in the human realm, and it killed a person."

Liam blinked. His wolf clawed at him, wanting to protect, to search. "What?"

"You heard me," Hunter snapped. "We aren't the only Pack on the outskirts of the human realm. We *are* the closest, though. And while lone wolves are out there, they're rare. *No* wolf is allowed to go rogue and kill humans. That's our number one law."

"What do you need us to do?" Alec asked. His best friend stood so he was shoulder-to-shoulder with him. Liam did his best not to shiver at the slight contact.

"Find the rogue," Hunter ordered. "Take care of it if you have to. Bring him back here if it's an option. Take care of it." He paused. "And figure out how to work side by side like you used to do, or things will have to change when you get back. I don't want to lose either of you. If whatever is going on between you makes it so *neither* of you can be my Beta or Tracker, then maybe we need another answer."

Liam's heart kicked at the thought of not being in his Pack...of not being with Alec even as Packmates.

"We'll find your rogue," Liam said after a moment. "We won't let you down."

Hunter met his gaze. "Good. Because you're both my right hands, and I can't imagine running this Pack without you."

Liam nodded, aware that Alec wasn't looking at him. However, he could sense his best friend at his side. Quiet. Unyielding. Like always.

No matter what happened on this hunt, he knew that when they came back, he and Alec would have to find a way to work together.

Apart.

Or as mates.

Either way, their time of cautious tension was over.

Finally.

CHAPTER 2

Alec rubbed at his jaw and contemplated growing a long beard and becoming a nomad. He'd add flannel and eventually end up in a cabin in the middle of nowhere where he wouldn't have to talk to another soul. Wouldn't have to see or think of the man that haunted him.

Maybe if he did that, the relentless ache in his bones would ease. Of course, knowing him, he'd just find something else to screw up along the way and end up searching for an ever-elusive peace that would never come.

His wolf nudged at him, and he sighed. He couldn't stand in his house any longer, staring at his duffle bag and not following his Alpha's orders. Hunter had told him that he needed to work with Liam to find this rogue, and that's precisely what Alec would do.

That didn't mean he had to like it.

Of course, he hadn't liked much of anything in far too long. The moment his wolf had done the unthinkable and told him that his best friend could be something more, he'd known things would never be the same.

He didn't deserve a mate, that was something he'd known since before Liam had come back into his life. He'd done things—taken lives and drew the blood of those he'd never thought he'd be forced to shed. Liam deserved someone with cleaner hands and a lighter soul. Things had been better when they were friends versus whatever they were now. He couldn't call them real friends, not anymore. They didn't talk about the important things, and they spent more time in tense silence than working towards a future that could help their Pack.

It wasn't lost on him that they were hurting those they were closest to because they couldn't let go of their pasts. He wasn't sure what held Liam back, but he knew it had to be something important to take down such a dominant man. If Hunter couldn't choose a Tracker and a Beta soon, if he couldn't rely on his friends, things would get worse before they got better.

How could he tell Hunter that he wasn't meant to be Beta? Wasn't meant to be trusted as Tracker?

Maybe it would have been better if he'd done what the

others in his family had and turned lone wolf. It was a difficult and solitary existence. If he had, though, perhaps he wouldn't have harmed his Pack.

Or maybe I can actually forgive myself and learn to be the man Hunter expects of me.

He let out a disgusted sigh and finished stuffing his clothes into his duffle bag. Maybe Hunter was right. Perhaps he needed time away from the den to get his head on straight. It wasn't fair to anyone if he kept going along as he was.

Only he wasn't sure the time away would help, especially since he wouldn't be alone.

He'd be with Liam.

The one man who confused him even more than he confused himself.

Pounding at the door pulled Alec out of his thoughts. The knock hadn't been necessary. He scented the man's approach. His wolf always knew when Liam was around, and that's what killed him every hellish time.

He grabbed his bag and centered himself for what would most likely be a grueling couple of weeks. Sadly, the fact that he was about to track a rogue wolf who had already spilled blood was only part of it. With a sigh, he made his way to the front door, opening it while keeping a neutral expression on his face.

There had been a time when Liam would have walked into Alec's home without bothering to knock. That had been before their Pack had almost destroyed itself, though. Before Alec's world had shattered, and he'd turned from Liam. Before Liam had drifted away as well, not saying a damn thing. Too many months and years where they hadn't spoken to one another about the important things and had done their best not to touch each other, as if too scared to do anything about what was left unsaid.

Liam stood on Alec's porch, his hands fisted at his sides, though he held his duffle in one. "We didn't decide what car we're taking."

Alec shrugged, though there was nothing casual about it. "You're here, so we might as well take mine."

"Good." The other man bit out the word, and Alec knew this trip was going to torture him every freaking moment.

As Liam stomped off without saying anything more, Alec finally let out the sigh he'd been holding and followed him, closing the door behind him. He hoped Hunter knew what the hell he was doing with this. Because if his Alpha didn't, this trip might end up with two dead wolves and no Beta or Tracker for the Pack.

Alec gripped the steering wheel as soon as he sat in his seat, then let out a curse. Liam was as stiff as a board, his jaw set, and his wolf right at the surface.

"Why did you even bother getting into the passenger seat if you're going to sit and growl like that?" he snapped. His wolf was on edge, and he barely kept his claws from sliding out of his fingertips and slashing the steering wheel.

Liam didn't bother looking at him, and Alec wasn't sure the other man could. He did *not* like giving up control. Ever. "It's your car."

"Then you should have driven over to pick me up for fuck's sake."

"I was being considerate." Each word was bit out, and Alec had to move his hands from the steering wheel, or he'd break it in half.

"Just fucking drive. Because God forbid you don't."

"I'll be fine," Liam growled.

"No, you'll just piss me off and backseat drive."

"It's not backseat driving if I'm in the passenger seat."

Alec let out a loud growl this time and threw himself out of the car. He stomped to the other side and almost ripped the fucking door off. Liam opened it instead. "I'm not going to be able to drive and deal with tracking the fucking rogue if you're going to be growly, moody, and bitchy from the passenger seat. Just drive, and let's get this trip over with."

Liam slid out of the car. Since he was doing his best not to meet Alec's eyes, he must not have noticed how close Alec was to the vehicle. The other man crushed against Alec's body, and they both froze.

That was when Liam met his gaze.

The raw hunger there almost brought Alec to his knees.

And even worse, he knew the same hunger was likely in his own.

Without a word, the two moved out of each other's way, their bodies tight as bows, each shaking with tension.

Hunter had been right, after all. If they didn't get this worked out, one of them would have to leave. There was no way Alec could be anything good for his Pack if he had to be near Liam and not *be* near him.

Silently, they got into their seats, and Liam started the car, making his way out of the den and the wards that protected them from any too-curious humans. While most of the realms within the worlds were connected by portals and other various magical means, wolves were slightly different. They were one of the only species that lived within the human realm, albeit secretly under ward protection. They weren't separated into their own realm through portals like the angels or demons or even the lion shifters.

It had gotten harder and harder throughout the years to keep their existence a secret, but the Conclave, the governing body of all the supernaturals, always had new and, undoubtedly annoying, ways of making it work.

Twenty minutes into the trip, they'd gotten far enough out of the forest that anyone looking at them wouldn't notice where they'd come from. As long as they kept going, too-curious humans wouldn't happen upon the wards. Of course, if those humans *did* notice, the wards and magic would push them away, their memories wiped, keeping the den safe.

"I need coffee," Liam grumbled.

Neither of them had said a word since they'd started the trek, and apparently, Liam's unholy need for coffee was going to be the thing that broke the ice.

"We just left my place," Alec said in a tone that he hoped was devoid of emotion. "You could have just asked for coffee there." He dared to look over at the other man who constantly invaded his thoughts.

Liam had his fingers around the steering wheel, much like Alec had earlier, the whites of his flexed knuckles prominent against the tan of his skin.

"I thought we needed to head out and find this rogue," the other man bit out. "I just wanted to get out of the den and get on our way. I don't know where the hell we're going. Hence, coffee."

"Hence?" Alec said with a snort. "Since when do you say hence?"

Liam pulled his eyes off the road for a brief moment, a familiar grin sliding over his perfect face for an instant before the other man must have thought better of it.

"Becca is teaching me the big words now."

Alec snorted. "I thought Becca only taught us the curse words."

"Truth, man, truth."

They drove a bit longer before Liam pulled over and swore. "I have no idea where we're going. How the hell are we going to find this rogue and make sure the Pack is safe when I don't even know where to point the damn car?"

Alec sighed. "You're going the right way. I figured we'd head to where the latest attack happened and see if we can catch a scent trail. You just happened to be going the right way as soon as we left the den, so I didn't comment on it."

Liam glared at him out of the corner of his eye. "Of course, you didn't comment on it. Why would you say anything?"

Alec gave him a sharp look and then forced himself to relax. They needed to get through this. Get over this. And they weren't going to do that if they didn't talk about it. However, going at it right off the bat probably wasn't the best way to start, especially since Liam needed coffee. Alec wanted to keep his head on his shoulders, thank you very much.

"Did Hunter give you any info on what we're going into?" Liam asked after another few minutes of deep silence.

"The rogue killed a college-aged girl on her way home from work one night."

Liam cursed while Alec's wolf clawed at him. Their wolves might want blood, but they didn't kill innocents. That was the difference between a rogue and a shifter in control of their animal. The way they controlled themselves might be different than other shifters in how they calmed themselves and even how they sometimes gave in to the wolf for their hunts. All shifters ruled by control.

It was the only way to keep their souls safe—as well as the rest of the realms.

"Who found her?"

"One of us." Alec let out a breath, calming his wolf. They would track, and they would hunt, and they would kill this rogue. That promise was the only way to keep his wolf sane at the moment since they didn't have a scent yet. "A pixie and her boyfriend found her."

"The pixie we know?" Liam asked as they turned the corner.

"No, Faith wasn't near this, though it's close to Dante's Circle." Dante's Circle was the bar where Hunter had met his mate. It was a familiar place to the Pack.

"Dante isn't handling this?"

"No, the dragon is letting us since it's a wolf. He said he'd be on standby if needed. Same with his mates and the rest of them."

"This is a wolf matter, so we'll handle it."

"That's the plan." A breath. "Turn off here. We're almost there." He directed Liam towards where the body had been found. Sweepers had come in to clean up the evidence, though they'd done their best to preserve the scent trails.

They got out of the car in silence, Alec's wolf at full attention. He inhaled, trying to untangle the mess of scents surrounding the scene. He could smell the burgers from the fast-food restaurant across the street, and pine from the trees surrounding the small grassy area where Kelly Martin had died.

No, *died* wasn't a good enough word.

She'd been gutted, pawed at, mauled, and left bleeding out with her entrails wrapped around her neck and her heart missing.

The fucking rogue had eaten the organ according to Hunter, and they only knew that because there had been saliva near her chest cavity. Licking for scraps, for blood.

No, the rogue wasn't human. Wasn't shifter. Wasn't even merely animal.

It was worse.

It was an anathema. The absence of life. Of hope. Of death. Of sorrow. It was the worst of all creation.

And now, Alec and Liam would be the ones to destroy it.

"Got anything?" Liam asked, and Alec shook his head.

"I need to untangle first."

Liam gave him a tight nod. "Same. Let's find this son of a bitch."

Alec pulled his gaze from Liam—something easier to do when blood ran hotly between them because of death and not lust or whatever the hell they hid behind—and went back to searching. The two of them moved around as one, each taking in scents and trying to get beneath the top layers of the trail and into what they really needed.

The rogue.

Alec could still smell Kelly's blood and tucked that away for future tracking. The rogue could still have her blood on its fur or skin since, in that mindset, it wouldn't be thinking of DNA and scents and safety measures.

Alec stalked down the path, leaving Liam in the clearing. He ducked under a tree, following Kelly's scent. Underneath that was a layer he didn't recognize until he laid eyes on it.

"Damn it," he growled, looking down at the mangled corpse of a raccoon. He knelt down near the furry body and sniffed, his muscles going as taut as a bow. No. That couldn't be right. That couldn't be the scent.

He lowered his nose and inhaled again, his wolf howling deep inside as he caught the familiar musk beneath the gore, rot, and insanity.

He knew that scent. Had grown up with that smell. It couldn't be the truth.

"Alec?" Liam asked from behind him, and Alec almost

jumped. It was only the fact that he always knew when Liam was near that he'd been able to sense him at the last moment. Not a safe thing when they were on the hunt. He needed to be on top of things, be better aware of his surroundings. Fuck. This couldn't be right.

"It's Charlie," he rasped, and Liam froze behind him.

Alec couldn't breathe, couldn't focus. It couldn't be Charlie. He knew that scent, even under the horror, he knew it like the back of his hand.

Liam put his hand on Alec's shoulder. He didn't react. He couldn't. Not when it was all he could do not to shift and throw his head back, howling at the world, at the irony of the injustice.

"It's Charlie," Alec said again. "It's my brother. The rogue is my brother."

And they were going to have to kill him. Soon.

CHAPTER 3

Liam stood up, rolled his shoulders back, and then held his hand out for Alec. "We should go. I've got the scent."

Alec just knelt there, his whole body still like a statue. Liam wanted to scream, shout, do *something* to help fix this. He didn't think there would be any fixing this. He remembered Charlie. Had never *liked* Charlie, though that was of no consequence. Because, in the end, he and Alec would have to kill Charlie. Kill Alec's older sibling, the one who should have been there this entire time to help, to be the big brother that could guide Alec through the darkness that had been their Pack.

Charlie should have been there for so much, only he never had. He had always been a selfish jerk that cared more about himself than his family.

The fact that Alec had always been far more dominant than Charlie had been a thorn in the other man's paw.

Liam had never understood why Charlie couldn't get over himself and just figure out what he needed. Instead, he wanted everything that he couldn't have. And, in the end, he'd left the Pack because he hadn't been able to take anyone being Alpha other than him. And Charlie was no Alpha. He had never been, and he never would be.

Now, all of that past was going to come back at them full force, and they would need to figure out what to do. Because, in the end, Charlie had to die. And Liam would be damned if he'd let Alec be the one to deal the final blow.

"Alec."

"I should've known." Alec stood then, ignoring Liam's hands before turning. His wolf was in his eyes, that golden glow that spoke of the dominance and the strength of not only the wolf inside but also the man that held the reins.

Liam wasn't worried, wasn't scared of the wolf he saw. Because even while Alec was all wolf just then, he was in perfect control. And maybe that was even more dangerous, considering what Alec could do in this state. What Liam had seen him do before.

"You have the scent?" Liam asked, ignoring Alec's words. He didn't know what to say anyway.

"Yes. I do. I know where to go. At least where he went

after the kill. He fucking *killed* a girl and a raccoon, and he couldn't even distinguish between the two, I don't think. He's that gone," Alec said, shaking his head. "He's *that* gone."

Liam reached out and gripped the back of Alec's head. They both froze at the contact. He couldn't help himself. He needed to do something. Alec looked in pain, as if he had the weight of the world on his shoulders. And maybe he did. Liam needed to do something, needed to fix this. He didn't know what to do, though. Didn't know how to fix this. Maybe there was no fixing it at all.

"I'm sorry. I'm so damned sorry it's him," Liam whispered. Alec's wolf pushed at Liam. He could feel it. It wasn't aggression, more like a longing. The same one that Liam felt within himself. Neither of them was more dominant than the other, and that was something they had always known. They were always on even ground there, even if they numbered themselves and put themselves into rankings to appease the Pack. They knew deep down that they were equals, even if they had this riding tension that they did their best to ignore—yet didn't do well at ignoring at all.

Liam slid his fingers along the back of Alec's scalp, the hair long enough that it curled over his knuckles. They both swallowed hard.

"I'm so sorry," Liam whispered again.

"There's no fixing it, there never has been. This was inevitable."

"Inevitable for Charlie, perhaps. Not for you. Not for me. We can walk away right now. Get Hunter to send someone else, or even get the dragon. It doesn't have to be you."

Alec met his gaze, and then, surprising them both, he leaned into Liam's hold just a fraction of an inch. Just enough that both of them noticed how close they were. Their heat blended together in an intoxicating way.

"It has to be me," Alec whispered. "There is never going to be anyone else. It has to be me."

"Okay, it has to be *us*. You're not alone in this. We're both here. Remember that. It's never just you."

"You say that, and yet, sometimes, it feels like it's always been just me."

"We need to go," Liam whispered, letting his hand fall. He saw the disappointment in Alec's gaze. This wasn't the time; they would come to a head with whatever the fuck was going on between them later. The fact that Liam could feel Alec in his soul. Now, they needed to find Charlie, had to make sure that no other girl or innocent raccoon or other animal or shifter died because they were too busy focusing on themselves rather than the rogue at hand. They would deal with that drama, and then they would deal with each other.

"I have the scent," Alec rasped. Pulling away.

"Same here. We'll find him."

"When we do, he's mine, Liam," Alec growled out.

Liam shook his head. "No, he's ours. We do this together. You don't get to put this all on your shoulders."

"And you don't get to tell me what to do."

"You know, while you're always stubborn, always a little hardheaded, you're *never* like this. You're never stupid."

"I'm not fucking stupid."

"Right now? Yes, you are. And I get why, so we're going to do this together. Like I said, Alec, you don't get to do this by yourself.

"Fine. Just don't slow me down."

"Like I ever could, dear Alec."

Alec snarled, and then the two of them were off, following the scent. Considering that the death had happened twenty-four hours earlier, if not more, the trail shouldn't have been this fresh. The fact that it was, meant that Charlie had come back. Liam frowned, a worrying thought sliding through his mind.

There were two types of rogues out there. Most rogues, the ones that lost control completely, tended to burn out quickly, their animal halves twisting to the point where they couldn't think. Therefore, they made mistakes and ended up getting themselves killed just by happenstance. Then there were the types of rogues that Liam was afraid Charlie had become.

The ones that could think, could focus on their prey, and sometimes remembered who they were and what their goal was. *They* were the more dangerous ones. They were the most powerful of all rogues. They had the thoughts of a shifter who once had dominance and control…and more.

"He came back," Alec said, echoing Liam's thoughts.

"Yes, he did. He came back, and that means he wanted to see his kill again or see who found it," Liam agreed.

"Fuck. I wish you were wrong."

They didn't speak. There was no need. They would have to figure out what they were going to do once they got to Charlie, even though the end result would be the same. Charlie could not go on living. He couldn't live in any of the realms. He'd not only killed the girl, the raccoon, and probably more, but he'd done it with a vengeance that spoke of insanity. He had risked the humans finding out what had happened. Keeping their secret was of the utmost importance. They would have to take the next steps to ensure that their people were safe and hidden.

They hunted for an hour, Liam taking the lead since he was usually the better tracker. Well, not always. Sometimes, it was Alec. That's why they worked together, why they were so good together. When they weren't fighting over the fact that they were both ignoring who they were to each other.

Liam just wanted to know why he wasn't good enough for Alec. Why Alec always chose being alone over what they could have. Of course, Liam wasn't any better. He wasn't going to think about that right then, though. He couldn't, not with so much at stake. That was always the case, wasn't it? There was always so much more to be done, so much more than the two of them. And that was why Hunter was threatening to kick them out of the Pack. Because they had focused on everyone else for so long, they had lost themselves. Now, they were likely going to lose the rest.

They came upon a stronger scent over an hour into their search, and Liam held his breath.

"Liam," Alec whispered, and Liam came to Alec's side, nodding.

"Charlie was here," Liam, said, his voice low.

Alec stiffened. "*Is*."

The growl behind him made the hairs on the back of his neck rise. There was no time for talking then. The rogue came at them, Charlie's scent wild and manic with a touch of decay.

Liam didn't know if the decomposition was from his kills or from his soul rotting. In the end, it didn't matter because it was *Charlie*. This had to be the end.

There was no other solution.

Alec twisted as the two of them fought first, with Liam bringing up the rear.

This was how Charlie wanted it, fighting his brother with whatever conscience he had left. He must have known that Alec was Liam's…maybe the scent. Who knew? No matter what he was thinking, Charlie wasn't going for Liam at all. If anything, he seemed to be avoiding him, keeping all his attention on Alec, letting nothing else distract him, even in his rogue form.

Liam ducked Charlie's single jab and then punched the rogue in the gut, his claws out. He froze at the sound of whimpering. He barely held back his strength, knowing the sound couldn't have come from Alec, even as the two pummeled each other, punch after punch.

Alec wasn't winning. Not yet. The problem with finding a rogue was that the toxicity in their brain made them up to five times stronger than an ordinary wolf or shifter. They had nothing to lose and used all of their energy. Liam or Alec might be able to take Charlie down, but it was going to take strategy, not just fighting.

That's why Hunter always sent two out on a hunt, not just one. It didn't matter that they were both strong and could take down any number of their Pack except for Hunter himself—and even then, Alec and Liam together could probably best Hunter.

A rogue on the verge of death and infamy could take out so much more than a single dominant wolf with skill.

However, that's not what Liam was focused on just

then. No, it was that whimper. The sound of someone young. And near where Liam had just punched.

Fuck.

Something small moved under Charlie's coat. Liam growled and looked over at Alec, who gave him a slight nod. They couldn't hurt or kill Charlie yet, not with whatever he was holding. Liam inhaled deeply, trying to catch the scent under the rot that was Charlie.

Fox.

A fox shifter.

Hell, it was a baby kit.

Motherfucker.

Liam distanced himself from the encounter and gave Alec a look, raising one finger. Alec nodded and then went one way, while Liam went the other. Charlie seemed to understand, and that was something that Liam and Alec had both known going in. Charlie would be able to understand their signals and know them.

Because Charlie had fought with them once as their Pack member. Now, he was the enemy. Alec grabbed Charlie by the throat as Charlie dug his claws into Alec's arm. Alec didn't growl, didn't wince. Liam knew that had to have hurt. Blood poured down Alec's arm, though Liam couldn't focus on that. He couldn't do anything but try to get whatever was in Charlie's coat out safely. It wasn't easy to do when the damn rogue kept moving, trying to lure Alec into a trap.

Alec squeezed harder, and Charlie's grip on the bundle under his jacket loosened just enough for Liam to claw at the garment, ripping it to shreds. A little bundle of red fur fell into his outstretched palm.

It looked up at him with wide, scared eyes, its little nose twitching. Liam wanted to scream at the world for daring to let this kit get caught up in this mess.

Charlie, realizing his lunch or whatever the fuck this kit was to him was out of his grasp, went at Alec again, clawing Alec in the face. Alec growled, but Liam couldn't help, not when he needed to keep the kit safe. Alec had moved a bit out of the way at the last moment, saving his eye and any deeper gouges to his face. Charlie must have known, even with the insanity of his rogue-ness, that he had to keep fighting. He leapt, running full-tilt away from Alec and Liam.

Alec's chest heaved as he looked towards where the rogue had gone. He didn't follow. Not when he was weakened, blood pouring from his arm and from the small cuts on his face. And not when Liam needed him. Because Liam had no idea what to do with this kit, and Alec was better with children.

Holy hell, this wasn't going to end well. Because Charlie was strong. Far stronger than any other rogue they had ever fought. And with the emotional connections, and this little baby in the middle of it? They would have to rethink how they went about this. First, Liam needed to make sure Alec and the kit were okay.

"Alec?"

"How's the kit?"

The little fox burrowed into Liam's chest, and he slowly slid his hand down her soft fur, trying to calm her.

"She seems unharmed. Her heart's racing under my hand. We need to get her somewhere safe. How are you?"

"I'll be fine. The dragon's lair is near here."

"Sounds like a plan."

Handing the baby fox over to a dragon might seem outlandish to some. However, Dante was mated to Jace and Nadie, and the three of them were wonderful parents. They could probably save the world. After all, they had already done it once or twice. They would take on anyone in order to protect their children. Would do anything to ensure their safety. And Liam knew that that protection would extend to any child, including this kit.

"We need to get you patched up."

Alec shook his head. "The kit first."

The little fox whimpered and buried its nose under Liam's arm. He kept petting the little fox, and Alec reached out with his uninjured arm and slowly stroked the baby, as well.

Their fingers tangled over the fox's fur, and the kit slowly calmed down at the feel of them, letting out a little yip before going back to normal.

"I'm sorry I wasn't strong enough to stop him." Alec growled, though his statement was pretty much devoid of emotion.

"You don't get to put this on you. It was both of us. We saved her. We'll save the next."

Alec didn't say anything to Liam, likely because there wasn't much to say. They had failed, and they would have to pay the consequences for that. This little kit didn't need to suffer for it.

They made their way to Dante's lair—in other words, his home.

It was surrounded by warding, though since they had been here before, they were allowed in. They walked past the empty guard stations that served to tell the humans that there was security. It wasn't manpower that kept the place safe, though. Eons-old magic held sway here.

Dante was a very old dragon and the most powerful in the realm.

His mate, Jace, was a Mediator for the entire Conclave, and a strong bear shifter in his own right. He would've probably led the bear shifters if his fate hadn't led him down another path. Nadie was one of the seven lightning-struck women and best friends with Becca.

Nadie was also a succubus and had far more magic than anyone knew. Liam had always been able to sense it, ever since he'd met her after she had mated Jace and Dante. She hid her power well from others. And that was good. It was always smart to be underestimated in a fight. And with war constantly on the horizon, especially within their own realms, she was a good asset to have.

Dante opened the door before they even had a chance to knock. Of course, Liam had figured the dragon knew they had arrived the moment they stepped onto his land.

"You're hurt," Dante growled out. Jace was there in the next instant, bandages in hand, tugging Alec inside. Nadie was there, as well, even as Dante's eyes roamed behind them, checking for threats.

Liam appreciated that since he wasn't in the mood to deal with more fighting at the moment. They needed to make sure Alec was safe, the same with the kit. His wolf rode him, wanting blood, needing to make sure Alec was okay. Craving to care for the young fox. He inhaled through his nostrils, trying to calm himself.

"Here, let me have her," Nadie whispered, her hands outstretched.

The kit burrowed into him more, and Dante raised a brow at Liam.

"All right. It's okay, little kit. Nadie's good. She's going to help you and make sure you're okay. Plus, you're going to need to shift back. You know it's not good to stay in your animal form for too long." He tapped her on the nose gently, and she nuzzled into him again before letting out a little yip and turning towards Nadie. Nadie smiled with kind eyes and took the kit from his arms, nuzzling her chin on the fox's furry little head.

"We'll take care of you. Our little babies are going to want to meet you, too. First, let's get you all cleaned up. You're so brave, little girl."

Nadie started walking away, and the little kit looked over her shoulder at Liam. He gave her a tight nod, not knowing when he would see her again.

"We're going to need to find that kit's family," Liam said.

"We will. And then you're going to tell us exactly what happened. And if you need my help."

Liam shook his head even as he explained what had happened.

"We can do this. We were just surprised about the innocent and needed to take care of that before we took care of the rogue."

"I can smell him on you. I didn't go down to the site, so I couldn't tell. He smells of Alec but not."

"I didn't realize dragons were so good at that."

"Dragons are good at a lot of things," the big man said, his eyebrow ring twinkling under the light. "I take it this rogue is family?"

"Blood—not family."

"Understood. If you need us, we're here. Any of us. I understand you need to take care of things in the family. Don't do anything stupid, though. At least, try not to.

And a piece of advice?" Dante continued, closing the door behind him. "Don't wait too long."

Liam froze. "Excuse me?"

"I almost waited too long because we were looking for our third. You're not waiting for a third. Are you?"

"Dragons really do know more than they tell."

"Sometimes. Figure your shit out, Liam. You're not doing anyone any favors by waiting."

And then the dragon stomped off towards the back of the house, probably to check his security.

Liam just stuck his hands into his pockets, wondering what the fuck they were going to do.

The rogue was still out there, and they couldn't stay for long. However, Alec needed to be healed, and without going back to their Pack to have their healer do it, it was going to take the night.

And that meant their hunt would have to begin again in the morning.

They were going to have to eliminate Alec's brother. Even if it might kill them both in the process.

CHAPTER 4

Liam made his way through the dragon's lair, doing a final perimeter check along with Dante. With any other man, with any other dominant now that he thought about it, they might have been a little annoyed that Liam was double-checking their work. Dante wasn't like that. He had his mates and his babies in the house, and therefore, any extra help and pair of eyes to make sure that the place was safe were good. At least, that's what Liam figured since the dragon hadn't roasted him for daring to question anything.

"I'm setting you and Alec up in the guest house," Dante said after a moment. Liam looked over and nodded. "Thanks. We can get our own accommodations if it's too dangerous for us to be here."

Dante shook his head. "We have a guest house for a reason, and I have really damn good warding." The dragon winked.

Liam really didn't want to think about what exactly would happen if someone breached the wards when they didn't have permission. Considering that Liam had seen Dante set someone on fire while still in human form just with the smoke from his nostrils, he really wanted nothing to do with that. It wasn't that Dante was cruel. However, if you messed with his family or his loved ones, you paid the price. And assassination attempts against his mates made for a very steep price.

"We appreciate it."

Dante nodded, his eyes narrowing. "Good. And I'm going to repeat my offer to help with this rogue if you need it."

"I would take you up on it if it were anyone else. This one? I think Alec needs to face it."

"I understand that. As someone who has dealt with family members who have been on the wrong side of the line regarding what is true and right, I completely understand."

"We'll be out of your hair in the morning, Alec should be healed by then."

"Jace and Nadie worked their magic on your not-mate. And your little kit is sleeping in the nursery."

Liam ignored the dig and the push from the temperamental dragon. "Is she okay there? Has she shifted back?"

Dante nodded. "Yes, to both questions. She's sleeping now. One of my twins is watching over her."

"Your child's not much older than she is."

"I have a dragon shifter and a bear shifter as children. They're always going to be protective of a little kit. The child hasn't spoken as of yet, but she's healthy and whole. She's sleeping now in her human form, and we had spare clothes for her." At Liam's questioning look, Dante shrugged. "We have a lot of friends with plenty of children. Our nursery is filled to the brim with spare clothes, toys, and food."

"I guess that makes sense." The Pack was like that too, though not in any parts of the den he regularly visited. Hunter was his only friend who had children. The rest were still single, waiting on their mates. Now that their Pack was functioning somewhat again, and the darkness had finally been clawed out, people were starting to find their mates and have babies again. Once Liam and Alec finally got off their asses and entered the circle to find their place within the Pack in terms of title, the Pack would become even healthier.

"I can start working on finding that little kit's demise. At first light, you need to take care of that rogue. I'd rather be with you, but I understand what needs to be done. Only with a rogue that thinks the way this one does, we're going to need to formulate a new plan, and Alec needs to be fully healthy."

"Totally understand. And Jace is already working on looking up where the demise was. The problem with fox shifters is they don't live in large groups. Only small families with a few members."

"And within our realm."

"Correct. Just like you wolves, they don't have their own realm."

"I always found that a little unfair."

"I haven't always been a fan of it either. However, you're at least closer to yours, while I have to open an actual magical portal to go back and visit the dragons. Or the Conclave. Not something I like to do these days."

"I don't think I'd be interested in doing much of that either. What happens if she can't find her demise?"

"Then we find another demise that can take her." Dante frowned, shaking his head. "The problem is that most fox shifters don't take in orphans."

"That's bullshit. True, but complete bullshit." Wolves had their own problems, his Pack more than most, but they didn't neglect young.

"It is. But it's not something I can fix. It's survival of the fittest, and if a demise is decimated and anyone's left behind, they're forced to start their own."

"She's what, two?"

"About that. Maybe three. Just small for her age. Either way, though, if we can't find her family, and no other fox shifters want her, we're going to have to find a place for her."

Liam stiffened. "There's not really an orphanage for fox shifters," he growled out.

"No, there isn't. There's not one for any of our kind." Dante paused. "Something I've neglected to think about until right now."

Liam's brows rose. "Are you going to open a Dante's Circle Orphanage?"

"I just might. If I tell Nadie and Jace about it, they'll be all over it. As for your kit, she's not going to be left alone. I can promise you that." He paused. "She's very attached to you and Alec, though."

There was a question in that statement, even if it didn't sound like it. Liam shook his head in answer.

"Let's not go there."

"Maybe you should. Maybe you need to fight for something other than what you've been fighting with Alec."

"And on that advice from a dragon, I'm going to head to the guest house and check on Alec."

"You do that. We did soundproof the area, and you're far enough away if you need anything. If you need privacy." Dante winked.

Liam shook his head, flipping the dragon off as he walked away. Dante laughed behind him.

"Well, a matchmaking dragon wasn't something I was expecting tonight," he mumbled to himself as he made this way to the guest house.

He passed the nursery on his way and looked in on the three children sleeping in a little puppy pile. Not that any of them were puppies. They sure did look comfortable. They had pulled all the pillows and blankets from their respective beds and had made a massive pile in the middle of the room. The little kit was safely ensconced in the warm arms of the dragon and the bear, each in their human form, clearly protective of one another.

The kit was safe here, and for that, Liam was grateful.

He kept going until he reached the back door of the house and headed towards the guest house. He could sense Alec there, could feel his frustration, his anger, and his healing. Alec would be safe soon. Well. And that's really all that mattered. Because in the morning, they would have to find Charlie and kill him. Something neither of them really wanted to do, yet something they would have to do, no matter what.

Alec was lying in bed in the small guest house that was more of a studio. It had antique furnishings and all the comfort you could want for an overnight stay when you were on the hunt.

His best friend and the person that he thought about

far too much sat up, shirtless, with blankets pooled around his waist. Alec didn't look any worse for wear. Liam figured even with the bandage on his arm, and the now mostly healed cuts on his face, they could probably go out right now to track the rogue. Darkness didn't matter, not with their wolf eyesight. However, he didn't want to start the hunt. Not yet. He needed to make sure Alec was in the right headspace. That they both were. And that meant taking their time for now and figuring out what they needed to do with the rogue. And with each other.

Others might have a different plan. But they were the ones on this hunt. This was Alec and Liam. Two names that had gone together for as long as he could remember, and yet they kept fucking things up. So, he was just going to have to fix that.

"You're looking better," he said as he cleared his throat and closed the door behind him.

"I feel better. I'm pissed off I got hurt at all. I wasn't thinking clearly." Alec looked down, and Liam wanted to reach out and touch him. He couldn't, though, so he fisted his hands by his sides.

"You're going to think clearly next time. You won't be surprised."

"I hope to hell he doesn't have another child in his grasp that we'll be trying to keep safe at the same time."

"That is true. I'm sorry I wasn't much help before. I needed to get little Kit."

"Do we know her name yet? Calling her *Kit* when she's a baby fox seems a little ridiculous and too on the nose."

Liam just shrugged. "She hasn't said it yet, not that I know of anyway. Maybe Nadie knows. We'll figure it out. And we'll find her family." There was a long silence. "Or another demise that might take her in."

"We both know that won't happen. Demises don't take in other shifters. Unless it's by mating or marriage."

"Well, maybe she'll be the exception to the rule."

"Maybe."

Neither of them believed that. You could tell just by looking at them.

"Since we're here, though, maybe we should talk?" Liam wasn't even sure he'd said the words until they were out.

Alec's brows rose, and Liam stuffed his hands into his jeans' pockets. "Or not. Sorry. I might have overstepped."

"No, no, not overstepping. I'm just surprised. Not that I should be. Because we do need to talk. Hunter sent us out together for a reason. And not just to find my twisted brother and kill him."

Liam winced. "Let's not talk about Charlie right now."

"What should we talk about?"

"I don't know."

There was more silence, and Liam knew if he didn't say something, he wouldn't. Because they were so worried about hurting each other's feelings, they constantly fucked up what was going on between them. And that's why they were on the verge of being kicked out of the Pack. That's why they were on this mission to catch the rogue to begin with.

As he looked at Alec, the thought of almost losing him filled Liam's mind, and he knew we had to say something. Because it hurt. *Everything hurt.*

He loved him. He had loved Alec for as long as he could remember and hadn't done a fucking thing about it because he'd been so scared of where he had come from and who he was supposed to be.

Because of that, he hadn't said anything. Alec hadn't either. If Liam didn't just open his mouth and say it, tell Alec what he was feeling, this would be it. There'd be no going back. He would lose his best friend and his soul mate.

Because Alec *was* his soul mate. His other half. The one person in the world who completed him in every way possible. And he was going to lose him if he wasn't careful.

He took a deep breath and leapt over the edge into the abyss.

"How about we talk about the fact that we're soul

mates, though we haven't actually said anything about it?"

Alec stiffened, and surprise wafted off him. The scent was spicy and filled Liam's nostrils. He inhaled deeply, wanting more of it. He just wanted more of Alec. He was crazy, he knew. He didn't care. They needed to figure this out. They needed to fix it. And if taking this leap was how to do it, then so be it.

"I can't believe you just came out and said that," Alec said, blinking.

"I can't believe I did either."

"Okay. Okay. *Goddess*."

Liam's brows rose at Alec's exclamation.

"I have no idea what you mean by that."

"I don't either."

"Okay, come on. I'll start. I think it all has to do with the fact that I haven't gone into the circle to fight yet."

Alec frowned. "What do you mean? How the hell are they connected?"

"I don't know who I'm supposed to *be*. Hunter wants me to be one thing, thinks I need to be the Beta to help lead the Pack, to take the position he once held. I don't think I can. You know what my dad used to do to me."

Alec nodded. "He forced you to fight when you were younger, forced you to use your claws and fangs well before you were supposed to. He put you into those dominance fights even though you weren't ready. You still came out on top. Still won."

"If I didn't, he would have killed me. Or it would have hurt Mom or someone else along the way. It didn't matter that she was his mate, he had twisted their relationship into something that was all about power and domination. That's why he's not part of the Pack anymore. That's why he's gone. Just like so many others on the council. They took what they thought was pure about being a wolf and a shifter and twisted it into their own amalgamation of power and dominance. And my dad was part of that. Every time I think about taking my first step into that circle, I think about what he did. And what he wanted me to be. I don't know if I want to be that person."

"And how do I fit into that?" Alec asked softly.

"You fit, because if I don't take that step, how am I supposed to have the courage to take the next step with you? What if I'm not good enough to be in that circle. What if it was my dad pushing me this whole time? And if I'm not good enough to be the Beta, how on this holy Earth am I supposed to be good enough to be yours?"

Alec just froze, his skin pale, the healing scars on his face standing out in stark contrast. "How can you think that? How on Earth could you ever think that you wouldn't be good enough for me?"

"You haven't made a move. I assumed that you were

either waiting for me to do it, or thought I wasn't worth it. What was I supposed to think? We've spent over a decade circling each other. I've known for a long time, ever since your scent changed, and I knew who you could be for me. Neither of us did anything about it. What was I supposed to think?"

Alec let out a laugh. It was hollow and devoid of emotion. "We are a pair, aren't we?"

"What?" Liam started to pace, needing to do something. His wolf clawed at him, wanting vengeance, wanting his mate. He didn't know what to do about it.

"I thought you didn't want me, so I stayed away. How fucking stupid is that?"

Liam whirled, his eyes wide. "And that's why you didn't make a move?"

"Honestly, I don't know if I am good enough for you."

"That's bullshit. You're the better of the two of us."

"And the fact that you think that makes me worry that I haven't done enough to show you who you are to me. Even if we just end up as best friends, you have always been a man of worth. A shifter who has done everything for his Pack."

"Right back at you."

"You know what I had to do when the Pack started to crumble after Hunter went missing. You know who was part of the crew that sent him to hell." Liam nodded. "It was your uncle."

"And I have no remorse for killing him. I would do it again in a heartbeat. And, in the end, I'm not going to feel anything when I kill Charlie either. Because I know my duty. Because of that, every time I think about it, I wonder how I could possibly be good enough for you. How can you want me when I have to be the one who kills? When I have to be the one who takes life and doesn't feel anything about it."

Liam stood, stunned, blinking slowly. "I don't understand."

"That I feel nothing?"

"That you can think that you feel nothing. Of course, you have something inside you. I can see it in the way you carry yourself. In the way you pull back from others. It might not be remorse for what you've done, but it's something. It weighs on you. And you protected our Pack. You stood by my side when we did it. We protect what is ours. We help our Alpha and his family. You have always been there. Of course, I'll always love you for that." Liam snapped his mouth shut as Alec's eyes widened.

"You love me?"

"I meant to tell you that a bit later." He slid his hands through his hair and started pacing nervously again. "I didn't really want to blurt it out like that. But, yes, I fucking love you. I've loved you for longer than I care to admit."

"And yet, we haven't done anything about it."

"Because we have our heads so far up our asses and are so worried about what the other might feel and what others have done to us that we've ignored it. Goddess. We're out here trying to protect our Pack and doing what others might find cruel and difficult. We're going to get it done."

"I don't know what to say," Alec said softly. Liam froze, dread filling his belly. What if Alec didn't feel the same way? What if he didn't feel the connection between them like Liam did?

"You don't have to say anything." A frozen pause. "I'll head back into the main house if you need some space." He turned, and the rustling of sheets behind him made him stop. And then Alec was behind him, his hand on his hip. Liam wanted to lean back, to feel the heat of him. However, he wasn't sure he could.

"Don't go."

Liam turned so they were facing each other, hip to hip, their breaths mingling. "Why?"

"Because you're not the only one who hid everything. I know you're my soul mate, Liam. I had to be a man worthy of you first. I think I made a mistake."

"You're not the only one."

"I've loved you for as long as I can remember. Ever since you smirked at me and threw me down on the ground as we fought just to see who was more dominant."

"I won that one," Liam said with a laugh.

"And I won the next. Because we've always been even. We've always been exactly who we needed to be for each other. And I should have told you long before this. I love you, Liam. And I shouldn't have hidden from you. I know you're my soul mate, and I will always regret wasting so much time worrying. Not saying anything."

"If you can regret that, then I can do the same. I want to put this behind us."

Alec nodded. "It's just you and me. Right now. 'Cause I don't want to wait any longer. I don't think I can."

"You're usually a man of few words."

"And you're usually the one taking action." And then Alec's lips were on his, and they both groaned. It was decades' worth of angst and temptation. There was no soft kissing, no tentative exploration. That would come later. They both knew that.

They ripped at each other's clothes, the rending of fabric splitting the air as Liam's shirt hit the floor. He didn't care, didn't want to think about what they were going to do in the morning. They would find Charlie, they would deal with the rogue, they would deal with Kit. They would deal with their Pack. All of that would come.

For right now, it was just the two of them.

Alec tasted like coffee and man. Like his best friend. And Liam wanted him inside him.

Alec groaned, and they both growled, their claws out as their wolves pushed at them. Their other halves wanted this, wanted the mating bond that had been so long denied.

"I've wanted this for so long," Liam whispered against Alec's mouth, and then he tilted his head as Alec bit down on his shoulder. It was a hard, fast bite, a claiming.

"No time for finesse," Alec growled out. And then Liam kissed Alec hard on the mouth and bit down on Alec's lip, just a gentle nibble. He loved seeing the surprise in the other man's face, and then he moved to Alec's shoulder and bit down hard, another claiming bite. They were each other's soul mates, and they were so close to being fully mated. He needed release, needed something. And then Alec's hands were on Liam's jeans. The snap was undone, the sound of a zipper, and then the denim was shoved down to his ankles. Liam tore off his shoes and socks and then shucked his jeans the rest of the way.

Alec was still wearing his pants, and Liam was standing there naked. Then Alec's hand was on Liam's cock, and they both groaned.

"You know, I've seen you naked before countless times."

"Because we shift in the nude," Liam said, rocking his hips into Alec's fist.

"Yes, then, too. And I've done my best not to stare."

Intrigued, Liam let out a slow breath. "I haven't been very good about not staring."

Alec raised a brow and squeezed, forcing Liam's eyes to cross. "I've noticed."

Alec reached down between them and undid his pants. He shifted to remove them completely. And then they were both naked, and Alec was groaning into Liam's mouth. Liam reached down and gripped Alec's thicker cock, and they rubbed against each other. He loved it. Hell, he'd been waiting his entire life for this.

"You think the dragon has lube in here?" Liam asked, and Alec laughed.

"I think he's married to a very large bear, and they have a beautiful wife that they have constant sex with. She's a succubus, after all. I'm pretty sure they have secret lube stashes in every inch of that house. And the guest house."

"I sure as hell hope so."

They tumbled onto the bed, and Liam crawled over Alec to search the nightstand. "Jackpot." He waved a bottle of lube, and Alec grinned, his hand on his cock as he slowly slid his fist up and down.

"Who's going first?"

Liam swallowed hard and looked down at Alec's girth

as he nodded. "Well, we both know neither of us is more dominant, so I say we just take turns."

And then Liam found himself on his back, Alec's mouth over Liam's cock as he swallowed him whole.

Liam didn't even have time to think before his hand was tangled in Alec's hair and he pumped up into his mate's mouth.

"You win, this time."

"You can take me next time."

And then there was no more talking. Alec's mouth was warm, soft, and he sucked like a dream.

Liam was almost to the point of orgasm before Alec pulled away, and then the sound of a bottle opening filled Liam's ears.

He couldn't think. He kept his gaze on Alec as both of them touched and loved and caressed each other. Alec worked him slowly, and then when they were both ready, Alec hovered over them and slowly, inch by inch, filled him.

They both gasped, the burn intense, the feelings more intense. They were chest to chest, touching everywhere, and it was everything.

Alec slowly worked in and out of him, and both of them groaned, holding each other. When they came, at the exact same time, the mating between them worked its magic, and they each sucked in a breath.

Liam could feel the bond snap into place, a slow ache

that had waited centuries upon centuries to reach them. They were mated, perfect halves of a whole, and he finally had his soul mate. His lover, his best friend, his everything.

They kissed again, slowly, methodically. Everything.

And when they fell asleep, only for a few short hours because they had to hunt in the morning, Liam held his mate close and knew he would never let him go again. Because he had waited far too long for this.

Tomorrow, there would be blood, there would be death. Tonight…*tonight* was perfection.

CHAPTER 5

Every time Alec took a step, he could feel Liam within his soul, steady, controlled, and on the hunt. *His*. Leaves crunched under their feet, even as they were as quiet as they could possibly be. The smell of decay was prevalent, rot along with the freshly mown grass from the park across the street. Birds chirped in the distance. Yet not a single one perched near. It was as if they knew there was a predator in their midst, and he and Liam were not that threat.

His wolf pushed at him, wanting to shift. They couldn't, not yet. They were far too out in the open to change into their wolf forms.

And that meant they had to fight as men, not wolves, and hope to hell that the human authorities didn't show up.

They couldn't use warding or spells to keep them safe, and that meant they needed to make sure things worked for them this way.

However, with each step, with each intake of breath, he could feel his mate.

They had wasted so much time. So much fucking time trying to make sure the other was good enough, that they were good enough for each other. They wouldn't be wasting any more time. Alec had his mate by his side, his wolf, his future Beta or Tracker.

First, they had to kill his brother.

Just the idea of having to end a life wasn't something he wanted to do. The fact that it was Charlie, his brother, the person who was supposed to be his best friend and someone he could always rely on, put a foul taste in his mouth. He couldn't go back and change anything, so he wasn't going to.

"We're almost there," Liam whispered, and Alec nodded.

Almost—*not* close enough.

"Close."

Then there was no more talking, they didn't need to, not when they had hand signals and could now feel each other within their souls. Hunter would probably like that because it meant they could battle better as a unit, as a team. And maybe, just maybe they wouldn't fight as much and annoy the rest of the Pack. They had to survive this first. They had to kill Alec's brother. He hated that he had to do it. Alec had long since given up on Charlie, though. Even though he had tried not to. Charlie had done the unthinkable. Long before this. That's why he had been banned from the Pack to begin with.

There was another crunch of leaves, and Alec froze beside Liam. That hadn't come from them. The scent of decay, the putridness of it, filled his nostrils, and they turned on their heels.

Charlie was there, blood splatter on his face, part of a liver in his hands. Alec inhaled, grateful and yet still sad that it had belonged to a deer, and not a human or another paranormal.

Charlie had officially lost his mind, even though that had likely happened long ago.

"Make this easy for yourself, Charlie. We'll make it less painful." Liam let out a slow breath, his voice low.

Alec didn't know if that was for him or for Charlie. After all, Liam had known Charlie just as long as Alec had.

"Never," Charlie growled out, and Alec's eyes widened. If the rogue could speak, if his big brother could still talk, he retained some functioning part of his brain. That meant he was the scariest type of rogue. The ones that could take over a Pack, decimate them, and make plans that could end them all.

Goddess. They needed to end this. And fast.

They leapt at each other then, no need for further communication. There was no going back from this. No words or peace talks would fix what had happened.

The rogue came at Alec first, just like they knew he would. Charlie swiped out, bloody claws prepared to rend. Alec ducked out of the way, then used his own claws to slash at Charlie's face. They had to be quiet, had to be discreet, even if there was nothing unobtrusive about what was happening.

The humans couldn't know, though. That was the whole point of this. The humans couldn't know.

And that meant that Alec and Liam had to make this quick, with the least amount of bloodshed and as little pain as possible. He just didn't know if that could happen. Not with the growls emanating from Charlie's throat.

Charlie ducked, going at Liam then, and Alec leapt at his back, trying to land a killing blow. However, with his rogue strength and whatever chemical imbalance made rogues increase in all attributes of brainpower, Charlie was faster, stronger, deadlier than Liam and Alec combined.

Liam punched Charlie in the head, only Charlie kept going, spittle flying from his mouth as he clawed and slashed.

There were no kits here, no innocents. Just Charlie. And they would have to end this. Soon.

It was like fighting five alpha wolves at this point, and they just weren't strong enough.

They kicked, swiped, growled. Blood flew. Alec went at Charlie's gut, trying to pull him away from Liam, but it was no use. While before, Charlie had gone solely after Alec; now, he only went after Liam. Some small part of whatever sane fragment remained inside Charlie's head knew that he needed to go after Alec's mate and not Alec himself.

He growled.

A swipe left, a gash to the chest. An uppercut, a black eye. A kick, a slash. Another growl.

All of it, and none of it was enough.

Charlie picked up a large branch and slammed it against Alec's chest. He landed on his back, his breath whooshing out of him.

Alec scrambled to his feet and screamed as Charlie dug his claws into Liam's chest.

Liam's eyes went wide, his whole body paling as blood seeped from the wound. Charlie just kept digging and digging. If Alec didn't pull him off, somehow find the strength to push at Charlie, Charlie was going to dig Liam's heart right out of his chest.

Liam met Alec's gaze and whispered, "I love you." Alec growled, rage filling him. His fist clenched, claws digging into his skin. His wolf howled.

He wanted to shift, wanted to use that strength, only he couldn't, not out in the open like this.

So, he got to his feet and moved.

Charlie didn't see him coming, and that was good. Alec leapt, clawed at Charlie's back, one slice, then another, and even as Charlie moved to try and fight him off, Alec was there. He wrapped his arm around Charlie's neck and squeezed. Charlie let go of Liam, and Alec's mate fell to the ground, his hands over his chest as he tried to stanch the bleeding.

Alec didn't think it would be enough.

After all of this, after everything that had happened, he was going to lose his mate.

He couldn't breathe.

His wolf wanted revenge, wanted blood, and Alec was going to give it to him. He squeezed Charlie's neck, even as his brother, his blood, someone who was supposed to be everything to him, dug at his arm, reopening the wound that Alec had finally healed. He could scent his own blood. It didn't matter. He squeezed, and with one twist, the snap of bone echoed in his ears. And then, Charlie was gone. The rogue was dead, his brother was no more. It didn't matter. He tossed Charlie's lifeless form to the ground. At any other moment in time, Alec would have probably wept, would have grieved for his sibling. Instead, he let Charlie fall and ran to Liam.

Blood spilled out of Liam's chest, even as his own inner strength as a wolf started to heal the wounds. Alec just didn't think it would be enough. Tears slid down his cheeks now. Not for his brother. For his mate.

He pulled Liam into his arms, covered his mate's bloody hand with his to try and stop the bleeding, and simply held him, even as they both shook.

They'd killed the rogue, they had found each other, but in the end, everything might've happened too late.

LIAM WOKE UP TO THE SOUND OF POUNDING IN HIS HEAD as if someone were building a house on either side of his and wouldn't let up.

His chest ached as if someone had stabbed him, and then he remembered, well…that actually kind of happened.

He tried to move and groaned, sharp pain slicing up his body, and burrowing down deep into his chest.

He could feel his heart beating, hear it with the pulse racing in his ears because he had moved. However, he still reached out, even through the pain, to make sure that his chest was still intact. He was covered in bandages, yet underneath them, he felt his heartbeat. Thank God.

"You're whole," Dante said from the side of the bed.

Liam turned his head to look over at the dragon. Dante had his leg crossed over his knee, and a large leather-covered book in his hand. He pulled off his reading glasses and set them on the table near him, along with the book. Liam frowned.

"I didn't know a dragon would need reading glasses."

Dante grinned.

"I don't. However, Jace said I looked hot wearing them, so now I can't help it. It's habit."

"Well, if it's for your mates, I can see it. Yet I don't see your mates in this room."

"Like I said. Habit. You're going to be fine."

Liam raised a brow. "Good. Though, hell, I can't believe I fell as hard as I did."

Dante shook his head. "I'm surprised neither of you was more seriously injured. Your Alpha was here. He'll be back later. They came to pick up the body."

"I slept through Hunter being here?"

Dante nodded. "Yes, you've been out for about twelve hours or so. Needed some time to heal. Charlie, your rogue, was quite possibly the strongest rogue Hunter has ever come across. At least, according to your Alpha."

"How the hell did that happen?"

"Hunter has a theory, mostly having to do with magic none of us want to cross."

"Charlie was working with someone else, then?"

"Maybe. We always knew there was an underground connection of rogues out there. And it seems it's not just shifters. Perhaps there are other paranormals, as well."

"Well, hell."

"Indeed. You will be fine. As will your mate."

Liam patted his chest. "I didn't ask, because I can feel Alec in my soul."

"I figured. He is, however, with your kit. Her name is Mili, by the way."

Liam raised his brows. "She's speaking?"

"Somewhat. She said her name before saying your names all at once, wanting you guys. She'll likely cry endlessly unless she has the two of you. There's some bond there."

Liam coughed, then winced at the pain in his chest.

"I don't know how that happened. It's not like we've been in her vicinity for that long. You, Nadie, and Jace have been with her longer."

"You can't decide who will be the other part of your soul. You should know that by now."

"I do." Liam snarled softly. "Did you find anything out about her family?" Liam asked, trying to sit up.

Dante let out a put-upon sigh, even though Liam knew it was fake, and then went to help Liam.

Even through the pain, Liam just breathed and found himself sitting up, the dragon fluffing his pillows behind him. He would have to tell Alec and Hunter about that later.

"Jace found the rest of her demise. They were wiped out by another one. Charlie must've come across it and found the only living member. She was hiding under a pile of blankets."

"Mili," Liam cursed. "Another demise did it? Foxes did that to each other?"

"Apparently, Mili's demise was encroaching on the other group's land. It's not unheard of, and there are Pack wars and dragon wars that prove that. It's not just them."

"Goddess."

"Exactly. We've been reaching out to who we can. However, no other fox wants her, not when her demise was the one that encroached. She has shame associated with her name, according to them anyway."

"That's bullshit. She's a baby."

"I agree."

Liam knew what he needed to say, even though he hadn't even talked to Alec about it. "She's ours now. We'll take her."

"I had hoped that would be the case." Dante grinned, though it looked more like a dragon's snarl than anything. Dante was one scary bastard.

"That is if that's what Mili wants. And Alec."

"I have a feeling that's exactly what's going to happen. However, I'm going to speak for all of us when I say that

Nadie, Jace, and I will be honorary aunt and uncles. Do you hear me?" A little tendril of smoke wafted from Dante's nostril, and Liam nodded. "I would have said yes, even without the threat of burning alive. Thanks for that image."

Dante shook his head. "I don't burn anyone alive. Not after what we saw."

"Jace's brother?" I asked, trying to remember the battle. It had almost been the end of the world as everyone knew it. Humans could have died in mass extinction if they hadn't fought against Dante's mother and the rest of those standing against the Conclave. Jace's brother, Torrent, had died. Burned to a crisp in front of them. An echoing scream from Jace and his family still filled Liam's mind sometimes.

"I'm sorry for bringing it up again."

Dante shook his head. "I don't know why it came to my mind just now either. We're healing. Jace doesn't talk about him every day like he used to. I'll always regret that we lost Torrent in our fight."

"We've lost a lot over the past few years."

"I've been alive for millennia. I know loss. I don't want to have it again." Dante sat up then, stretching his back as he did so. "I'm glad you have your mate. The mating bond shines brightly between the two of you. And soon, you'll have your child. Mili is special, that one."

And with that cryptic statement, Dante stomped out

of the room, smoke trailing behind him. Liam didn't think Dante could help it sometimes. He liked being mysterious, and the smoke helped.

Liam was just about to swing his legs over the side of the bed when a sharp voice permeated the air. "Don't you dare think about getting out of that bed."

He looked up as Alec strode in, a little girl with light brown skin, dark brown hair, and honey brown eyes in his arms.

Liam's heart clenched at the sight. He couldn't help it. He loved that man so much that it hurt. And now Mili... Their daughter. *If* it all worked out. He still couldn't quite believe it.

"I was just getting up to come and see you."

"Well, now I'm here. So, don't get up and hurt yourself."

Liam settled back against the pillows, holding back a wince so he wouldn't worry Mili. Her wide eyes were fixed on him, her little nose twitching like a baby fox's.

Hell, she was so damn cute.

"Hi there," Liam said. Feeling awkward, "I'm Liam."

"Hi," she whispered, her voice high-pitched.

"She doesn't say much. I think she's a little too young to have full-on conversations with us."

Alec kissed the top of her head, and she nuzzled into him, her eyes closing.

"Hell," he whispered, hoping Mili hadn't heard. If he had ovaries, they would have burst.

He finally understood that joking statement.

"Dante told me what you said."

Liam's brows rose. "And?"

"It seems neither of our places is going to work. We're going to need a bigger place for the three of us."

Liam's heart practically burst as Alec came to sit next to him on the bed. Liam scooted over just a bit, and then Alec was there, leaning against him, with Mili sleeping in his arms.

"I'm sorry about your brother," Liam whispered.

"I'm sorry I almost wasn't fast enough."

"You don't get to blame yourself for that. You heard what Dante said. Something's happening."

"I know. I just wish we would have been able to figure it out faster."

"Me, too."

"There's no going back," Liam whispered.

"I never thought there would be. I love you."

Liam let out a little growl, his wolf reaching towards its mate and the girl who could one day be their child in truth. "I love you, too."

They had so much more to work out, but they had time to figure it out. After all, they'd had centuries to work out who they were as a couple, as friends, and as men.

Alec was his, had always been, and Liam had almost lost him because he had been too afraid, and had ignored things for far too long.

There is no going back, he reminded himself. And as he looked at Alec and Mili, he knew he never wanted to.

CHAPTER 6

Alec fisted the sheets, sweat beading on his brow as he groaned, pushing back into Liam. Liam gripped Alec's hips so hard that Alec knew there would be bruises in the end, and he didn't care.

Another thrust, another shout, and they kept going, moving as one, Liam filling him up so completely that he knew he wasn't going to last long.

And then Liam was reaching under him, gripping his cock, pumping hard.

He came on a shout, Liam following right after, and then he was boneless, unable to even keep himself up on all fours.

They lay there, sweat-slick and laughing because they weren't really on the bed anymore. Somehow, they had rolled off to the side of it, sheets on the floor, pillows on the side table, barely missing knocking over the lamp.

"Well, then. That's one way to start the morning," Liam said, kissing Alec's shoulder over their mating bite.

They had been back in Alec's home for two days, and Liam was fully healed. News of their mating had already spread throughout the Pack. The den was excited, awaiting their mating ceremony later that night. First, they needed to finish another ceremony.

Later today, they would officially be given their titles, having fought in the circle the day before.

Only it wasn't what anyone had thought.

And that just made Alec grin.

"We should go, Mili's going to wake up any second."

At the sound of Alec's voice, Mili let out a sharp cry, and Liam chuckled.

"I swear, it's like you're attuned to her."

"You're the same way, Papa."

"I don't know if I want to be called Papa," Liam said as they cleaned each other up.

"I think Dad and Daddy work. Or maybe Father?"

"We'll work it out." Alec smacked a kiss on Liam's lips, loving the way his mate blushed.

He liked surprising Liam with small displays of affection, little tastes.

They had a long way to go to figure out how they

were going to work as a couple, but in the end, they would find their path. After all, they had spent far too long hiding from it. Except that meant that they had years of learning each other's secrets, needs, and desires.

Now, they would put them to the test.

Alec quickly pulled on some pants and went to pick up Mili from her crib. It was a borrowed one from Becca's stash, and right now, the kit was in Alec's office rather than her own room. But the den was already building a house for them, and he had a feeling it would be done within a week, given how quickly they were working. It was a little ridiculous how fast they were getting everything done. With a little touch of magic, anything was possible.

"Well, hello there, Mili girl," Alec said, picking her up. He nuzzled the top of her head, and she snuggled right back.

Mili. His daughter.

He hated that she had come into their lives in such a way. And that she had been abandoned by her own kind. Sometimes, fate happened for a reason, though, even if he didn't like the thought of that. So, he would take what he could, and give her everything that he was able. She would be cherished, loved, and his.

Thanks to Dante, and the rest of the lightning-struck, there were plans in place to never let this happen again.

The lost would be found. At least, that's what he hoped. There were so many realms, so many children without homes, hidden away and scared.

And Alec had already offered his services to help in any way he could. They were just far-fetched plans at the moment, but he trusted the dragon to get it done.

He fed Mili, changed her, and got everything ready for the day. They didn't have a routine down—not in the slightest. That would come later. With two men who had never lived together before and a baby, as well, things were a little complicated.

Today, however, was mating day, and their mating ceremony would occur as soon as the moon rose.

He couldn't wait.

First, though, came the big news.

"Ready to go?" Liam asked a little bit later, and Alec nodded. "I and the pumpkin are ready," Alec said, jiggling Mili a bit so she laughed.

"Pumpkin?" Liam asked, brow raised.

"What? At least we're not calling her Kit all the time, right?" he asked, kissing Mili on the nose.

"I kind of liked Kit," Liam said, kissing Mili on the cheek and then Alec on the lips.

"Let's get there."

They headed to the circle where the rest of the den was already waiting.

Today was a big day for more than one thing, and he was more than ready. It was past time, and the den felt it.

It wasn't only the den and the Pack there. All of the lightning-struck had shown for the occasion, and they would stay well past the mating ceremony, according to Hunter. They had been instrumental in keeping the Pack healthy and safe, as well as saving the world more than once. Dante and his mates were there, as were a couple of angels, a demon or two, a lion, a pixie, a wizard, and a few others.

Everyone had brought their children, as well. Today was a fantastic day. Everyone was excited, laughing, and there wasn't going to be any bloodshed.

Because Alec and Liam had already stepped foot into the circle.

They didn't need to fight, the magic of the stones had already done the work for them.

And it was nothing like they had planned or imagined.

"Quiet down," Hunter said, their Alpha's voice booming.

The crowd quieted at once.

"For the past few years, we have all known that we would have a Beta and a Tracker when the time came. We all knew that I would be Alpha, and I fought in this circle, bled for you both here and in hell itself to make sure that happened." There were murmurs, memories whispered, yet no one spoke too loudly. They all knew the story.

"We all thought we would have our Beta and Tracker in the positions we'd always placed them in." Hunter raised a brow at them, and Alec and Liam just shared a look. No need to get in trouble again, they had wasted enough time on too many things.

"We were wrong." Murmurs, mostly because nobody knew what was about to happen next.

"We thought that Alec would be our Tracker, the one who would find those rogues, the one with the best skills for the scent. We thought he would be the one to stand apart, to keep our Pack safe from outside forces that came against us. But we were wrong."

More murmurs.

"And we thought Liam would be our Beta, the one right under me, my second in command. The one to handle the Pack's needs, to find the threads within our Pack and balance those ideals. But again, we were wrong."

Now there was full-out talking, speculating.

Alec held back a smile.

"So, we don't have our Beta and Tracker?" a woman asked, and Hunter shook his head as everyone shushed her. They wanted answers, and they were about to get them.

"We were wrong because our own biases got in the

way. The goddess has spoken, and so have we. Meet our new Tracker, Liam."

There was silence and then shouts of happiness and surprise.

"He has always been the one at Alec's side, training right along with him. He is the one who we have been waiting for, for what feels like centuries. He's the one who will keep us safe from afar."

"Finally!"

Alec didn't know who said that, but he just grinned.

"And our Beta, he has always been here, as well. The one who will listen to you, who has always listened. The one who is a bit calmer than the other." Hunter winked, and Liam blushed, considering Liam was anything but calm most days. A personality trait that was needed for the Tracker, but not the Beta.

"Meet your Beta, Alec." There was shouting then, howls, and Alec just shook his head, bouncing Mili on his hip as she laughed and giggled and clapped her little hands.

Liam leaned forward, brushed a little baby hair from her forehead, and then whispered into Alec's ear. "You ready?"

He met his mate's gaze, knowing that this was it. This was the start of their future. "Always."

He had his home, his Pack. A family. He had thought he'd lost it all when he was forced to kill his uncle and then his brother. When the Pack disintegrated, everything had changed.

But then he had fallen for his wolf, his mate who wasn't the Alpha, but an alpha wolf in every way that mattered. He had fallen for his best friend. And that, in the end, was always going to be a fate worth fighting for.

AT LAST SIGHT

CHAPTER 1

Jonah wasn't used to taking nights off. It wasn't that he was overworked, but he tended to stay in his own realm so he could be close in case something happened overnight. Not that it was *his* realm. It was the one he'd chosen, the one that had chosen him. This was his home now, no matter where he might have once come from.

As for leaving his ward? He wasn't sure he should have. He'd seen what had happened far too often when one lost sense, control, or let their guard down. He'd lost his leg because of such a thing. Had almost lost his ward, the darling child Penelope, because others had tried to break their words and their bonds.

What would happen if he wasn't there?

"If you keep grinding your teeth, I'm going to have to

pay for replacements, aren't I?" Malik, Jonah's employer, Alpha, and friend asked from his side. "Wait. Do jaguars grow them back like lions do? That would make things simpler."

Jonah scratched his cheek with his middle finger, and Malik's mate, Eliana, laughed from the other side of the booth. They were at Dante's Circle, a bar owned by a dragon friend. A place that had changed the lives of almost everyone in the room.

A few years ago, lightning from *on high*—or rather the Conclave some might say—had struck seven friends under the bar's roof and changed everything. Each of the women had not only had a hand in saving the realms more than once during these passing years, but each had also found their mate or mates *and* had unlocked their supernatural DNA in the process.

Eliana had been born human but was now a phoenix. One who had literally risen from the ashes. She was his Alpha, as well, mated to a lion shifter who ruled their realm.

"I'm not grinding my teeth," Jonah said after the pair had quit laughing. "And I can grow them back. Slowly."

Malik winced but, thankfully, didn't look down at Jonah's leg. Most shifters could grow back limbs, as well, but he'd almost died when he was injured, and the magic involved hadn't been truly shifter-based. His leg had remained how it was, and he'd learned to fight and live far differently than he had before the war. It had been so long that Jonah barely remembered what he had been like before.

"What are we drinking?" Dante asked as he sidled up to the table, his long, black-and-blue hair pulled back from his face. He smiled as he said it, and Jonah figured the man's perfect timing wasn't a coincidence. The dragon was good at soothing awkward situations...as well as decapitating anyone who dared hurt his family, but that was another perfectly logical and needed trait.

"A beer sounds great," Malik said and leaned over to kiss his mate on the temple. "Feel like it's been forever since we just came out and did this, you know?"

Eliana smiled widely, her heart in her eyes. "I know, we've all been so busy. And I'd love a beer, too. Anything you have special on tap. You know us."

Dante just grinned, nodding. "I do." He looked over at Jonah. "What about you? What are you in the mood for?"

Jonah just shrugged. "I'm sure you can figure it out, dragon."

"That is true. But I like to pretend that I give you guys a choice in these matters."

"You're very scary, you know that?"

Dante flashed a smile that was all teeth, and Jonah just laughed. If Dante weren't his friend, he might actually be scared. In fact, any other dragon? There would probably be a Jonah-shaped hole in the door on his way out. He was a warrior, a soldier, had fought until his feet were bloodied, and his soul was marred, but fighting a dragon? Not his favorite thing to do.

"I've a really good pumpkin ale that we just put on tap."

Jonah scrunched his nose. "Pumpkin?"

"'Tis the season and all that."

"I wish pumpkin season was every month of the year," Eliana said, her voice dreamy, like when she spoke of Penelope.

"You and those pumpkin spice lattes," Malik said, shaking his head even though his lips quirked into a smile.

"I am surprised you're not wearing UGGs and a North Face jacket right now," Jonah said dryly, and Eliana flipped him off.

"Hey, that's not very queenly," Jonah said, and Eliana flipped him off with her other finger.

"Queen this. And don't make fun of being basic. It's what I like."

Jonah nodded. "Yeah, I have a North Face jacket, too. There's nothing wrong with being basic. I just like making fun of you."

Eliana grinned, and Dante just snorted from in front of the table.

"And, Eliana?" Jonah asked. His Alpha's mate leaned

forward to look at him. "There's nothing basic about you."

"Stop flirting with my mate," Malik mock growled and then kissed Eliana square on the mouth, a little too enthusiastically. Jonah had to move in his seat just to get out of the way.

Dante rolled his eyes and then went off to presumably get three pumpkin ales.

That's when Jonah saw her.

Her. The new bartender.

He swallowed hard, trying to slow his heart rate down even as he looked at her.

Dante had staff members coming in and out of the place often. Mostly because he took in those who needed help, even as he needed the help behind the bar, as well.

Becca, one of their friends, had been a bartender for a while. Now, she was mated to a wolf shifter, an Alpha no less, and had her own family responsibilities.

There had been a few other bartenders since then, but this one? This one was all new.

And he couldn't stop staring.

Her skin was a dark brown, soft, illuminated under the lights of the bar. Her black hair was in curls all around her head like a halo, and the style just highlighted her sharp cheekbones.

She had on a purple top that bared her arms, and silver bangles that went up both wrists to the middle of her forearms. They jangled as she worked, sounding like music to his ears.

He could see from the side of the bar that she wore jeans that hugged her ass, but he tried not to look there because he wasn't that much of a lecher.

At least, he didn't think so. He hadn't thought so before this moment anyway.

She worked with an efficiency that told him that she had likely done this before, or perhaps was just a fast learner. But while she worked, her smile didn't quite reach her eyes. And her gaze constantly darted towards the door.

Maybe she *wasn't* so proficient at this. Perhaps she was new but knew precisely what she was doing.

He couldn't stop staring at her, and when Malik cleared his throat beside him, Jonah pulled his gaze from her, grateful that the woman hadn't seen him staring. It was bad enough that he was staring at all. He didn't want to be caught doing it.

"That's Poppy," Eliana whispered from Jonah's other side.

Jonah looked towards her and shrugged. "New bartender, then?"

He hoped he sounded casual. But from the look that the mated pair gave each other and him, he knew he had been anything but.

"She's a quick learner. Dante said she didn't really have any experience before this."

"That's good. Good. Think she's pulling our beers now," Jonah said, having found his gaze right back on her. He couldn't help it. But he truly needed to stop.

"You should go over there and ask her out," Eliana said, and Malik snorted.

"Jonah? Ask out a woman? Well, I would say it'd be a cold day in hell, but I don't actually know if hell has only hot seasons."

"You are friends with a demon, as well as Lucifer's son. I'm sure you could find out," Jonah added wryly.

You know, I just might text them," Malik said, narrowing his eyes at Jonah. "If you don't ask her out, at least go over and say hi. You know, make an introduction."

Jonah just shook his head. "I'm fine.

"You're not," Eliana said. This time, her voice was soft.

Jonah swallowed hard and then did his best to look like he was fine. "Seriously, Jonah. You rarely take days off, and even though I love that you are such a warrior for my daughter, you're allowed to have time to yourself."

"I'm here with you, aren't I?"

"Because we dragged you out bodily," Malik said.

"Yes, you did. Maybe it was because I didn't really want to encroach on date night. You two rarely go out."

"We go out," Eliana said, shaking her head. "We go out

often. You, however, are constantly back in our realm, being a loving nanny to our daughter."

"I'm a caregiver, I don't like being called a nanny."

"You like it," Malik said. "You're the one who calls himself a nanny."

"Fine, I don't mind the word, I just don't like it when you get that look in your eye whenever she calls me that," Jonah said to Malik, and his friend just grinned.

"What? I find it hilarious. Mostly because I like to get under your skin. Nothing much gets under your skin these days, Jonah."

"And if we're going to continue getting all introspective about my life, I'm going to need that beer."

As if Dante had been waiting for that exact moment, the dragon set down three pints of pumpkin ale, and Jonah's mouth watered.

"You're going to like it," Dante warned.

"Was that a threat?" Malik asked, and Jonah just grinned before taking a sip. Flavor burst on his tongue, and he held back a moan.

"Told you," Dante said before he went off to help another table.

"This is amazing," Malik said, practically whispering into his beer so nobody could see.

"Oh, yes, I think this is my favorite."

Eliana held the pint with both hands and smiled into

it as she wiggled in her seat. "I think I could drink this whole thing."

"Do so. Have as much as you want." And then Malik whispered something into her ear that made her blush, and Jonah averted his gaze.

He didn't mind being the third wheel. He was usually the odd man out when it came to them. He was Penelope's guard, not just her nanny as they put it. And though he had the evening off, and she was surrounded by five of his most trusted soldiers, he still wanted to go back and make sure that she was safe. He couldn't help it, he had lost too many people before, he wouldn't let anything happen now.

"So, is Poppy human?" he asked, the question out of his lips before he could even fully think the words. Humans who worked at the bar didn't tend to know the secrets of the paranormals, but sometimes, they did. They had to tread carefully. And even though they were all talking aloud about lions and dragons, the magic within the bar itself helped keep their secrets.

Malik just grinned like a cat in cream, and Eliana clapped her hands in front of her after she'd set her beer on the table. "She's not, but I don't know exactly what she is. You know it's not nice to ask."

"I can go over and see," Malik said.

"Don't use your little shifter senses to figure it out. I'm still new to the whole supernatural game, and I don't even know if phoenixes are supposed to be able to sense what other paranormals are."

"Phoenixes are a rare breed. I'm sure after a time, you'd be able to figure it out. And, no, none of us should go over there to uncover the mystery. That would be rude." Jonah resisted looking over at Poppy again. But he could feel her, sense her. And that worried him. He had never felt like this before, and he didn't want to know what it meant.

"You should still go over and talk to her," Eliana said, pulling him out of his thoughts.

"No, I really shouldn't."

"She's the first person I've seen you look at like that. Ever."

He ignored Malik's words.

"There are good reasons that I don't." But he wouldn't. He wouldn't even look at her again. At Poppy. Such a bright, happy name for a woman who didn't smile.

As he forced himself to look away, he remembered the color of her eyes. A pure silver that had beckoned him. Because from his first look into those silver eyes, he had been lost. And he was damn worried that if he looked again, he wouldn't be able to pull himself out like he had before.

This wasn't something he needed. He had a job, a life, a ward. Penelope needed him. Eliana and Malik needed him. They had given him purpose after a life he had thought he'd lost. He didn't want to risk that again. Didn't want to risk what was deep inside of him. The haunted part that he had hidden for so long.

So, he wasn't going to look.

Eliana and Malik seemed to have noticed the change in his mood, so they moved the subject to Penelope and the rest of the seven.

He liked the seven, the seven lightning-struck women who had become a core part of his life. He didn't get to see all of them at the same time often, not when each of them lived within their own realm, either ruling it or working with the monarchies. But he liked them, liked the way that, no matter what, they were always there for each other.

They were some of the most powerful supernaturals in any of the worlds, and he was blessed to be a part of the outer circle.

They finished their beers, and then the couple kept leaning forward, whispering to each other. Jonah finally rolled his eyes and cleared his throat.

"Okay, you two, go get a room. Or, you know, you have your own. You even have a few homes in the human realm. Why don't you use one?"

"Because we're here with you," Malik said, even though he was looking at Eliana.

"Go. Have fun. Though I bet you'll go hug your

daughter tonight first because you guys can't stand to be far away from her either."

The couple looked at each other and grinned. "Sorry," Malik said, sliding out of the booth, holding out a hand for his mate.

"No need to be sorry. You guys need time for each other, too." He paused. "Thank you for coming out with me. And forcing me to be here."

"Always. You're family, Jonah. You always have been. And you're going to be until the end of our days."

"Let's hope the end of our days is a very long time off," Eliana added, and they all looked at each other and smiled softly. Each of them had almost died multiple times, and Eliana had actually died once.

They didn't want to deal with any of that again.

Malik reached for his wallet, but Jonah shook his head. "I've got this one."

"We're the ones who asked you to come."

"Then I'll take this one. Next time, you can pay."

"That means there's going to be a next time," Eliana added.

Jonah shrugged. "Maybe. But go."

The two nodded and then went off with each other, fingers entangled as they leaned into one another.

"Oh, I was going to see if you guys needed another round, but I guess…your check?" a soft voice asked from the side. Jonah swallowed hard, doing his best not to react. His hair stood on end, and all he wanted to do was lean forward and sniff her. His jaguar prowled, and he pulled it back. He would not shift. Wouldn't lay claim to her.

But as he inhaled her sweet scent, he knew exactly what she was. Knew exactly *who* she was.

She was a Medusa, a gorgon as some called them. One under full glamour since her hair looked normal. She didn't have snakes showing—her pets, her prodigies, her death. No, she had gorgeous curls and a silky voice.

But she wasn't just a Medusa. No, she was *his*. His mate, his other half.

After centuries, he had finally found her.

And from the way she froze as he looked at her, those silver eyes going wide, she knew as well.

But he didn't want to mate. Had seen firsthand what happened when you cared too much for someone, and then you lost them. He didn't want that.

But he didn't even have a chance to say that, to even fully feel that or convince himself it was the case.

Instead, Poppy just smiled wide and set down the check. "Well, got to go. Have a good night." She scrambled away, leaving Jonah lost, wondering what the hell had just happened.

Jonah frowned at his empty beer glass and at the check on the table and wondered why she hadn't even let him answer—or order another drink. Instead, she'd had the tab ready, and then had run.

Run from him.

He shook his head, put some cash on the table, a nice tip for Dante and her to share, and slid out of the booth. He would go home, check on Penelope, and then spend the rest of his evening off alone in his home, wondering what he was going to do next. Because he loved his work, adored his job, but he was tired. So tired. And he knew he couldn't come back here, couldn't come and see Poppy again.

If he did, he wouldn't be able to hold back. Wouldn't be able to do the right thing and say *"no."*

Dante wasn't around when he headed out towards the parking lot, so he didn't say goodbye to the dragon. He hadn't seen Poppy behind the bar either. Instead, there was another person there. He figured Poppy must be on break. Or maybe she had run from him like he was doing with her.

Well, apparently, they were a perfect match, after all. Fate be damned and all that.

He slid his hands into his pockets and made his way to the car, but then a familiar scent hit his nostrils, and he heard the sound of a scream.

He growled, his claws ripping through his fingertips as he slid his hands out of his pockets, his jaguar prowling.

Poppy. That was Poppy's voice, Poppy's scent. And he'd be damned if anyone hurt her.

He ran to the other side of the parking lot where the lights were dimmer, and the shadows crept.

Three large men surrounded Poppy, the tight coils of their hair sliding in and out of their glamour as their snakes came at her. One had Poppy by the arm, the other by the waist, the third with a dagger in his hand.

"Let go of her," Jonah growled, and the three gorgons froze, looking over their shoulders at him.

"Be gone, animal."

"Wrong answer." He jumped then, fighting like a warrior of old.

And he was a warrior of old.

He sliced at the biggest gorgon, getting him in the side and kicking him in the knee at the same time. The gorgon fell, clutching his ribs as blood pooled. But Jonah didn't pay attention. Instead, he went to the other gorgon, wrapping his arm around the man's neck and twisting. He didn't break his neck, didn't know if he deserved death yet, but he did incapacitate him enough that he passed out.

Jonah looked towards Poppy, her eyes narrow, silver slits even as she tried to fight off the other man. She punched at him, kicked, but he was bigger. And he was the one with the knife. She didn't have the skills, and she was young. Too young to learn centuries' worth of fighting techniques. One day, he would teach her. His mate would fight by his side as a warrior. He pushed that thought from his mind because she wasn't going to be his mate. He had to remind himself of that.

And so, he went to the other man and clawed at the gorgon's back. Before the assailant could slice, Jonah reached out and gripped the gorgon's wrist, tightly enough that the other man dropped the knife right into Jonah's hand. And then he stabbed, right into the underbelly of the gorgon. He screamed, and Jonah slid the dagger back out as he looked over at Poppy.

"Are you okay?" he asked, his jaguar in his voice and his eyes if the glow surrounding them was any indication, blood dripping from his claws.

Poppy looked at him, her eyes wide.

In answer, she ran.

CHAPTER 2

Poppy did what she did best.

She ran.

Her heart raced, pulsating within the cavity of her chest, and she knew her glamour was fraying at the edges. She couldn't focus on both at the same time, at least not perfectly, but she did her best. She turned the corner, her feet pounding the pavement as she closed her eyes for a moment so she could focus on the glamour.

The disguise was what kept her safe. No, that wasn't right. It was what kept *others* safe. Because if the glamour fell, her snakes would show. Her little vipers that were death incarnate, but also *her*. They weren't her children per se, but they were part of her. It would break her if they were ever hurt, but she also couldn't let them harm anyone else. That meant she had to be careful. She refused to kill again because of lack of control. She didn't want to see the life drain out of someone's eyes as they turned to stone because of who she was.

She couldn't let that happen, and that meant she wasn't going to. She ran her hand over her hair, thankful that the tendrils slid against her palm, not the coolness of her snakes. The glamour made it so she could feel the coarse texture of her hair rather than the snakes themselves.

And anyone else who touched them would feel the same—not that she wanted anyone to touch her hair without permission. However, she knew they wouldn't feel the snakes even though they were there…waiting.

Because they could turn the viewer to stone. Her snakes *and* her silver eyes.

There were no contacts invented in all the realms that could protect people from the silver of her stare. Her glamour, however, protected her snakes….and the outside world from their existence.

Her glamour back in place, she turned the corner, only to freeze as a man jumped from the roof of the building next to her and landed right in her path. She knew him. Had talked to him in the bar. He'd saved her life. But…why? Why would he be here?

"Poppy? Are you okay?"

He knew her name. It made sense in a way that he

would. He knew Dante and the others. Only the word coming off his tongue worried her. *Did* something to her.

She swallowed hard and took a step back. She hadn't meant to, hadn't meant to show that weakness. She was just *so* tired. She'd thought she had found some semblance of peace, but apparently, she'd been wrong. Because how could she be at peace when they would always be searching? She hadn't even been safe in the lair of a dragon. Where else could she hide? Where else could she run?

"I'm Jonah. I'm friends with Dante. The man you work for."

"I don't think I'm going to be working there much longer," she said, the words out before she could stop them. Her job wasn't the most important thing to mention, after all.

"Well, we can talk about that later. For now, let's get you somewhere safe."

She shook her head and took another step back.

His eyes narrowed, and then he lowered his shoulders as if trying to look smaller, less dangerous. Only she didn't think he could ever look less dangerous.

"I don't know if there're more gorgons around. Clearly, they are after you for a reason, *and* you're running. Let me at least get you somewhere safe."

"Why?" she asked. Why was he helping her? Why was he here? No one had helped until now. No one until

Dante had even given her a job. And now the dragon's friend was here to help her again? It almost felt like a dream. She was just so *tired*.

"You know why."

She did, she could feel it. That one instant of eye contact at the bar and she had known. Known that he was hers, just like she could be his. That he could be her happily ever after, her true half, her mate.

But she didn't want that. How could she?

She was death personified, the Grim Reaper in all its glory. Of course, she wasn't an actual legendary reaper that came from the shadows of time and myth. No, she was a murderer. She was the hand of death.

"Poppy. We need to go."

She shook her head and then froze when she scented the gorgons on the wind. *They were coming.* They were following her. They would always come for her.

Because she had broken the most important rule of a Medusa. Honestly, she had broken all the rules in the end. She had no line, no family. She had nothing.

Except for a job given by a dragon who had taken a chance on her.

Jonah cleared his throat. "I have a place somewhere close."

She shook her head. "I don't even know you."

"You know Dante. You saw me with him. We're friends. You can trust him. You can trust me."

She shook her head again.

"Then come with me because you know exactly what we are to each other. At least who we have the potential to be. It's better to be safe under a roof of protection, rather than out here in the open, especially when we don't know where the gorgons are coming from."

Those words got to her more than anything. She didn't know Jonah, didn't know this man, this jaguar, but maybe she could figure out what she needed to do from somewhere that wasn't out in the open. Because she didn't think she should go back to Dante's Circle. What if she did and the gorgons followed her? They wanted her dead. They wanted her beheaded, the rest of her body burned. Then they wanted to keep that head on a spike or perhaps even a silver platter. They wanted her death to be a symbol, to become something of myth and legend.

The legends had been wrong. Medusa hadn't been evil, hadn't been cruel. She had been brutalized. Taken advantage of by the gods who'd once sworn to protect her. And then she had been cast out in sin for the others to remark upon.

The truth didn't matter to the other gorgons—didn't matter to the royal line. They wanted Poppy as their new symbol. They wanted her because of her power, and because of what others couldn't have.

She knew that. She knew that was why they had come after her to begin with. And she knew she couldn't stop them. She hadn't been able to fix anything, and right now, she needed to figure out what to do.

Jonah growled, and the sound went straight to places she did not want to think about. She didn't have time for this. Didn't have time for feelings or anything that would stop her from running. She was just so *tired*. That exhaustion made her do the unthinkable. She slid her hand into his and swallowed hard. "Just for a few moments."

He nodded tightly and then tugged at her arm. They were running then, Poppy trying to keep up with his much longer stride. He was a jaguar, after all. In shifter form, he would be able to outpace her quite easily. In human form, though, it felt like he was just as fast.

Gorgons weren't the best runners in all the realms, nor were they the best athletes. Personally, she was not the best fighter, either. She'd never had cause to learn. Right then and there, she promised herself that she would train. She didn't want to be helpless. She hated that. But she hadn't been raised to be a fighter. She had been a scholar, had been someone who thought she'd had a future. She had been wrong.

"Where are we going?" she panted, annoyed with herself since he wasn't even the slightest bit out of breath.

"Somewhere close," Jonah growled out. He looked over his shoulder, and she knew he wasn't going to tell her exactly where since someone could overhear. This was insane, trusting someone she didn't know, but she didn't have a choice. She needed to figure out how to save herself because hiding and running wasn't working. Clearly. And so, she *moved*. She ran.

They turned the corner and kept going until they found themselves in a quiet neighborhood. Jonah leapt over a fence near the end of one street, and she just blinked at the wooden planks, wondering what the hell he expected her to do.

And then his face was over the slats, then half of his body, and he held out an arm. "Sorry, I forget that not everybody can jump as high as I can."

She didn't know if he was blushing, couldn't tell even in the moonlight, but she heard embarrassment in the tone of his voice.

She jumped as high as she could, and he gripped her hand and then pulled her over with ease. So quickly, in fact, she didn't even touch the top of the fence as she sailed over it.

His strength was amazing. She knew that most shifters were that strong, but for some reason, he felt stronger. Or maybe that was just the bond that wanted to flow between them, making her hormones act crazy.

Jonah got them inside a two-story house, and she looked around the dark home, wondering where she was, and how exactly she had gotten herself into this situation.

"Let's not turn on the lights just yet," he whispered, and she jumped, not realizing that he had gotten so close.

"Where are we?"

"My home."

"You live here? In the human realm?"

He shook his head. "No, I don't live in the human realm at the moment. However, I do have a home here. At my age, it's good to have backups in case something happens. And it's always good to have a connection to the human realm. After all, it's the realm that connects all the others."

"At your age?" she asked and felt heat rising in her cheeks.

Jonah just smiled softly. "I'm a few hundred years old. Not too old for a shifter." He paused. "How old are you, Poppy?"

"Twenty-five," she whispered. So young compared to him, but that didn't matter in most cases with the supernaturals.

Jonah let out a harsh breath. "Ah, well, that makes sense."

She narrowed her eyes, feeling like she should be insulted. "Why does that make sense?"

"Because you have no fighting skills whatsoever."

Affronted, she frowned. "Hey, I punched."

"And you had your thumb in the wrong position. If you had used any strength at all, you would have broken your hand."

She scowled, even as she *knew* she blushed even

harder. "I'm not that bad."

"You are. But if you want, I can help you."

"Why? Why would you do that?"

"For many reasons."

"Tell me." They had more important things to worry about, but she couldn't stop this train of thought.

"How about the fact that I don't want to see someone get hurt? Or that Dante hired you and, therefore, you're sort of part of our circle."

"Our?" She didn't want to sound jealous, and that feeling wasn't for another woman or man. It was for the fact that he actually had a *group*. She'd seen him laughing with his friends over a drink. She'd tried not to watch, but her gaze had continuously been pulled in his direction. The long, lean lines of his body, the strong line of his jaw. The way he constantly watched the entrance of the bar, a protector at his core. She loved the smoothness of his skin, and the stubble on his face. She had watched him all night, and she had wanted him.

And she hated herself just a little bit for it. Because she didn't have time for feelings. She didn't even know if she deserved those emotions.

"I'll also help you because of what we are."

There was a pause when she tried to think of what to say. "And, who am I to you?" she whispered.

"You're really going to make me say it?"

She shook her head, knowing one of them needed to

say the words. They both knew what pulsed between them. It was a feeling. A knowing. And there was no mistaking it. Not for them, at least. Perhaps for others, but not for them.

"I'm in no position to find my other half. My mate," she said quickly, looking down at her hands.

"I don't think I'm in that position either."

The words were soft, yet she felt as if he'd shouted them, the blow shocking.

"Oh," she said, her voice a whisper.

"But I don't think anyone is truly looking when it happens, are they?"

Her gaze shot up.

"I don't know what this means, I don't know what any of this means. But why don't you tell me first why the gorgons are after you. And why you were hiding in Dante's bar."

"I wasn't really hiding," she lied.

"I've been a soldier for over two centuries, almost three. I have seen more war and bloodshed than you could imagine. I know when someone is hiding."

Her head snapped up. "Don't tell me what I can imagine."

He nodded. "You're right. I'm sorry. Humans live but a fraction of our time, and yet they have eons of heartache in those moments. I shouldn't disregard your feelings because of your age."

"Thank you. Because you don't know what I've seen."

"Maybe one day you'll tell me."

Maybe one day she would. And perhaps one day she'd figure out exactly why she wanted to tell him. Why she wanted to divulge the secrets that she should hide.

"You should tell me why the gorgons are after you. It'll help us figure things out."

"By *us,* do you mean you and me? Because I can do it myself. I've been doing just fine on my own."

"You have. You're alive."

"Are you placating me?"

He shook his head. "No, I *know*. Those three gorgons were strong, warriors of your people. And I'm sure there are probably others after you. Am I right?"

She nodded.

"And you have survived. That counts for so much more than you think."

"I don't know what I'm supposed to be doing. I'm just so tired."

"I've been there. Tired, weary."

She swallowed hard, hating the fact that he could understand when she didn't even get it herself. "How did you get better?"

"I found a purpose."

"And what is that?"

He smiled then, laughter filling his eyes. It made him

even more handsome. "I found a job. I work for the Alpha of the lion realm."

Her gaze widened. "Not the jaguars?"

He shook his head. Sadness washed over him, and she wanted to reach out, but she didn't know him. She had to remind herself that. She didn't have that right.

"Malik has been my friend for over a century, though it feels like far longer. When he needed help protecting his mate and child, I stepped in. I had been on my own for a while. I wasn't part of the jaguars anymore," he whispered, and she knew there was more to the story.

She didn't have the right to ask just then, though. And, honestly, she wasn't sure she wanted to. Not only did she want to stay separate from him—as long as she could tell herself there was distance, she would be safe—but she also didn't want to hurt him. And she had a feeling that asking that would hurt.

"The Alpha protects his mate, and I help, but my first job, my first duty is to protect Lady Penelope, their daughter."

"You protect a child?" She warmed, trying to imagine this rough jaguar soldier with a baby lion cub.

"Yes, and she has me wrapped around her little finger." He grinned. "My friends call me a nanny, and I don't even mind it."

She laughed then, and then put her hand over her mouth. She didn't know she *could* laugh. She had thought she had forgotten how. And yet, here she was, laughing with this man.

Who was he? And how had this happened so quickly?

"Now, tell me. Why are the gorgons after you?"

She lowered her hand and swallowed hard. "Because I killed someone."

His eyes widened marginally, and then he narrowed them. "That can't be all."

No, it wasn't, but she'd never told anyone the story before. She'd never had anyone *to* tell. She looked up at him then, his body so close, the heat warming her too-cool skin. "I feel like I need to tell you, why is that?"

"We already went over this. Because of who I am, how we are connected. I can't protect you if I don't know."

"I didn't ask for your protection."

"It's freely given."

And she knew that. Deep down, even though she had just met this man, she knew that. If she ran away right now, he would still protect her. And he wouldn't ask for a single thing. He was a man of honor. It should worry her, but it didn't.

Plus, she was just so tired. She knew she needed to tell him. Even if he left after she did. "You know the stories of Medusa."

"I've met a few gorgons in my time."

"I'm a Medusa, not just a gorgon."

"What's the difference? I didn't know there was one," he asked, frowning.

"It means I'm at a higher level than most of the realm. I was born this way. I can't change it. I'm even different than my parents. They're all gorgons, but I was born a Medusa. It means I need a stronger glamour, but I have more control over it than most. It means while *some* gorgons can turn others to stone with just their snakes and their eyes, it takes them longer. They have to be forceful. I don't have to do much at all. Unless you are my blood or my mate, if you look at my eyes or the snakes look upon you, you will die. Turned to stone in an instant."

She swallowed hard, but he just kept looking at her. So, she continued.

"They banished me from my realm because I killed a mortal when I was nineteen."

Jonah nodded, and his voice was soft when he spoke. "It was an accident, though, wasn't it? You were nineteen. And you say you have so much power, didn't they help you with control?"

She shook her head. "It is a Medusa's *honor*,"—she spat the word—"to learn control. To have that power comes with great responsibility, they say. I had to learn how to protect myself *and* others. I'm the one who learned to glamour, even though someone should've taught me. In the end, however, I lost control, and I killed my boyfriend. I was nineteen, and with one touch, one look, killed the boy that I loved."

She didn't cry, she couldn't. Not anymore.

"Poppy."

She shook her head. "And it would have been fine, they would've covered it up, but the king of our lands has three daughters." She said that wryly, and he frowned. "Three daughters who don't have my power but want it. Women who didn't have my boyfriend but wanted him. They drugged my water one night while at a court dinner. The drug took away my glamour in the heat of the moment. If I felt satisfaction, if I felt happiness, if I felt any strong emotion, my glamour would fade. And I loved that boy, I loved Alex. And he died. Because I loved him."

Jonah cursed under his breath, but she didn't stop. "My family disowned me. The realm banished me. Because those three girls wanted my power, and they couldn't have it. They convinced their father, the king, that I was a plague upon our realm. That if I wasn't caught and murdered, if I wasn't beheaded, then I would be the end of our realm. *Their* realm." She corrected herself. It wasn't her home anymore. "The king loved his daughters, and in the end, he banished me."

"Banished you, but didn't kill you," Jonah added, his voice a growl. "Yet the gorgons after you tonight wanted your head. I saw the knife."

"At first, it was banishment, but then the king died," she whispered. Jonah's eyes widened. "I haven't been in touch with anyone to know what he died of, but the timing makes me think it wasn't natural. His eldest daughter, now queen, Mina, asked for my head. Demanded it." She shook her head. "I'd had hope. Thought I could just live as banished in the other realms, with the humans or maybe another paranormal, but this year, Mina came after me. She sent her goons, and I can't run anymore. I'm just so tired."

And then Jonah was there, her face in his hands as he growled, his forehead against hers. "We will fix this."

"We can't." She wanted to believe him, wanted to do something.

"We *can*. I might not be a king or the most powerful shifter in the world, but I know leaders. I know those with power. And I have strength of my own. We will fix this."

She couldn't say anything, didn't have the words. Before she could even think of something *to* say, the sound of an explosion slammed into her ears, and fire engulfed the house. Jonah roared, throwing his body over hers.

CHAPTER 3

Jonah's jaguar came to the surface, wanting him to shift, clawing for action against the inside of his skin, only Jonah couldn't let the cat out yet. He needed to be in human form to get out of the burning home as well as carry Poppy if he needed to. She wasn't a cub where he could just use his mouth on the scruff of her neck to drag her out.

They were both on the floor, the house burning around them. He didn't have a single feeling within him for anything in the house other than the woman below him. Nothing within the walls was personal or had anything to do with him other than providing a place to sleep and shelter.

As it turned out, it hadn't been a place for shelter at all. He hadn't scented those who laid siege to his place.

No, he had been too focused on Poppy and had missed the warning signals.

He scrambled to his feet, ducking low as smoke billowed overhead. They had *bombed* the house, windows shattered, planks of wood splintered all around them. Poppy lay on the floor, a thin trickle of blood trailing from a cut on her head, but he could feel her pulse, even as his jaguar growled, wanting revenge for someone having dared to hurt her.

He quickly lifted his head, trying to scent any intruders, but there weren't any about. They were waiting outside, watching. He would get to them, but first, he had to make sure Poppy was okay.

"Poppy," he whispered, checking her body for burns or other injuries. There was just the head injury it seemed, and there wasn't anything *just* about it.

He growled low, sliding his hand over her skin to make sure that she was whole and unmarred everywhere else. Her glamour faded in and out, and he let out a shuddering breath as one of the snakes wrapped its body around his wrist. It looked up at him, its beady eyes searching.

The baby viper didn't bite him, and he blinked, realizing that he hadn't actually turned to stone. He was her mate, after all, and she wasn't looking directly at him with those silver eyes. He would be safe from her snakes. In fact, the snakes she wore like a crown now seemed to look at him for help, as if wanting to wake their master and unable to do so.

He understood that, because he needed her to open those pretty eyes, as well.

"Poppy," he growled again and went to pick her up.

She slashed out with her hands, her eyes wide. Suddenly, he found himself staring into those silver pools, her snakes all around her, hissing at him.

He hadn't turned to stone, hadn't ended right then and there.

Because he was hers. Something he could not ignore. Neither of them could ignore it.

She quickly closed her eyes and slid her hand over her snakes, whimpering.

"How…I didn't…are you okay?"

"You're the one bleeding."

"You're not stone."

"I'm your mate." His tongue tripped over the word, but it was getting easier to say. After all these years, after everything he'd lost, he could at least get the word out. "You're safe with me. And I'm safe with you. But we need to get out of here. The flames are getting worse and closer, and we're going to die of smoke inhalation if we're not careful."

"Okay, I'm okay." Her snakes still writhed around her head. She hadn't yet put on her glamour.

"Keep your glamour off," he ordered, and her silver eyes widened.

"Why?

"Because it's a good defense against those that are coming after you."

"But what if there's an innocent?"

"Then close your eyes and pull your glamour up quickly. But I only scent smoke, fire, and those three damn gorgons. Apparently, I didn't stab the bastard hard enough."

He ground out the words, and her eyes widened for a minute before he lifted her to her feet, both of them coughing.

"Let's go."

She nodded.

They made their way out of the burning home, and he felt a tinge of regret that he was losing the place, but it didn't matter. His true home was in the lion realm, as was his heart. No, that wasn't the case anymore. Because the person beside him could also hold that organ. Just like baby Penelope already did as his ward.

"Can you fight at all?" he asked, and Poppy shook her head.

"I don't know the moves. My parents didn't want me to fight, thought it wasn't in my nature. And not all gorgons are as violent as the current court and these men after me. And it won't be just these three. The queen has far more."

"I figured as much. Sending her entire army out at once would be idiotic. We'll get out of this. I just need to know your skills."

"My only skill is death," she whispered, and he reached out and squeezed her hand. He hadn't even realized his claws were out until she looked down, her eyes wide.

"Sorry," he grumbled as they ducked under another fallen pillar.

"No, don't be. You didn't scream at the sight of my snakes. I'm not going to do so at your claws."

He held her hand and pulled her through the damaged house. Soon, they were outside, hidden behind a tree, both coughing up smoke and whatever else had gotten into their lungs.

They were paranormals and would survive this, but Poppy was far younger, and therefore would take longer to heal.

Jonah looked at the wound on her head, grateful that the bleeding had stopped, but he still ran his hands over her body to make sure she was okay. Her snakes didn't hiss at him, they just stared at him curiously.

If they were in any other situation, he might have quirked a smile or tried to reach out to say hello to introduce himself. That would come later. For now, he needed to keep them alive.

"I'm okay," she whispered, and he really wished that were true. But there wasn't a lot of time to ask and make sure.

The scent of gorgon intensified, and he knew they were out of time. Suddenly, they were on them, all three of them, and two extra little buddies. The gorgons had their snakes out, but they weren't as strong as Poppy's. They weren't Medusas, so he might be safe from turning to stone as long as he didn't let them focus for too long.

Poppy threw herself in front of him and screamed. "You know the laws. You do not use your powers within the human realm."

"Yet you have your snakes out, your glamour gone. Maybe you're just as weak as the rest of the world thinks you are," one of the gorgons spat. Blood covered him, and he was limping, but he had caught up to them. Had hunted them.

These gorgons would die. By Jonah's teeth and claws if he had any say in it.

"Will they hurt me?" he whispered, so low that he knew the gorgons wouldn't be able to hear him, even with how close they were.

"They're of lower rank and power. They can't actually use their hair like a Medusa can. It's only for show."

"Truly?" he asked, surprised.

"We don't speak of it outside the realm."

The closest gorgon must have heard the last part because he snarled. "You dare defy our laws? You're a murderer, a slayer of innocents, and now you're telling our secrets to an animal?"

"And that is enough of being called an animal," Jonah growled. And then they moved. He trusted Poppy, maybe not enough to defend herself because she didn't know how—something that would change. However, he trusted her because, deep down, he knew that she wanted him to survive just like she wanted to survive.

He moved then, the soldier deep inside clawing at him, ready to fight for what was right, just, and *his*.

Five gorgons were on him at once, seemingly ignoring Poppy. Did they want her dead, or just incapacitated so they could bring her back to the queen? He wasn't sure, and he wasn't going to find out.

He slammed his fists into one of their jaws, and the gorgon spat blood. His snakes bit at Jonah's hand, and he really hoped the damn fuckers weren't poisonous. Venom wasn't something he needed to deal with at the moment.

Another gorgon came at him with a knife, trying to slice him from behind, and Jonah ducked, spun, twisted the first gorgon's arm behind his back and used him as a shield.

The gorgon that had been coming at him stabbed his friend, and they both growled, shocked, before falling into a heap as Jonah kicked them both from behind so they were on the ground in a blink. Jonah could move fast, even with just one leg. Not that anyone knew exactly what was beneath the leg of his jeans. They didn't know that if they took out his prosthesis, they might have an advantage. He had been fighting with the fake limb for nearly as long as he'd been at war when he was whole.

He knew what he was doing.

The end of his stump hurt as he pressed all his weight onto the metal and other materials that made up his prosthesis, but he ignored the bite.

Because he needed to fight.

He leapt away from the two as they clawed at one another, trying to stanch the bleeding, still growling at him. He ignored them. At least, for the moment.

Three others came at him, one with a knife, the other two with their fists. And Poppy was there at his side, her hands outstretched, her snakes coiling and hissing around her head.

"Stay back," Jonah ordered.

"You don't get to do this alone."

And then she opened her eyes, and the first gorgon in front of her spat, screaming. Stone slid up his calves, his knees, his hips. He clawed at it, screaming as blood seeped from his eyes, his nose, his mouth. The stone crept up his chest, and then down his shoulders to his fingertips, wrapping around his neck as if a vise. The snakes hissed, growled like they were shifters rather than snakes, and they spat at him, but then they were all stone. Dead.

Poppy shook at his side, her body swaying. He grabbed her, holding her close as she closed her eyes, sweat pouring from her.

It must have taken such strength to do that, even as she had more power than a normal gorgon. He didn't want to think about what would happen if another gorgon tried to do what she had just done. But she had been beautiful, so strong, courageous. He wasn't going to let the pain that he knew she had to be feeling from doing that to one of her own be in vain.

The last two gorgons came at them, and Jonah wasn't playing anymore. He sliced out, twisted, jabbed again, tucking Poppy behind him, thankful that she could at least still stand. His jaguar was out in full force, taking over but still letting him stay in human form. Poppy shook against him, her eyes still closed, and he was glad for that. He didn't want her to use any more strength, didn't want her to harm her soul any more than she already had by having to kill. He knew she didn't like it, but it wasn't like he did either. However, this was a necessary means to an end, something he was used to. He had been a soldier for so long that he had forgotten what it felt like to not have those scars on his soul.

He slashed out, one strike to the jugular, a twist of the

neck, and then there was nothing else. No more screams, no more sounds of fighting. Just the spark and crackle of fire behind them as the house burned. There were sounds of humans outside his home, sirens, but the warding he'd put on the place would keep it safe for a few more minutes. Not long enough to stay safe for long, however.

Jonah looked at the carnage and knew they'd have to clean this up soon. Perhaps not the two of them, though. Not when others could come after him and Poppy. One gorgon stood as stone, death within marble. The others were on the ground, blood pooling, death taking them.

"We need to get out of here," he growled, knowing that even though the battle had taken no time at all, it had taken long enough that the authorities would be on their way any minute.

"Where do we go?"

He took out his phone, grateful that it had survived everything that had just happened, and dialed Malik.

"We're on our way," Malik growled, and Jonah's eyes widened before it hit him.

"The wards?"

"We felt them go off, but we're still a couple of minutes out."

"I need to get Poppy safe."

"Poppy? Are you okay?"

"We'll be fine. One's stone, and there are four bodies, and my home is on fire."

"Dante's close, as well. He's going to be there to take care of any authorities. We'll glamour what we have to." A pause. "Wait, stone?"

"They're gorgons. They're after Poppy." Jonah paused. "She's my mate, Malik."

Poppy let out a little gasp, and he shook his head. He would explain Malik and everyone else later. They didn't have enough time now.

"Well, damn." He could hear someone else whispering, but then Malik was back on the phone. "Go to the place on Fifth. It's protected behind wards, and you'll be safe from the other gorgons. And then you're going to tell me exactly what's going on."

That was an order from an Alpha, not just a friend, but Jonah understood. "Yes. Of course. Just make sure the humans don't find out. We weren't exactly quiet."

"We never are when we're protecting our mates. I'm glad for you, Jonah."

Jonah couldn't say anything because he had no idea what to feel. Adrenaline coursed through his system, so he just cleared his throat and said, "thank you," before hanging up.

"There's another safe house. This one's an *actual* safe house rather than a home. It's hidden deeper beneath wards and is harder to get to."

"Was that the man from the bar earlier?"

"Yes, my friend and Alpha. They're on their way. We'll be safe."

"You said I was your mate."

"I'm staring at your snakes right now, and they're not killing me, I am not stone. I *am* your mate. We can discuss exactly what that means later, but first, we need to be safe."

"Okay, you're right. It's just a lot to take in all at once."

"Yeah, I get that."

And then he tugged at her hand, and they were off again.

They ran through the alleys, and while he probably could have stolen a car or something to get them there faster, he didn't want to risk it. The humans had no part in this. He didn't want them to have to deal with a stolen vehicle or motorcycle if he took one.

They kept going, even as Poppy lagged behind him. She had to be exhausted, using that much power to turn another gorgon to stone, and she had said that she was tired before the battle. He could pick her up and carry her, but then his hands wouldn't be free to fight if needed.

By the time they got to Malik's place, he knew Poppy wouldn't be able to see it, but he could. He was Pack. He could sense the home behind the wards. So, he sliced his hand using his claw, even as Poppy gasped beside him. Then he slid his palm along the wards, creating a doorway. He pulled Poppy through as he closed the opening behind them.

"That was...I've never seen that kind of magic."

"It's Pack magic. Others have it, too. Do the gorgons?"

She shook her head. "The gorgons don't have much. They're so secretive that they don't evolve in powers and magic or align in treaties with others. They keep trying to find new Medusas so they can replenish their powers, but we're dying out. Centuries of forgetting the rest of the world. We're dying."

"You're not dying today."

"I feel like I just might."

Alarmed, he moved forward. "What is it?"

"You're not supposed to turn another gorgon to stone. It hurts, takes more out of you. She slid her hand over her hair, now under full glamour. "My snakes are sleeping. They're exhausted, too. They'll be fine, but we need to rest."

"Then that's what we'll do."

He pulled her inside, locked the doors behind them, and checked the security system. Magic and technology didn't always work together, but in their safe houses, they had found a way. Malik was a genius at protecting what was his.

"Thank you," she whispered. "Thank you for saving me. I hate that I couldn't save myself."

His gaze was on her, his jaguar rising to the surface

again. She didn't move back, though, and he was grateful for that. "You did everything you could, and you saved me. I was able to do what I did because you were there. I wasn't alone, and you fought. I can teach you self-defense. I can teach you how to use more than your powers. And you'll learn. But don't negate the power that you have."

"You want to teach me?"

"Of course, I do. You're my mate." And before he could stop himself, his hands were on her face, her silver eyes wide, and his mouth was on hers. Consequences be damned.

CHAPTER 4

Poppy's body shook, but it had nothing to do with the escape, the bombing, the fights, or the other gorgons. No, it had everything to do with the man in front of her, the jaguar who held her close, his hands on her face, and his mouth on hers.

She shuddered in his touch, wanting more, craving him. She didn't have an animal inside her, didn't have a beast clawing its way through her in order to escape. She *was* that beast. She was a Medusa, and the magic within her pulsated, arcing out of her so it could wrap around the man in front of her.

Her glamour fell, and she heard her snakes hissing, moving around her head as they stared at Jonah. She pulled away, gasping. She *never* lost control like this. She could have hurt him or someone else just then. If they had been in public? No, she didn't want to think of what could have happened. She'd have to remember that part of her control, make it rote.

Jonah looked at her snakes and laughed. "I've never kissed a Medusa before, should I introduce myself to them, as well?"

"Are you making fun of me?"

He shook his head. "I'm not making fun of you at all. I don't know the proper etiquette, just like I wouldn't know the proper etiquette for kissing a dragon."

"So, you and Dante never kissed?"

Jonah threw back his head and laughed. He was beautiful when he did that. "First, pretty sure that dragon could kill me with one single bite. Second, his mates could do far worse."

"That *is* true. As for my snakes, no, they do not have names, but they are mine." She slid her hands through them, and they coiled around her. "They're not pure reptilian. They're a part of me. It's hard to explain. They feel what I feel, even though they do have personalities of their own."

"So, you don't have like a sled of puppies on your head, as Penelope would say." He said it softly, and it made her smile. Apparently, he knew she was nervous. She'd spoken of her snakes before. They were part of her, but she'd been forced to hide them even within the gorgon realm. It was hard to let go of those secrets, even to a man that she knew deep down would never betray her.

She smiled, though, thinking of baby Penelope. "No, I don't. No sleds here. I haven't named them truly. Others have, but mine are just a part of me. They haven't wanted names yet, if that makes sense." She paused. "But I think they like you."

He studied her snakes, his jaguar in his eyes. "The one on the right coiled around my wrist when you were passed out after the attack."

"I figured. That one likes to wrap around wrists and other things...mostly because it can strangle."

He arched a brow, but there was still laughter in his eyes. "That's good to know."

"They're a part of me, and I can put the glamour back up." She ran her hand over her snakes, and they slithered along her palm.

"You don't need to wear a glamour if you don't want to."

"Maybe not, but they might be in the way." She caressed her snakes, mostly to make sure they knew they weren't in trouble, even if they would have been able to feel it from her directly. Then she turned her glamour back on so she was only skin, and hair, and nerves.

"What are we doing?" she whispered after a moment of silence. Not awkward, but filled with *moments*. Anticipation.

"Living." A simple answer that was anything but simple.

"I don't know what to feel. I've never felt like this before in my life."

"I don't think you were supposed to. I'm your one and only."

"I don't even know you."

"You could. Here." He rubbed his fist over his heart.

"If we do this, we'll be bonded for eternity. There's no going back," Poppy said, swallowing hard.

"And I know we should take time and not rush into it. I know we should figure out exactly who we are, but I want to know more. I want this. And I know it's fate pushing at us, and it makes no sense, but I'm going to protect you till the end of my days."

"You don't even know me," Poppy said, laughing.

"I would protect you even if you weren't my mate. Because I protect the innocent."

She shook her head. "I'm not innocent."

"You are. But it'll take more than my words to make you believe that. Until then...we wait. We wait to bond. We figure out who we are, but first, we need to protect you."

She let out a shaky breath, needing to do something but unsure what to say. "Will you teach me how to fight?"

Jonah nodded. "First, let's teach you how to punch. Do not tuck your thumb in."

"I thought that was the best way to do it," she said, looking down at her fist.

"Like I said, that's the best way to break your thumb."

"Oh."

He slid behind her, and she sucked in a breath, the heat of him almost too much.

"This might be a bad idea," she whispered, but he didn't say anything. Instead, the growl in his chest reverberated through her.

She could feel her snakes quivering above her head, and she knew they wanted this as much as she did. More like they wanted emotion, and she was the one who gave it to them. In a weird Medusa way, but that was who she was.

"Okay, how do I punch?"

He was right next to her ear. "You have to move your body with it, not just your arm."

"Show me."

It wasn't a question, but thankfully, he did. He moved with her, showing her the motion, and she did her best not to tuck her thumb into her fist.

He had one hand on her hip, his front pressed firmly to her back. She could feel the long, thick ridge of his erection, and she swallowed hard.

He moved away then, and she turned in his arms, even as she let out a shaky breath. "We're not going to bond tonight," he whispered.

"Is that a euphemism?" she asked, and he laughed.

"We're not going to have sex. We're not going to bond. We're going to get to know each other. We're going to stay safe behind these wards."

She couldn't focus, but she knew it was the right decision. "Who are you, Jonah? Other than the man from the bar that saved my life more than once tonight."

"I'm a jaguar, a soldier, and, if we dive into fate, I could be your mate."

"And you're not going to tell me? The stories."

He looked down at his hands. "I want to. I will."

"It's a little heavy, though, right? I mean, I told you mine, but that was because we were on the run from parts of my past. We could take a minute before we talk about yours."

"We can. But I want to tell you. I haven't told many people. Malik knows, but no one else."

"Why is that?"

"Because it's my past. But my past has to do with my present somewhat." He leaned down, and she frowned as he pulled up his pant leg.

She saw the metal there, and her eyes widened.

"You've been fighting all night. Are you hurting?"

Jonah nodded. "Yes, I should probably rest it for a bit. I've been fighting on some form of prosthesis for half my life at this point. You think I'd be used to it."

"I didn't realize that shifters could lose limbs." She

closed her eyes and groaned. "Don't comment on that. That's a horrible thing to say."

Jonah took her hand and led her to the couch. He sat down, and she did the same. She hoped she wasn't going to say the wrong thing.

"I've been intrusive. I'll stop."

"No, you're not. When I'm not wearing shorts, it's hard for me to bring up the fact that I lost my leg in battle."

"Oh."

"It doesn't hurt anymore. It's been long enough that the scar tissue feels like just normal skin and muscle at this point. But thanks to some magic that went against nature, I was unable to grow my leg back the way a normal shifter would."

"I'm sorry."

"I am, too. However, I learned how to fight with one leg—or three if I'm in my animal form. I'm still a good soldier, and I can still protect Penelope."

Poppy shot up to her feet. "Penelope. Shouldn't you be there? Protecting her? We need to go. Or you can go, and I can stay right here for you, but you need to get back to the realm, don't you?"

"I do." He held out his hand, and she looked down at it, swallowing hard. We can both sit down, Poppy."

She did.

"I've been texting with Malik, Penelope is fine. She's with her mother and her guards."

"How many? Doesn't she need like a battalion to keep her safe?"

"It's good that you're worried for her, it means you're a protector just like I am. There are seven guards with her right now."

The way he said it made her think. "How many guards when it's just you?"

"There is no need for other guards when I'm there." He looked smug, yet still serious.

"I see. Full of yourself, aren't you?"

Jonah smiled, and she did, as well. "Sometimes, others are around, but it's mostly just me and Penelope and her mother and father. Right now, we're on high alert because of the gorgons after you."

"I don't want anyone else to get hurt because of me."

"I said it was the *gorgons* after you, not you who was the issue. We will figure this out, and Penelope is safe in her bed in the lion realm."

She wanted to ask him why it was the lion realm, why it wasn't anywhere else. But she didn't. She didn't want to ask about him being a jaguar yet. Instead, she tried to change the subject just a little.

"Will you show me what you look like as a jaguar?" she asked, her voice soft. "After all, you've seen me in my full Medusa form. You've seen me turn someone to stone. I've always wanted to know what a jaguar looks like."

"I can do that." He paused. "I'm going to have to get naked to shift, though. I don't have a change of clothes here, so I can't shred these, and it's not that easy to shift while still attached to my prosthesis."

"Oh, could you do it on the other side of the couch or something?" She knew she blushed, and he laughed.

"Yes, that would probably be a good thing. Getting naked in front of you is one thing, getting naked in front of you and not being able to touch you? That's going to be a little difficult."

"We hardly even know each other, Jonah."

"Exactly. But the mating urge is riding us: your Medusa, my jaguar. We can hold it off. We're strong enough. But I'll still show you my cat."

He pulled off his shirt then, and Poppy swallowed her tongue. He was all muscle, every ridge of his eight-pack defined, every hard line of his chest. He had that V that went down below the waistband of his jeans, and she swallowed hard, trying to catch her breath.

"Wow."

"Thanks," Jonah said, winking. And then he stood up, and she watched his back as he moved, each muscle perfect, strong. A warrior's form.

She wanted to learn to fight like him. Didn't want to have to rely on anyone else.

But somewhere deep down inside, she knew she could rely on him.

And that should worry her, but the magical aspects of her nature told her that she didn't need to be concerned.

He crouched down behind the couch, and she heard some rustling, and then there was the sound of skin against skin, and then fur against fur, and then a jaguar walked around the side of the sofa. She stood up, her eyes wide, her hand over her mouth.

"You're beautiful," she whispered. And he was.

He was a golden yellow with dark black and brown spots all over him. He was muscular, his head large, his ears twitching.

He had a long tail that helped him with balance, and she could tell that he used it differently than many jaguars might. It helped offset the fact that he didn't have a back leg. He walked with a regality that spoke of royalty, rather than a soldier as he'd called himself.

She didn't know his story, but she hoped one day he would tell her. She swore Jonah preened.

"Am I allowed to touch you? Pet you? Would that be weird?"

This time, she *knew* the jaguar rolled his eyes. In answer to her question, he butted her palm with his head. She sank her fingers into the soft fur and smiled. "You're so soft."

She slid her hand down his body and over his tail,

even as it coiled around her wrist, the same as her snake did.

As if knowing that she was thinking about them, they undid her glamour and hissed.

She knelt in front of Jonah so her snakes could look at the jaguar in front of them, and she swore she could feel them purr right along with the big cat.

It was so odd, so different. Gorgons and Medusas were usually stuck in their own realm, not able to mix amongst the humans, other than when she was younger, and her parents let her go to school in the human realm for college.

It had been a mistake, she had killed Alex, but she had learned so much, too. And now, she was learning even more.

She let her hand slide over his body again, but then he tensed, a little growl sliding from his throat.

He was in front of her in an instant, and she whirled towards the front door. A man didn't walk in. Instead, a majestic lion prowled through, its mane thick and wonderful. He stalked proudly into the room, two guards having opened the door for him.

She knew who this was without even having to ask.

This was Malik. Alpha, king.

And Jonah's best friend and boss.

"Wow," she whispered. Jonah narrowed his eyes at her before turning back to Malik.

Jonah let out a rumble, and then Malik did the same, except Malik's seemed to shake the whole house.

Jonah once again narrowed his eyes at her as if he knew what she was thinking, and then he padded behind the couch again. She saw him stride to the back of the house, clothes tucked neatly into his mouth. One of the other lions followed with Jonah's prosthesis.

She looked back at Malik, who she had a feeling was laughing at her. One of the guards slid clothes into his mouth, and Malik padded off right behind Jonah.

Well, this was an interesting way to spend the evening.

The guys came out together, both tugging their shirts over their heads as they walked in, jeans undone, bare feet slapping on the hardwood.

She had known that Malik was gorgeous, but damn, seeing him standing next to Jonah?

It was a feast for the eyes.

And she was suddenly very hungry.

Jonah's brows rose, as Malik's eyes filled with laughter. She wanted to bury her face in her hands. Instead, she double-checked that her glamour had been put back into place as soon as the door opened.

She didn't want to turn anyone to stone, especially not people Jonah loved. Particularly not the king.

"Poppy, this is Malik, my Alpha."

"And friend," Malik said. "I would reach out to shake

your hand, but in the throes of the mating urge, Jonah would probably bite my arm off."

Really? She shouldn't feel delighted at that. "Hi, I'm Poppy."

"It's good to finally meet you."

"Did you get to the house?" Jonah asked, coming to Poppy's side.

He slid his arm around her, almost a claim, but more likely just because he wanted to touch. And she didn't mind.

"We were at the house. The whole thing's lost, Jonah."

Jonah let out a growl, and Poppy reached around to pat his chest with her hand. "I'm sorry."

"You do not get to apologize for them again," Jonah growled. "The place wasn't my home, and I'll rebuild or find something else. My home's in the lion realm."

She didn't have a home, so she understood not having connections, but she still blamed herself.

"I need to go back to my mate and child, but I'm going to leave some of the lions to guard and protect you and Poppy."

"Thank you very much, Alpha," she whispered, feeling as though she'd walked into a dream.

"Call me Malik."

"Sorry, I'm not really good at the rules of etiquette with other realms. I was never taught."

"You have time to learn. You can always call me Malik.

You're Jonah's, therefore, you're family. Jonah, stay here as long as you need to. If you have to come to the realm to stay safe, do that, but I have a feeling that you'll want to take care of it here."

"I'm not leading the gorgons to the lions."

"No, we can't do that," Poppy added quickly.

"I figured as much. Take care of it quickly, and then come home." Malik looked at her. "If the lion realm is where you choose to stay." She didn't know if he was talking to her or Jonah, but this wasn't the time to dwell on it.

"We'll help you however you need," Malik said.

"It's the queen though, she wants me dead."

"Do you deserve death?"

Poppy opened her mouth, but Jonah was the one who answered. "No, they're the ones that caused this, and now they want her head for their own mistakes."

She swallowed hard. "That might technically be true, but it's not the whole story."

"It's enough of it. So, we're going to figure it out," Jonah put in. "Thank you, Malik. You didn't have to come here in person."

"If I didn't, a certain lion cub would have tried to scratch my face off with her tiny little claws. Fix this, the both of you. We will have your back if you need it. And you know Dante is already here to help."

"Dante?" Poppy asked.

"That dragon considers you part of his hoard." Malik rolled his eyes.

"Really?" Poppy asked.

"Yes, you're one of us now," Jonah said.

"Seriously, it's like a cult."

"It's not that bad," Malik said. "You won't be alone in this. My men will be here for you, and any of the seven and their mates will be here, as well. There's a lot of us here that can help. Protect yourselves, and then come home when you're ready. But I have a feeling that you two have more to talk about than just a fight to the death."

And with that, Malik nodded and walked out, his guards following. She could sense other lions near, but only just. She was learning that part of her powers.

Jonah had his hand on her hip as the others left, and she turned in his hold, swallowing hard.

"They'll help you, no matter what. They don't even know me."

"They don't have to know you. You have the chance to be mine, so of course, they're going to help. That's who they are. That's who *we* are. We protect those in our circle, we safeguard the innocents."

"I already told you, I'm not innocent."

"You *are*, Poppy." He kissed her again, and she swallowed her words, just wanting his taste, wanting *him*.

"I should tell you more about me, and then this will make more sense," he said as he pulled away.

"How?"

"Because Malik was there for me when no one else was, and I want it to make sense for you. Why I am how I am."

And so, she let him lead her to the couch, and he squeezed her hand.

"You told me your secrets, so maybe now I should tell you a few of mine."

She leaned closer and wondered if this was her next path set by fate. If somehow, amongst the darkness, in between the running, she had run smack into her destiny.

CHAPTER 5

Jonah hadn't told his story. Ever. Malik had gleaned it, had been part of the end of it, the resolution, but Jonah had never gone through it all step by step, day by day for anyone before. But he would. For this woman that he hardly knew but felt as if he had known his entire existence, he would. Is that what soul mates did? Is that what true halves did in this world of supernaturals and paranormals?

He hadn't seen it happen with Eliana and Malik, but their mating had been far different than anyone else's. After all, she hadn't been a paranormal when they met. The way the lightning worked, meant that she wouldn't have changed until she was bonded to her mate. And a lion shifter couldn't mate to a human, so they were in a constant state of flux until Malik could mark her as his.

So, no, while their connection might have always been there, it wasn't like this. At least, he didn't think. Maybe one day he would ask, but would that be too personal? Did he have a right to ask?

"What are you thinking?" Poppy asked, her hands at her sides.

He knew he needed to tell her, and he would. He just needed to figure out exactly where to start.

"I'm not as old as many of my friends, but I've been through a few wars."

"You mentioned that. You call yourself a soldier. And I can see some of what you've lost in the turmoil."

He shook his head. "My physical scars and losses are only part of it." He reached out and ran his knuckle down her cheek. She leaned into his touch, and he held back a smile. He wasn't even sure she realized she'd done it.

As soon as she did, her eyes widened, and she leaned back again, a small smile playing on her lips. "Sorry."

"Don't be sorry," he whispered. "I've been a soldier my whole life," he continued. "I was born into the jaguars, and I fought for them. I grew up in the rankings, just like most jaguars my age. I was not of royal stock, but I wasn't a commoner either. So, I went into our military, just like all boys and girls of my age and rank did."

"It was required?"

He shook his head. "More like there wasn't much else to do. I didn't have land or a real income, and the best way for me to make sure I could take care of my family was to join the military."

"Your family."

It wasn't a question, but he still answered.

"My mother and my two sisters." He knew his voice was a little soft, but he held back anything that could potentially make him break. It was hard to think about them. But he was doing his best to live on and honor their memory.

"My father died in battle when my mother was pregnant with my youngest sister. We were fighting against other jaguar clans at the time. While some Packs and clans around the supernatural world have been at peace for long enough that there aren't as many wars, the jaguars have never really been able to settle down. They don't like to be in groupings, but they also can't be by themselves for too long. Meaning, there's constant infighting and blood battles. It doesn't help that, during the time of the war where I lost so much, most children didn't make it past the age of two."

Her eyes widened. "What?"

This was where it got complicated. "Long ago, a wizard family cast a curse. A wizard who had married into one of the jaguar families." This wasn't a story he liked to tell. It wasn't something the jaguars liked to think about.

The fact that one of his friends was a wizard, meant

that Jonah had been forced to deal with the repercussions of knowing and trusting someone such as he. But it wasn't Levi's fault that he had been born a wizard, just like it wasn't Jonah's fault that he had been born a jaguar. He wasn't even sure Levi understood what had happened all those years ago. Not everyone did, and not everyone needed to.

"A wizard family that was mated in to the jaguar clan put a curse on all children so they had to fight for survival."

"They cursed children?" Poppy asked. Her snakes popped out, hissing.

He nodded and slid his hand over a snake on the right, the one that liked to coil. It licked at his finger, and he raised a brow.

She blushed under the darkness of her skin, and quickly put her glamour back on.

"Sorry. I usually have much better control. You just bring the lack of it out of me sometimes. It's a little dangerous."

"You've only had trouble when we're alone."

"Maybe. But it's still a little embarrassing."

"Well, then we'll just have to make sure it doesn't happen around others."

"Good. Now, back to your story. Sorry."

"Don't be sorry. It's given me a little bit of time to figure out what I need to say next."

He raked a hand through his hair. "The curse was broken later when the wizard family died out, but the resentment is still strong within the jaguar clans. I'm friends with a wizard now. He's one of Dante's friends, as well. I don't have the anger like some do, but it's taken time. The curses that came from the wizards meant that children past the age of two had to be strong enough to survive any ailment that came at them. During that time, many illnesses came all at once to test the child. My family was strong enough, but only barely. My youngest sister will always be frail because of what she suffered."

"That's horrible." Tears filled Poppy's silver eyes, and he wiped away the single drop that fell down her cheek.

"It is. One of the worst curses I've ever heard of, and yet we don't let anyone outside of the realm know what happened to us in the past. They can't know we were ever weak." He still wasn't sure he agreed with that, but it wasn't his place. Not anymore. He was of the lions now.

"So, you fought them? This clan that did this?"

"We all did. It was one of the worst battles and wars in the history of our histories. And one that isn't written down in the books. Because if it were, the atrocities that came from both sides would destroy the realm in every way possible. Its foundation shaken to the core."

"What happened?" she whispered.

"We went against the wizard and their clan, and we lost." Jonah looked down at his hands, fisting them in front of him on his lap. "We lost. They used magic along with teeth and claws, and I lost my leg in the process. It was ripped from me, and the magic in the air sealed the wound shut. The limb couldn't grow back. I couldn't heal completely. I was lucky I didn't die like so many others did."

"Jonah. I…I'm so sorry."

He nodded, not knowing how to take the comfort she offered. He'd been closed-off for so long, other than with the family he'd chosen to protect, that he wasn't good at this. "I barely survived. A quick-thinking healer saved my life. Yet they weren't able to save the lives of those closest to me."

She froze. "What do you mean?"

He swallowed hard as bile filled his throat. "While some of our enemies fought us on the battlefield, others went to our homes, our villages, and they burned them to the ground. Our strongest fighters were on the battlefield, and we left some behind to protect the innocent, but it wasn't enough." He let out a shuddering breath. "My mother and my sisters were murdered, as were my wife and my unborn child."

Pain seared him at the memory, and his hands shook. Poppy's glamour was once again gone, her silver eyes wide.

"Your wife? Your…child?"

"Everyone's gone. We were newly married, but not

mated." He was firm in his voice, hoping she would understand. "She was not my other half, not my mate like what you could be. But she was my *wife,* and I loved her. And I was going to be a father." His voice cracked.

"My God, Jonah...how could they do that? How could they take her from you?"

"I couldn't understand then, and I still don't. The jaguars who fought alongside me and survived took out the other clan. I wasn't even able to avenge their deaths until I could be healed. And by then, the others had already taken care of it for me. We won the war eventually, but it took so much that I'm not even sure it counts for anything."

"Jonah, I'm so sorry." Her hands were on his face then, slowly rubbing his temples, moving down his cheeks. No tears fell—he didn't cry anymore. He didn't need to. He had already grieved, wept, and raged. He was whole, but just barely. He wasn't sure what he had left for Poppy, as he'd always thought he'd be alone forever. However, an instant recognition of souls had changed that.

"I have a family now. One I've made, not one of blood."

"The lions," she said, her tone understanding."

"Malik and Eliana and Penelope. They're my family now, they're the ones that helped to save me."

"I'm so sorry you went through that. It's not fair that our worlds have to be so violent, so evil. And it doesn't seem like I can find peace regardless of where I go. There's so much heartache, so much pain."

"There is. I left the jaguars and went to the lions because of Malik. I went back to the jaguars when I had nothing left, and then met Malik centuries later during *another* war. He was helping the jaguars as a young cub on the brink of adulthood during his roam—a time when most cats leave their realms to search and gain an understanding for the meaning of time and life. I never had that, as I was too busy fighting in wars. Malik, however, survived the battles. And then I was able to, too. He was *so* young, not even a full adult yet at the time. I was far older than him."

"So, you were more like a father?" She understood so much for a woman who had been on the run and hidden for so long.

"A little. The lions took me in, and I worked for them in other ways than on a battlefield. Now, I'm more part of the family than I was before. And I do not mind that at all." He paused. "I think that, no matter what realm you find yourself in, that *any of us* find ourselves in, we have to look for the goodness, for that laughing child or the man that saves another. For the woman who does the same. I thought I lost everything on that battlefield, and not just a part of myself. Everything. But I only had to look up and wander until I met Malik. And now, I've met you."

She was silent for long enough that he was afraid he'd said too much. His history was awash in blood and heartache, and he didn't know how to change who he was. He wasn't sure he could.

Or if he wanted to.

"What are we doing, Jonah?"

He shook his head. "Getting to know one another. I don't want to rush this. I've never rushed anything in my life. And I'm not about to start now with this."

"Good, because I feel like I'm in a dream, and I don't want to feel like that when I take the next steps."

"Deal," he whispered. He was just about to lower his head when his jaguar perked up, and he growled.

"We aren't alone," he whispered.

"No, you really aren't," a woman with dark hair and a cruel smile said from the doorway. Blood saturated the bottom of her dress and sleeves, and she just licked her lips. "I was going to use my powers like you did, dear traitor, but I know the rules of the lands. One does not turn one to stone when you're outside of the realm."

Jonah was on his feet in an instant, growling, his claws out. "Queen Mina, I presume?"

"Oh, it seems the traitor does tell tales. You killed my men, animal. The others are injured, and I'm not happy about my losses." She snapped her fingers, and two other women that looked just like the queen walked in behind her. "Madeleine, Marci. You see? I told you we had to do this ourselves."

"Did you kill everyone outside?" Jonah asked, seething. If those men and women outside had died because of him, he would never forgive himself. And he'd be damned if he let Poppy blame herself. He searched for their pulses and scents while keeping his attention on the women in front of him. He held back a sigh of relief at finding them all alive. He didn't know the extent of their injuries, but from the blood on the queen's clothes, it likely wasn't good.

"No, they're just a little hurt. It took a spell or two, and then they didn't even notice that I was ripping them to shreds."

"Spells," Poppy said on a gasp. "You used spells?"

"I'm quite adept at it," one of the sisters said, wiggling her fingers.

"You should know that, dear traitor," Mina added.

"So, you admit it. You used a spell against me." Poppy shook at his side, and he wanted to murder the three women where they stood. However, he couldn't, not when he didn't know what would happen if he did. He'd be damned if Poppy got hurt because of his recklessness.

Mina shrugged. "It doesn't matter if we do. You'll be dead soon, with only Madeleine and Marci to back up your claims."

"And we would never do that," the other sister said.

Jonah didn't know which one it was, and he really didn't care. Because they were going to die right then. All of them. Even if it caused an inter-realm incident. He didn't care.

"You took everything," Poppy whispered. "And yet, you still want more? Why?"

"Because you don't deserve to live," the queen spat. "Because you are an abomination. A Medusa with too much power."

"I always knew you were jealous of me, but I didn't know you were stupid."

Jonah's brows rose.

"How dare you?" the queen screamed.

"You know that Medusas are needed to keep the realm healthy. Just their presence brings the realm more power and stability. Something we have long lacked over the years with so much infighting and segregation. And then you did that? Apparently, you're not strong enough to handle it on your own. You're the queen, but you aren't a Medusa. You're a gorgon."

"You're a gorgon, too," the queen snarled.

"I am. And I have always been proud of it, I was always proud of who and what I was, until you made me feel like I was different. Like I wasn't enough. You took everything. You took Alex, you took my family, and you're trying to take the realm. I tried to run, I attempted to keep out of it, but you sent your people after me. Why? What good will my death do?"

"I don't leave stones left unturned. I don't let threads stay unwoven. You are the final piece. Once you're gone, I'll be queen in truth. Nobody can try to take my throne."

Poppy threw up her hands, and Jonah just looked at the queen aghast. "I never wanted your throne. You have killed so many, hurt countless others for something I would never do."

"You don't deserve to be here. You never bowed, never scraped. You weren't the one who was supposed to have the power." Mina took a step forward, and Jonah growled. For an instant, the queen looked scared, and he was glad for that. Just the slight widening of eyes and the tightening of her mouth belayed her fear. Good. She should be scared.

"You were always my princess, your father always my king. The only thing I ever did wrong was exist. And that's not on me. That's on you. Don't make me do something we'll all regret."

"You already did something. After all, you killed that human boy. You don't deserve to live."

"I didn't mean to hurt him, you were the one who drugged me. Spelled me," Poppy said from Jonah's side. He wanted to reach out to console her, but this wasn't the time for that. He could sense the other lions prowling around the house, all six of them. None of them had died, even though the queen and her sisters must've used some form of spell to dampen the sounds earlier. They weren't using it now, and he didn't think that the queen could hear them. No one had died, but he could tell that one or two of the guards were injured by the way their breaths came in labored pants. They were going to help though, if he needed them. There didn't need to be any more bloodshed today. He didn't want that. He wanted Poppy to be free. However, if that meant bloodshed, he'd do what he must.

"You can't actually beat me," Poppy said, her snakes out now. She had let the glamour fall, and he had never seen her look so beautiful. While he hadn't known her for more than a handful of hours, he knew right then and there that this was Poppy at her best. Protective, stunning, and powerful.

He hated that she was going to have to use her powers, though.

"You are nothing," Mina growled out, and Jonah took a step forward.

"You would do well to watch your tongue with my mate."

The queen's eyes widened. "Mate? You mated with an animal?" The queen threw her head back and laughed. "Of course, you did," she said, still laughing. "Of course."

"You really do want to die tonight, don't you?" Poppy asked, coming up to his side. She slid her hand through his, gave his fingers a squeeze, and then let go, knowing that she would need both hands to fight. Or, at least, that's what he hoped. He didn't want her to avoid touching him out of fear.

"Once you're dead, things will go back to normal. And that's all that really matters." And then the queen threw her hands out to the sides, and her snakes writhed around her head.

Jonah closed his eyes, but Poppy just laughed.

"Breaking the rules, are you? But the thing is, you're not a Medusa. You can't turn anyone to stone. You never could, and you're never going to be able to."

Jonah's eyes widened, and he looked over at Poppy.

"She just has her fighting skills and her magic?"

"She used spells to hurt the others, she doesn't have the skills." Poppy laughed then, but there was nothing cruel about it, just weariness. She had been running for so long. She had to be exhausted.

And he was tired of it already.

"You should just go," Poppy said. "I won't hurt you. I'll never come back to the realm. But I'm done. I'm done running."

"And I'm done listening to you." The queen turned to one of her sisters. "Marci, use your magic."

Marci grinned, and there was pure darkness in her eyes. She began to whisper something, but Poppy threw herself in front of Jonah before she could finish.

"Stop doing that," he growled.

"Let me fix this," she muttered, but then there was a commotion. Madeleine pushed Mina out of the way and threw herself on top of Marci.

The queen looked stunned, just like Poppy and Jonah did, and he was confused at what the hell had just happened.

"What do you think you're doing?" Mina asked.

"No, no more magic. It was eating your soul, can't you see that?" Madeleine asked. She scrambled to her feet, and Marci stood up with her, shaking.

"Stop it. Just because you're too weak to do anything, doesn't mean you have the right to hurt us."

"I am not weak," Madeleine said, her voice shaking. And then she let the glamour fall, and Poppy cursed.

"Close your eyes, Jonah," she whispered.

He did so, confused. He trusted her, though, so he didn't even hesitate. "What the hell is going on?" he asked.

"Madeleine, she's a Medusa," Poppy whispered.

"No!" Mina growled out.

"I'm done hiding. You killed our father. And you're going to kill Poppy. I'm done." And then Madeleine screamed.

CHAPTER 6

Poppy staggered back, the revelations far too much for her to even breathe just then. Madeleine was a Medusa?

How did she *not* know? How had nobody known?

Of course, Mina and Marci had always made sure to push Madeleine down, to hide her as the youngest sister, the one that didn't matter. They had been just as cruel to her as they had been with Poppy her entire life.

She had missed the fact that Madeleine was in pain just like she was. That she had to hide just like Poppy did.

"You think you can hurt us?" Queen Mina screamed. "You've always been nothing. So what, you think you're a Medusa? I'm sure you just used magic like Marci did. Is that how you did it? Because it can't be true. You couldn't have been a Medusa all this time."

"She has, though," Poppy said, not knowing if it was actually the truth or not. Although, it seemed like it *had* to be.

The queen raised her chin, her eyes narrowed to slits. "What do you know?"

"I know that if there was a magical way to create a Medusa, you would have done it long before this. You would've found a way and killed anybody in your quest to do so. That's why you're here, isn't it?"

"Enough of this," Jonah growled, his eyes were still closed, but his claws were out. He was one second away from shifting to end this, and Poppy didn't blame him. She could sense the others outside, but she wasn't sure that any of the gorgons and the other Medusa in the room could.

In fact, she was pretty sure that these three women were oblivious to the fact that the lions were prowling around, ready to come inside the house at any moment to help.

But Poppy didn't want anyone else to get hurt. Between Marci's magic, Mina's tenacity and cruelty, and Madeleine's Medusa powers, she didn't know if she could keep everyone alive if anyone else joined them.

"You'll die, just like your little friends," Mina spat.

Poppy cursed again, her powers fluctuating as she figured out what to do. Madeleine had her snakes out, her eyes wide, they were a darker silver, almost gray and matte, but they still had some of the Medusa power in them. How had Madeleine hidden that for so long?

Poppy didn't know, and this wasn't the time to find out.

Instead, she let her snakes hiss and shouted, "Stop now, and you can live. I don't want to kill you."

"You're going to die anyway," Mina growled.

"Stay back," Jonah ordered, and Poppy knew that was directed at the lions. With two Medusas in play, they would die just by being in the wrong place, and she didn't want that. She couldn't stand by and let Madeleine die, nor would she let Jonah do all the work for her.

Marci had her arms out, muttering some incantation, but then Jonah was on top of her, his claws slashing. Marci ducked, screamed, and threw a *curse* at Poppy. Poppy ducked out of the way, the death curse that would've killed her missing her by a bare inch. Marci must have had a warlock or someone teach her that curse. Someone had infiltrated the realm like everyone had once feared, but it was Marci who had succumbed to the temptation and hurled death magic.

Jonah growled so loudly the windows shook, and then Marci was done screaming. He snapped her neck in one quick movement, and she fell to the floor, a pile of dusted bones in a long dress.

Poppy's eyes widened.

"You use a curse that takes a life, you're going to lose

your own," Jonah spat. He wasn't looking up, just down towards where Marci's bones were.

So, using magic required a sacrifice, and since Poppy hadn't died, Marci was the one who paid. Jonah just helped that along. But he had to keep his eyes closed, because Madeleine's eyes were still open.

"You're going to hurt someone," Poppy called out, needing Madeleine to stop, to pull her glamour back.

"I can do this," Madeleine rasped, her whole body shaking.

Poppy didn't think she could. Madeleine might be a Medusa, but she was even more untrained than Poppy was. Even more powerless.

"You were always nothing, just like little Poppy. You'll deserve the death that comes for you." Queen Mina held out her hands and grinned.

"You might have bested the witch, but you can't best me. I'm the queen."

"And you have no power. No power over me, and no power over the realm." Poppy let her snakes hiss again, and her eyes widened. She felt her power wash over her.

Mina's mouth gaped as Poppy let the full force of her Medusa out.

Jonah growled, and she knew he was right beside her, she could feel his hands on her hips as if he were trying to help her by giving her some of his own power and strength. She leaned into him. She didn't have to do this alone, even if he couldn't help with this one thing. Because the lions, if able to, would walk right in. They would help even if she was a stranger. Because they were good, and they did what was right. They were not Medusas, they were not what Mina had made their realm. Treacherous.

Mina reached out, her hands outstretched, but under the combined Medusa powers of Madeleine and Poppy, she wasn't enough. The stone slid up her dress, rose to her hips, wound around her chest and her arms, and eventually reached her neck. Mina tried to let out one last final scream, but it wasn't enough. The stone slid around her body, her snakes, *everywhere.*

The queen of the gorgons was gone.

Madeleine fell, her eyes shut, her glamour back on as she passed out, her energy spent. And Poppy just leaned into Jonah, shaking.

"What...? I can't believe..." she whispered, unable to do anything else. Her glamour was quickly back in place as the lions finally came in, ready to fight.

"Jonah?" one of them asked.

"It's over. For now. Be careful with the one that's still breathing, she could still turn you to stone."

"I don't know what to do now," Poppy whispered. The immense relief that she thought would've come from knowing that she could go back to her realm if she wanted, *didn't* come. Nothing did.

She was numb, and she didn't know what to think. But as she leaned into the man, the one who could be her mate, she knew she needed to breathe, needed to think. She just didn't know where to go from here.

"We will take care of this, because you are ours," Jonah began. "And I think, right now? I think we should go see a certain cub. She can help you with anything. Give you a little respite."

Poppy turned in his arms and smiled.

"I can come see your home?" Poppy asked.

"I think you should. And then, when the time comes, we'll figure out what to do next. But you need to rest, Poppy. After all this time? You need to rest."

As she looked down at the tattered remains of what had once been her enemy, the woman who had once tried to take so much from her, she knew Jonah was right. She was ready to go to his home, and maybe if she believed in fate, it could be her home, as well.

EPILOGUE

Months later

Poppy groaned, wanting more, but not sure what to do. Jonah smiled down at her, his lips on her jaw, then her neck.

"It's been months," she whispered.

"Months, I've gotten to know you. Every inch of you. And now you're mine."

"I'll always be yours," she whispered. "Six months? Don't make me wait any longer."

They had waited in the months since the attack. Since her freedom had been found. Because they needed to get to know each other. Although they had each told one another their deepest, darkest secrets the first night they met, Jonah was a man of old deep down in his heart, and had taken the time to court her.

There were flowers and chocolates. There were little notes. There was the soft touch of his fingers on her cheek. The way he played with her hair...and her vipers. There were days that he would just stare at her and smile. Times when she found her favorite book on their bed, waiting for her.

So many little things, tiny glances. So much time where he could be hers and everything that mattered, and she got to know him in more ways than just their deepest and darkest secrets. But in a way that took him straight to her soul.

They were in the lion realm now, and she was learning to fight, learning to be with Jonah.

She would protect baby Penelope and any children that came from her and Jonah's union along the way. Because she wanted to be by his side, even if they were no longer in the realm of their births.

She knew that he would take her to the jaguar realm someday, but he didn't want to go there for himself. So, she would wait, even if it took a century or two.

And she could go back to her original realm to see the gorgons, to see what had come of Madeleine and her new realm. Because Queen Madeleine was a just ruler, one who wanted people to enter their realm and be happy, to find peace. And Poppy knew the gorgons were on their way to a new world. Once Madeleine found her mate, everything would change once again, and the queen would be able to rule in full.

That time would come, and Poppy knew she would help, but it was no longer her home.

Because her home was with Jonah, the jaguar who smiled at her, who helped her protect herself. Who taught her what it meant to be part of something more than who you were when everything was taken away from you.

And now, after months, she was ready to be his.

A bond in truth, a mate forever.

"Are you sure you're ready?" Jonah asked, his voice soft, deep.

"If you don't get inside me right now, I'm going to scream."

Her snakes came out for just an instant, hissed, and then went back under their glamour.

Jonah laughed and then took her mouth hard. "I'm afraid your little vipers are going to bite me if I don't make you an honest woman."

"They're ready for me to be mated. And you need to mate with me right now, mister. Be mine, Jonah. You're already mine in everything but bond. Love me."

"Always, my Poppy. My precious, my mate. Always." And then he slid into her, and she groaned.

He licked up her neck and then kissed her again

before going back to her shoulder, his fangs piercing her flesh in the mating mark. Even as he did, he thrust in and out of her, his cock thick, hard, and pulsating with need. She groaned, wrapping her legs around him, wanting more, needing more.

As the mating mark burned, it sent them into oblivion. She knew this was it, the moment she had been waiting for. He spun them so that he was on his back with her riding him, his hands on her breasts, his fingers pale against the dark brown of her nipples.

She grinned down at him, arching her back just slightly so he could go deeper. And when his thumb moved down to her clit, rubbing that little nub just so, her whole body clenched, and she shook, calling his name as she came.

Jonah gripped her hips and thrust in and out of her, harder, faster, until both of them were shaking. She screamed again, her hands on her breasts as she plucked at her nipples.

He came inside her, deep and hard, fast. The bond between them slid into place, perfect, everlasting. She couldn't do anything, couldn't breathe. It was all she could do not to beg for more.

Then she was on her back, and Jonah was sliding in and out of her, once, twice, and then again.

She held onto him, her hands sliding down his sweat-slick back. His lips were on hers, and she was lost.

She had found her mate, her love, and even though she had been the one on the run, she hadn't known where she would land, let alone that it would be with him.

AFTERWARDS, THEY CLEANED EACH OTHER UP AND THEN got ready to head to work. After all, she still had a job to do. When she wasn't training so she could protect baby Penelope and the others she loved, she was still a bartender. Dante the dragon still needed her until he could find a replacement, and she didn't mind in the least.

She went back behind the bar when they got there, and Jonah went to the large table in the corner where the seven lightning-struck were sitting with their families. It was one of the baby's birthdays, and even though it might feel weird to have a birthday for a child in a bar, it didn't here. It was daylight, and Dante's Circle was open for everybody. Plus, no humans were around. It was just the supernaturals. So, when a baby dragon and a baby bear started wrestling on the floor, nobody thought much of it. Poppy wanted to take a picture and never forget.

When Jonah walked up, baby Penelope in his arms, she just grinned.

"Poppy!" Penelope babbled, her hands outstretched, her little arms waving around.

Poppy reached out and plucked the baby from Jonah's

hip and held her close. She smelled of powder, innocence, and sunshine.

A little baby lion cub, one that she loved with her whole heart. And as she looked over at her mate, she grinned. One day, they would hold their own child, and she couldn't wait. But for now, they could breathe, and she was safe.

She was no longer running from anyone, only to a future she could have with her mate.

They had a child to protect, a future to pave, and as someone called out for another beer, she knew she also had a job to do.

Because Dante's Circle was open to everybody, and those who stayed had a home, a family, and, in her case, a future.

BLOOD'S FIRST KISS

CHAPTER 1

The shark came out of nowhere.

Caly swore, one day, her tombstone would have that exact phrase. She used to be far better at remembering to look over her shoulder when a shark was near. She used to be able to sense them. However, recently, she'd been a little busy, a bit focused and in her head, and she kept missing the fact that, yes, she probably should be aware of her surroundings when she swam underwater.

After all, she was a mermaid. She lived deep down under the sea. She wasn't friends with a flounder or a crab. However, she did have to worry about the aforementioned shark.

She snarled, angling her fin out of the way of some very pointy teeth. It was not a shark shifter, but a regular old hammerhead that wanted a little bite of her. And it wasn't like she could actually hurt the damn thing because she didn't want to hurt an innocent fish.

It was just hungry, and her fin was shiny. Apparently, the taste of mermaid was what was for dinner.

She swam quickly, swishing her fin again as it tried to nibble on her once more. She sighed, tired. "Stop it," she muttered under her breath, bubbles of water and air escaping her lips.

She couldn't actually talk to sharks, or really any sea life under the ocean. Her brother was better at it. Sometimes, she could if she tried. However, right then, the shark clearly wasn't listening to her. It was hungry, and she didn't have a weapon other than her brain to get herself out of this jam.

Considering she hadn't even noticed the shark was upon her until it tried to nibble at her, her brain apparently wasn't doing too well right then either.

"Okay, you asked for it." She shot down to near the bottom of the seafloor, picking up a piece of driftwood that had sunk over time. It was waterlogged, not exactly good enough to do any real damage, but she didn't really want to hurt him. She just wanted to stun him.

She twisted, smashing the shark between the eyes with the piece of wood. Unlike in some monster movies, sharks couldn't swim backwards—though a few shark shifters she knew liked to try. The shark froze, seemed to shake it off, but swam away quickly, hopefully realizing that she was the superior predator.

Not that she really believed that, but at least the shark was gone.

She roamed her hands over her body, making sure she hadn't actually gotten nicked by the shark.

In her mermaid form, she had gills on the sides of her neck, but not webbed fingers like some myths indicated. She wore a shell-shaped bra, mostly because it was easier to swim when she didn't have to deal with flowy shirts underwater. Sometimes, she wore tight shirts with sleeves or other tops, but she'd felt like going Ariel today. Her green and blue tail with its touch of purple shimmered under the light that shone from the nearby underwater house, but she didn't see any blood.

Frankly, she really just wanted to get home, so she was grateful that the attack hadn't been worse. She had papers to pore over, and her brother and his mates were going to be there along with their son. She missed Seth and his family, and she just wanted to feel like she had a family of her own. She hadn't really had much of that recently.

She quickly pushed those melancholic thoughts out of her mind and headed home. She waved at a school of young mermaids and mermen and then gestured at a couple of warriors. They gave her a strange look as if surprised to see her, but she shook it off.

She wasn't supposed to be anywhere, was she? No, she just had to do some research and spend time with her family. Right?

She swam under the large dome that was her home and traversed the tunnels until she came to a pool. There were a few around her house where even humans using magic could find their way into her home. They acted as front doors as well as actual pools in the house. She loved them.

Her head breached the water, and she sucked in oxygen, her lungs now working as a human rather than a mermaid. She levered herself out of the pool and grabbed a towel. She shifted back into her human form and wiggled her toes, grateful that her legs were back. She loved both forms, but sometimes, she just really wanted to stretch her feet, and she couldn't really do that with a tail. She wrapped a towel around her waist, the top half of her suit still on, and then got to her feet.

"What are you doing here?" her brother Seth asked. She turned, screaming.

"It's my home. But you're here. I'm so glad you are. I've missed you, Amara, and Tristan so much." She ran to him and hugged him hard.

"I've missed you too, big sister," Seth said as he lowered himself down to give her a big hug. Her little brother wasn't so little anymore. He was a big guy with a heart of gold, two wonderful mates, and a baby boy.

She was an auntie thanks to him, and he made her so happy.

"Okay, where's the rest of them? I can't wait to hold my nephew." She clapped her hands together and then went to go get her clothes from the bench.

"I'm going to ask you again. Why are you here?" he asked, and she frowned.

"What do you mean? I live here."

"I know you do, darling, but you're not supposed to be here."

"What?"

"Amara is putting Eli down for a nap, but Tristan is at the Conclave meeting. You know, the one you're supposed to be at."

Caly's eyes widened. "Oh, my goddess. How did I forget?"

She ran her hands through her curls and shook out her hair, knowing it was futile to want it to dry since she was going to have to head back into the water now. "How late am I?"

"Well, probably about ten minutes by now. They likely haven't even started yet if the elders are just bumbling on about the good old days of the Conclave where they didn't have to worry about the lower species."

He wasn't wrong about that. "Crap crap crap. Okay, I'm going to have to use a portal to get there. I don't have time to swim to a main one on land that'll use less magic."

"I'm on it. You know you're going to have to be in mermaid form when you're there."

Caly rolled her eyes. "I know. Everything has to be tradition. Even though Dante doesn't have to show up as a dragon. And none of the shifters are in animal form."

"No, but the first mermaids showed up in mer-form during the original Conclave. Therefore, you have to at least start the meeting in your nice little pool on your pedestal.

"I hate it. I literally feel like a fish in an aquarium."

"Well, you are, Calypso."

She stuck out her tongue and then pulled a ruffled shirt on over her swimsuit top. She didn't like the way some of the older Conclave members stared at her boobs when she was in her mermaid form. Just because she liked her curves and the way she looked, didn't mean she needed to be oversexualized by old dudes who would never touch her.

"Amara says we will have dinner for you when you get back with Triston."

"She's doing the cooking, right?" she asked and went up on her toes to kiss her brother.

"You know it. You're bringing a bag with all your work?"

She nodded. "Yep, and it's waterproof. And I also have a pair of pants so I don't have to stay in my mermaid form the whole time.

"You just hate the way they stare."

"True. I love both forms, I don't like others."

"The family motto," Seth said, rolling his eyes.

She punched him in the arm and kissed where she'd hit him, and then went to the portal that Seth had opened for her. She hadn't changed out of her towel yet, so she sat down at the edge of the portal that she would dive into, changed back into her mer-form, and then undid the towel.

"Good luck," Seth said.

"I guess I'll need it."

And then she dove. Magic swirled all around her, and she shimmered, her body shaking. She hated traveling by portal. She would've preferred to go to one of the other sanctioned areas where she didn't have to touch so much magic and have to travel in her mer-form, but she was late because she had forgotten the darn meeting. All for a Conclave she'd once loved being a part of.

The Conclave was older than most of the realms themselves. Each of the realms had their own governing body, their own knights and kings and queens or Pack leaders and Alphas. It depended on the realm and the type of shifter or magical being they were and how they lived. After centuries and millennia of wars and strife and loss, a Conclave had been created.

It was her job to fine-tune the history and the lineage of those within the Conclave, and those of importance to the governing body. So, she knew more history about it than most. However, she wasn't allowed to speak about the majority of it.

Two members of each of the realms met for the Conclave so they could discuss any important business. Namely if there was a war going on or like, at one point, if the seven lightning-struck women—one of which her brother had married—needed to be wiped from the face of the Earth or not.

She had been against that, and had, in fact, wanted to ensure that they stayed safe. Not just because of Seth, because at first, she hadn't even known her brother would be mated to one. No, because it hadn't been their fault that the gods had decided that they needed to change the way the face of the Earth lay.

Since her tenure as a Conclave member, she had dealt with countless wars, ridiculous infighting, and even the sanctions of a new realm. It was a realm of shaded magic that wasn't actually as dark and evil as their name might suggest. She didn't know much about them, but she was learning. Just like she was learning about all the realms. Including the brownies, dragons, bears, and all the others.

It was an exhausting job, but she loved it. Most days.

She found herself in her glass bowl on her pedestal after she slid through the end of the portal. She sucked in some air, trying to be as discreet as possible, but a low chuckle sounded from beside her.

She narrowed her eyes at Reynard, her second, who just shook his head. "Knew you'd forget," he muttered.

She flipped him off. She wasn't a huge fan. She used to have another merman next to her, but he had retired a few years ago. Now, she was stuck with Reynard. The merman who liked her boobs, and that was about it.

However, he did get shit done when it came to the Conclave, so he wasn't all bad.

"What did I miss?" she asked, leaning against the edge of her bowl. He leaned against his, and she did her best not to let anybody's stares bother her. No one else was truly in their shifter forms except for them, and she hated it. Loathed being on display. But she couldn't fix it, not until after the minutes of the last Conclave were read, and she could change into her human form and sit on the edge of the bowl if she felt like it. She had done that more often than not recently, and she planned on doing it tonight, too.

"They're about to start the minutes. It seems that a few of the elders were late, as well."

Her eyebrows rose. "Why?"

"Probably because they like to keep us waiting."

"You know, I wouldn't put that past them."

There were murmurs, and then the minutes were read. As soon as they were, she quickly shifted back to her human form and dressed. Reynard stayed in his mer-form, but he didn't have to deal with the stares as much as she did. Usually anyway. Some of them liked to look at his tail just as much as hers.

They went over the agenda, and she was kind of grateful that nothing seemed too important. It was mostly just rehashing what had gone on at the last meeting. That meant that, at the moment, there weren't too many wars and battles happening.

"I take it you took care of the rogue situation," one of the elders said to one of the wolf Conclave members.

The Alpha of the Nocturne Pack nodded. "My men took care of it. You won't have to deal with it."

"And you took in that fox kit?" another elder asked.

"Yes." The Alpha of the Pack glared over at the fox Conclave members, but the foxes didn't seem to notice or care.

"Wonder what that was about," Reynard whispered as the talks moved to something else.

"Don't worry about it," she whispered. "Seriously."

He just looked at her. She knew exactly what that was about, and what the gorgons had been doing as they were questioned, as well. Not because it had made Conclave news before this, but because it all had to do with friends of friends and the fact that her circle was growing as Seth's circle seemed to. She didn't mind knowing as much as she did, and she liked having people in her life because, sometimes, it got a little lonely with what she was doing.

"If that's all, we can end our Conclave," the elder said, his voice low.

There was a commotion from the front, and the large —at least four-stories-high—gold, gilded doors slid open, smashing into the walls as a man with dark hair, a smirk, and a long, leather trench stormed in. He strode confidently forward, his head held high. Everyone started to shout, glaring at him.

"Unauthorized entry. Who let him in? Where are our guards?"

People started to move, ready to fight, but the elders held up their hands.

"Stay in your seats. What is the meaning of this?"

"You're having a Conclave meeting. Shouldn't you have all species represented?" the mysterious stranger asked.

Caly moved forward, trying to sense what he was, but she felt like she hit a brick wall when she tried. She had no idea what type of supernatural he was. And she was usually pretty good at sensing those things.

"I don't understand," the elder growled out.

"No, you don't seem to understand much. But I just need to make sure you understand this. You have left out a prominent species based on your hatred. Let me join as a Conclave member, along with one other as per your rules, or suffer the consequences."

There was an uproar, and she moved forward, trying to understand what was happening.

A new species? That hadn't happened before. At least to her knowledge. The shades weren't a new species, they had once been on the Conclave long ago, but everyone had thought they'd died out. When they showed up again, they had been allowed on the Conclave.

However, she didn't know of another species like that.

Who was this man? And why couldn't she pull her gaze from him?

"Be ready to run," Tristan, Caly's brother-in-law, said from her side.

He was fae, one of the Conclave members. His friend, a wizard named Levi, was at his side.

"Why would we run?"

"Because I don't have a good feeling about this," Dante the dragon said from behind her.

She turned and almost fell into her bowl, but Tristan held out a hand for her. "Seriously, this doesn't look good."

Dante hummed in agreement. "Hunter and the wolves will be gone, as well. Our friends will be safe. But I don't trust this stranger."

Caly looked at Dante, then back down at the man who

wasn't any supernatural species she'd ever known. "What is he?"

"That, I do not know. And that worries me more than I care to admit."

Considering that Dante was millennia old, she didn't blame him. She'd thought he knew everything there was to know about the realms.

"You can't just come in here and issue ultimatums," the elder snapped. "You are nothing. A figment of the imagination. You should go before you suffer the consequences. You are but one against many."

The stranger tilted his head. "You know exactly who I am. Your lies and deceit can only last so long. And you know what I can do. You know what I represent. Let us have a voice, or remember exactly what happened the last time you ignored us." He looked around, winked at her, then shrugged.

What. The. Hell?

"I'll be waiting outside while you make your decision." He strode off just as he'd come in, and she was honestly so confused that it took her a moment to catch up.

"Well, that was interesting," Tristan said, shaking his head as the rest of the Conclave fell into an uproar. "We need to get back to Seth and Amara. I have a feeling that this isn't going to end well."

"We can all meet up later if needed," Dante said, but

before Caly could agree, not even knowing if she was truly invited, one of the elders called out her name.

"Calypso Oceanus. Come. You are needed."

She froze, and Reynard looked at her. "Should I go with you?"

"No, go home with Tristan and the others. You don't want the elders' eye on you if you can help it."

"You shouldn't go alone," Tristan said.

"I don't really think I have a choice." She squeezed his hand and then jumped off the edge of her bowl so she could make her way to where the elders sat.

She looked over her shoulder as Tristan and her friend stared, clearly ready to fight if needed. She really hoped it wouldn't come to that.

"Sire," she said, not kneeling, but she did bow her head in respect. She might not like the elders, but they still helped rule the Conclave. Not that the Conclave truly had leaders per se, but the elders did hold sway. And if they asked to meet with you, you met with them. Their powers were legendary, and she didn't want to face that. After all, she was just a mermaid. She wasn't even sure she had any real powers to begin with."

"Calypso."

"Yes?"

"Talk to that man and figure out exactly what he wants. In detail. It is your job of lineage to figure out who this imposter is. Find him, or you will lose your job as a

Conclave member, as a lineage maker. You don't want to be shunned by the mermaids, do you?"

The elder spoke so quickly, she felt as if she couldn't keep up.

"What?"

"You heard me. More is at stake than just your connection to your realm."

"You're threatening me?" She fisted her hands at her sides, but the elder held up a hand.

"No, merely making a promise. That man isn't going to wait much longer. You will speak for us, but make no decisions."

Then they were gone, leaving her alone, wondering what in the goddess's name had just happened.

"What was that?" Tristan asked, coming towards her.

"They told me I need to talk to him. And figure out what he is."

"Alone?" he asked, and she shrugged.

"I have a feeling if I don't do it alone, they're going to do something far worse."

"They're not allowed to have that kind of power."

"It seems they do. I'm going to go figure out who and what he is."

"You shouldn't. Not without help."

Caly just shrugged. "I'm okay. I promise. I'm not going to do anything stupid."

And then she chased after the man, going back the

way he had come through, past the large, gilded doors. She really hoped like hell she knew what she was doing. Because, honestly, she had no idea what to do other than just come right out and ask him.

"Looking for me, pet?" a deep voice asked as soon as she was outside the large marble building that housed the Conclave.

She skidded to a halt, her heart racing. "You. What do you want?" she asked, looking at the man with the dark hair and hooded eyes.

"Well, things just got interesting, didn't they, pet?"

Before she could ask exactly what he meant, he winked once, then vanished into thin air.

CHAPTER 2

Misha slid between the shadows, thankful for his glamour. No one could pierce through it, not even another of his kind. Although his kind *could* detect if a glamour were being used, just not who was beneath it. Thankfully, no one who knew him or could ever know him, was near.

Not that he enjoyed the idea that he was alone, but he was used to it.

This time, however, gave him time to look at her. A mermaid. Of all creatures, she would be the one to call to him. Well now, that was interesting.

He had spent centuries alone, helping his people, trying to keep them alive, but he had never truly searched for a mate. After all, what was the point when they would just die long before he did?

Because he was already dead, at least according to legend. Why add life to it?

"So, are you going to stand in the shadows all day, cousin?"

Misha smirked, having sensed his cousin Broderick near him right when the man glimmered. Glimmering was how his kind went from one point to another. It was another form of transportation, but it took immense power that not all had.

The truly strong didn't need to see the end point of their glimmer in order to end up there. Some, most of the young, and those who had used far too much of their power over time couldn't glimmer without knowing exactly where they were going. Others of their kind couldn't glimmer at all, but Misha and Broderick were not those.

"I think I made my statement," he said, ignoring Broderick's taunts.

"And what kind of statement would that be?" Broderick asked, his voice low.

Misha looked over at him. "It's whatever we need it to be."

His cousin sighed. "I don't know. I don't trust any of this. We've been hidden for eons for a reason. The Conclave has never liked us, even in whatever iteration they were in when they knew we existed in the open."

"I think two of the elders knew exactly who and what

I was, even though they lied about it." That worried him, but it shouldn't. He wasn't too surprised.

"The elders of the Conclave, lying? Shocking."

He raised a brow at Broderick. "They will be our elders if we join the Conclave like we want."

"I still don't know why we have to. We've been fine alone." Broderick looked off into the distance, worry in his tone.

"That is a lie, and you know it." He turned to face his cousin.

"We don't need them. We never have."

"We have *always* needed them, and you know that. We've done fine on our own because we've been forced to, not because we've *thrived*. Our members are dying, and there's no coming back from that without protection and treaties and a *realm*. The best way to accomplish our goals and keep our people safe is by letting the Conclave know we exist. By joining their numbers. By having a voice."

"So you say."

"Don't growl," Misha said, looking over at his cousin. "We all voted on this. We've spent years fighting over it, trying to find a better way. But this is it. This is our legacy. And we need to protect our young, Broderick. You have a child, a mate. Do you want them to die because we're not strong enough to protect them?"

"You question my strength?" Broderick asked, his eyes glowing red.

Misha shook his head. "You're one of the strongest people I know, but the two of us together aren't enough to protect everyone. We've known that for a long time." And he hated himself more every day because of that glaring fact.

"I still don't like it."

Misha held back a smile, his body tense, ready for whatever would happen next. "I don't like it either. But we'll figure it out."

"So, you went in there, did a little show, and then what?"

"I told them they'd have to recognize us or I'd do what they feared the most."

His cousin was silent for a moment. "You would really tell the humans who we are?"

"I would do anything to protect our people, and threatening to do that is only the first step."

"It's against all our laws," Broderick growled.

"I know. I don't want to do it. And, hopefully, they won't make us. I would do anything for our people," Misha whispered.

"I know. You've sacrificed so much for us over the years, and I will be forever indebted to you."

"There's no debt between blood. You know that."

"So," Broderick said after a moment of silence, "Is the plan the same? To make friends with the dragon?"

Misha frowned and stared over at the large building where the Conclave was held. It had been dismissed after his announcement, so most people had already left, including Dante the dragon—the one that Misha had always admired from afar, though the two had never truly met. It was safer for his kind, and himself, if he stayed away from Dante. Dante was one of the most famous of all of the paranormals. He'd saved their worlds countless times over his eons of existence.

The plan had been to meet up with Dante and try to form an alliance with him and his mates. It was said that the seven lightning-struck women were all connected to him, as well. If Misha and his people were to join forces with them, maybe the Conclave would recognize his kind as having the right to exist. And if that happened, then his kind would finally be safe. Or, at least, on the way to becoming so.

"I think...I've found another way in," Misha said, his chest growing tight.

Broderick frowned. "Better than the dragon? Who does the Conclave look up to more than the dragon?"

"I don't think anyone, but I might have another connection to the Conclave. Someone close to the elders."

"Oh?"

"I found my mate."

Broderick's eyes widened. "What?"

"My mate."

"You were only gone like thirty minutes."

"And, in that time, I went to the Conclave, told them our demands, and I found my mate. It's been a productive day." He still couldn't quite believe it.

"I'll say." Broderick paused. "So, your mate? What the hell? What are you going to do?"

"That remains to be seen. However, she's young. A mermaid."

Broderick blinked. "One of our kind with a mermaid?" Broderick said, contemplating. "You know, that works."

Misha looked over at him, his brows raised. "Really?"

"Well, it does. If you think about it. We're both myths, ones that the humans think they know are true. And there's that whole breathing thing."

"Yes, the breathing thing would be interesting. However, I'm not quite sure what I'm going to do next."

"So, wait. You're going to use your mate to get us into the Conclave?"

He frowned. "I don't like the word *use*."

"Well, what other way would you say it? Because we need to protect our people. And you said yourself that you would do anything for them."

"And use my mate? Am I truly that bloodthirsty?"

Misha looked over at his cousin, and Broderick just rolled his eyes at the joke.

"I believe you'll do anything for our people, including using her." Broderick was silent for a moment, so Misha looked over again.

"What's with that tone?"

"Our people need peace. They need a home. They need the right to exist. Just don't taint your soul in the process, dear cousin."

Misha stared at his cousin and shook his head. "You say that as if I've ever had a soul."

"You know you do," Broderick said, shaking his head. "Don't give in to the lies about us and the darkness just because we're on the brink of destruction."

"I will do whatever I have to in order to protect your young. To protect *all* of our people. And if that includes finding a way to use my newfound mate, I will."

"Would it be better to fight?" Broderick asked. "To fight the dark ones?"

"We've been fighting them for centuries. And we're losing." He shook his head. "No, it wouldn't be better. We have to find another way. We'll die if we don't."

"And how will your mate help?"

"She works for the Conclave," Misha said simply.

"Really?"

"I believe she's a council member, one of the

mermaids. And she was sent to find out exactly what I am."

Broderick's eyebrows rose to his hairline. "Well, that's going to make things very interesting for your courtship."

Misha snorted. "There might not be a courtship."

"Don't ruin your fate."

"If I don't protect my people, I won't have a fate. But I won't be too much of a complete bastard."

"So, you're going to change your entire existence, then?" Broderick asked and then ducked Misha's punch.

"You're the bastard, dear cousin."

"Yes, but I'm happily mated and have a child. You are about to fuck up your chance."

"Well, I do have one chance at happiness and all that other crap that comes with mating. However, before I can ponder too hard on any of that, I need to make sure my world can actually survive. So, I'm going for a swim."

Broderick's eyes danced with laughter. "Really? A swim?"

"She's gone home with her family. That means, I need to follow."

"Don't ruin your chance," Broderick repeated.

"What's a chance without a little danger?"

"You're not that much of an idiot."

"Sometimes, I truly feel like I could be. But, no worries, I won't hurt her. Only if I have to use her to protect our people. Then, so be it." And before Broderick could say anything else to that, Misha glimmered and followed the scent trail of his mate.

Like shifters, his kind were trackers. It was how they hunted their prey and found their food source. After all, sometimes, those two weren't the same.

He followed the path through the portals, using his glamour to get through any barricades in his way, and then found himself at the edge of the mer-realm.

The realm itself had an above-the-sea section. It wasn't all under the sea, not like a realm that you just plunged into the depths of the ocean. Although, that would be a deterrent for anybody who dared come to their lands uninvited.

However, the mer-kin knew that some of their mates and friends would not be able to breathe underwater without a special charm or the kiss of life as some were able to give.

Misha himself didn't need that. After all, his kind didn't need to breathe.

Oh, his lungs functioned just fine, and he even breathed in and out when he felt like it. He could scent and needed that to hunt. He could enjoy the smell of a flower, or freshly brewed coffee. However, he could also hold his breath indefinitely if he needed to.

It was just the way his kind worked. And probably why so many were afraid of them.

That was, if they knew they existed at all.

So, being a mate to a mermaid? Well then, perhaps it was fate, after all.

He looked down at his tattered black jeans and Henley, as well as his leather work boots, and wondered if he should have changed before he decided to dive in. However, there was no time for that now. He had a mate to find, and one he needed to convince to help him. Whether she liked it or not.

He rolled his shoulders back and then dove off the cliff that he stood on, right into the ocean below. Perhaps if he had a submersible or fins, he would have been able to make the trek faster. However, he did swim faster than a human. So, he kicked and used his arms and slowly made his way down below, tracking his lovely mate's scent.

He ducked out of the path of a shark, one that was just prowling and hadn't really noticed him. However, he really didn't want to be shark bait at the moment, so he kept his distance. There were a few mer-warriors on patrol, so he did his best to avoid them, as well.

They had a great defense system. However, he had spent his life amongst the shadows, in the darkness. They would never be able to catch him. However, if he were going to mate with this woman, he would do his best to train those soldiers better than they were. After all, his mate needed to be safe. What if he wasn't around all the time? They needed to be able to sense that he was near and not let an enemy into their midst.

He'd been to the mer-realm before, though it had been decades. He'd met with another of his kind who had been on patrol within the realm itself. He hadn't talked to any of the true inhabitants of the realm, much like he hadn't done with many of the other paranormals.

His kind lived in the shadows, much like the magic users of that particular realm. Secrecy even amongst the secret kept them alive.

However, the time had come for change, and Misha was going to be on the forefront of that—and, hopefully, with a mate who could aid him in that quest.

He followed his mate's scent towards an underwater dwelling that seemed to have multiple sections with bubble tops so the entire place could either be open to the sea's viewing, or fully opaque. At the moment, he couldn't see through the tops, but he could sense a few heartbeats within. He passed over what seemed to be a family of four, one of them a small child, and made his way to the other wing of the large home.

His mate moved around the room, her heartbeat strong.

Misha swam under the large dome and came up through a pool on the other side of the room where his mate stood. He couldn't sense anyone else around, but he still kept his predator senses on alert. It wouldn't be good to get in a fight now when things were just getting interesting.

The place looked welcoming, even if it felt like he was also in a fishbowl under the ocean. He wasn't quite sure how mer-kin lived like this all the time, but he wasn't one to judge. After all, his people literally lived within the shadows, constantly ducking from one enemy after the other. Usually, within their own ranks.

He pushed those thoughts from his head for the moment, though. Right now, he needed to focus on his mate. He walked past the bedroom, thankful that a towel had been placed on one of the benches so he could at least begin to dry off. He did his best to walk softly along the path so as not to make too many wet sounds on the tile as he walked past her bedroom to where she currently was.

The fact that she was in the shower? Well, this was officially an interesting way to introduce himself to his mate, beyond how he had outside the Conclave.

Nerves crept up his body, but he ignored them.

This was just like any other meeting. She had something he needed, and hopefully, he had something for her. The fact that he had never done anything like this before, and never thought he'd ever find a mate notwithstanding. In fact, he wasn't going to think about that at all.

Because it wasn't safe for her to be his. Not until they figured out exactly how to protect his people.

He made his way past the door to the bathroom and grinned as he saw her standing there, a towel around her back as she dried off.

She whirled, her arms outstretched, the water in the tub as well as in the sinks pouring out as she stretched her fingers.

"You," she whispered.

Misha grinned. "Me."

"How dare you just show up at my house. How did you get past the guards?" Her eyes widened. "Oh, goddess, did you hurt Seth?"

"Seth?" he asked, tilting his head as he studied her, the way her dark hair slid over her body. He purposely tore his gaze from a droplet of water as it trailed between her breasts.

She was all curves and heat, and he had to hold himself back from wanting more.

The predator within him wanted her, needed her.

Sadly, there wasn't time for that.

He needed to get the Conclave to understand his people. And that meant he needed to use this mate of his.

Even if it hurt them both in the end.

"Who is Seth?" he asked, his voice low.

"My brother, you asshole. You better not have hurt him."

The water trailed over her, and he grinned. Ah, she was a water bearer. Not all mer-kin could move water like she could. But perhaps it was only when she was beneath the depths of the sea and not out in the realms. After all, she hadn't used water against him before.

"I have not harmed anybody. Nobody can sense me, so they are safe. Is Seth the one with a family at the other end of the home?" he asked, honestly curious.

"If you hurt them, *any* of them, I'll kill you."

"And if you kill me, then you'll never discover what the Conclave seeks."

She narrowed her eyes and lifted her lip in a snarl.

"Tell me what you are and what exactly you want from the Conclave so I can get rid of you."

"Is that really what you want?"

He moved closer, and she raised her chin. She didn't back up, and he liked that.

"What do you want?" she asked again.

"If I were to say *you*, what would you say?"

"I'd say you're delusional," she snapped.

"Well, then, I'll just have to live in those delusions for a while longer. I need your help, mermaid."

"My name is Caly. Use it."

Caly, he liked that. She looked like a Caly, and he could imagine saying her name as he plunged into her wet heat, but he pushed those thoughts out of his mind. He had other things to worry about.

"I will tell you what I am, but first, I need your help."

"That doesn't make any sense. If you don't tell me, and

if I don't figure it out, I'll go back to the Conclave empty-handed. And then they'll take everything from me. Do you understand that? They'll take the one thing that I've been striving for my entire life."

He shook his head. "If that's the case, perhaps you need more in your life."

He didn't know why he was being such a dick to her. In fact, he didn't know why he was being an asshole at all. Just her presence got under his skin, though. He didn't like it. How was he supposed to protect his people if he had to deal with this? He didn't feel like himself.

"Excuse me?" she growled.

He winked. "I like when you growl. It's cute." And then he leaned down and lowered his lips to hers. He hadn't even realized he was doing it until he was kissing her, and she had her hands on his chest, the pressure increasing with each passing moment.

She tasted of the sea and home, and he wanted more, his predator pushing at her. She pushed at him again, and he freely took a step back, knowing he was in the wrong.

"What the hell was that?" she snapped.

He was surprised that she didn't wipe her mouth. "Well, I might as well be honest."

"That would be different."

He grinned. "You're my mate. And I'm going to have you. But first, we need to help each other."

He didn't even register the slap until he blinked, and

she looked down at her hand. "Did you just hit me?" he asked, a little perplexed, and a lot turned on.

"Don't throw the word *mate* around. How dare you say that? You come into the Conclave and throw your weight around as if we're supposed to fear you. You break into my home, you tease me, you kiss me without my permission, and now you're calling me your mate? All the while, you want something from me. Who are you?"

He raised his chin and smiled at her. "I am Misha, one of the last of my kind. And, yes, I am your mate. If you look beyond the turmoil within your soul, you'll feel the connection. And I will tell you exactly who I am, and *what* I am. First, though, as I said, I need your help." He paused as she blinked at him, rubbing her hand along her chest, her towel sliding just a bit. "I need your help to make sure my people are safe. Even from the one who is one of us."

She blinked at him then and shook her head. "What do you mean?"

Right then, he knew he needed to trust her, even if he had only been baiting her before. Because his people were dying, and he didn't have time to court her, didn't have time to play around.

He needed her to save his people, and then maybe, save his soul.

CHAPTER 3

Caly did not trust this Misha as far as she could throw him. And considering this unknown paranormal was insanely built, she wouldn't be able to throw him very far.

As soon as she had put on clothes, thankfully out of Misha's view, she had taken him to another part of the underwater world. She hadn't wanted him to be anywhere near Seth or his mates. Or the baby.

Oh, this man might be her mate, though she wasn't a hundred percent certain on that, but she didn't know his true intentions. After all, he'd shown up out of nowhere, was a cocky son of a bitch, had threatened the Conclave, and was the person standing between her and a job she loved.

So, no thank you, Misha. If he truly was her mate, he

wouldn't be an asshole. Right? Wasn't that the way things worked? Mates were once in a lifetime. Considering that supernaturals could live for thousands of years, that was a long time to be alone if you never found your other half.

Seth had been lucky, he'd not only found his mate, he'd also found another part of his soul along the way. His mates were sweet, loving, and could kick the ass of anyone who dared come after their family.

That was something she had always secretly wanted deep down, though she had never voiced it.

But now, this man had shown up, threatened so many, and was now claiming that she could be his? No, she didn't want to believe that. And, frankly, she wasn't even going to try.

"Nice cave," Misha drawled, sounding like the egotistical asshole he probably was.

"Not to your liking?" she snapped, her nerves on edge.

"It's just fine, Caly. I understand that you want to keep your family safe, and I don't blame you. I'm just trying to keep my family safe, as well."

Her gaze shot to his. "What's with the nice tone? Are you trying to lure me into a sense of security?"

Misha ran his hands through his hair and growled before he paced the cave. The cavern was underwater, but they were in an air pocket where he could breathe. She was back on two legs, having brought an extra pair of clothes so she could change after they had swum. She didn't know how he had made it down to where she lived, and she hadn't needed to use the kiss of life on him during their swim.

What kind of supernatural could breathe underwater like she could? Or perhaps he didn't need to breathe. She didn't know, but she was honestly a little worried. She didn't know this man, didn't know what kind of magic he had. However, something deep within her wanted her to trust him. And considering who she was, and the power she held, she didn't ignore that instinct. Because sometimes she could see prophecy, could sense the future. It wasn't a significant part of her powers, but it was enough that she knew when she could trust others. And the fact that her senses were telling her that she could trust him worried her. Because she didn't know him, and she shouldn't feel like she could trust him at all. But here she was, alone with him, with no one else around, somewhere he could hurt her without anyone knowing.

And yet, she stood here. Oh, she might be a warrior, able to fight well, and she had fought endless wars for other realms—even once for her own—but this man, this stranger, seemed far stronger.

"What do you want?" she asked again.

"I need to protect my people, and to do that, I need to tell secrets, things that we have hidden for countless years."

"Why tell me? Why are you here?"

"I have other plans," Misha said, continuing to pace. "I was going to talk with that dragon, Dante. He seems to hold a lot of power, and I thought maybe he could sway the Conclave to help my people."

"And who are your people?"

He didn't answer. "But then I saw you, and I knew exactly who you were to me."

"I'm nothing to you."

He met her gaze, his eyes glowing red for an instant, and she froze.

"What are you?" she whispered.

"You can feel it, can't you? Who we could be? It's not just one-sided. It can't be. You know that not everybody can feel that pull. Sometimes, it takes years for it to grow between people. But a bond can be made, and it didn't even surprise you. I feel it already, and I've only been in your presence for moments. We have the potential to be true halves, mates in truth. But I didn't plan on this. I didn't plan on you."

She swallowed hard, trying to ignore the feeling inside. Because she felt the tug, that pull. The fact that he could be the one person to complete her soul.

But she didn't want that. She couldn't.

"It doesn't matter what I feel, not when I have a mission. And that is to find out exactly what you want, and who you are. You keep neglecting to mention that, so, why don't you tell me?"

"I haven't told anybody who we are for so long, it's hard."

"Just say the words, and then we'll figure this out. Though the fact that you threatened the Conclave means you're not on the right side. You're the one I need to protect my people from."

"Your Conclave has ignored my people for centuries because of their prejudice."

"I am *part* of the Conclave. So, watch your tone."

"My apologies, Caly. I was merely speaking of your elders. The ones who hide their secrets."

"Everybody's allowed to have secrets," she whispered.

"And yet you want me to divulge mine?"

"Because you're playing games. You want your people to be recognized by the Conclave. And you threaten to do it. Yet you won't tell anybody, you won't tell me what kind of supernatural you are. How are we supposed to want you to be part of us and give you a voice when you won't even make your true intentions known?"

"You've got me there, but the elders know who I am. The fact that they sent you on this wild goose chase means that they want to look as if they're trying."

She froze, blinking. "They can't know, they wouldn't have done that." But she knew she was lying. She didn't like the elders. Never had. They had forced some of the

Conclave members to do things that nobody in their right mind would ever want to do. They'd stayed back from wars when it served them, and they hid behind their shield of power.

It was only because of the lightning-struck, and Dante himself that the actual apocalypse had ended before it began. The elders would have let it happen, stating that nature needed to run its course.

"I'm an immortal," he said, his eyes narrowed.

She rolled her eyes. "Oh, that's a good one. We're all immortal, you asshole. That's what being a supernatural means."

"No, the supernaturals appear immortal. I'm a true immortal."

She froze. "You can't die?"

He shook his head. "You can't kill what's already dead, can you?"

Fear crawled up her spine. "Tell me what you are."

"I'm not what they say I am."

Before she could question him further or shake him to get the answers she wanted, there was a sound behind him, and he whirled, the red of his eyes lighting up the cave.

"Damn it, he found me."

"You brought danger to my realm?"

"I thought *I* was the danger," he drawled, and she cursed under her breath.

"Who is it?" she asked, ignoring his taunts. He was on edge. And if he was, she needed to be.

"One of my kind who wants to eradicate the rest of us. And then wipe out the rest of you. He's dark, but I won't have you hurt."

"Because you want answers from me? You want help?"

He looked over his shoulder and shook his head. "Because you're mine." And then he jumped, and a blur moved across her vision.

She let out a shout as a man in dark leather pants and a leather jacket came at Misha, his hands outstretched, clawed fingertips slashing.

She slid the water from the crevices around her and let it wrap around her arms and legs before she pushed it at whatever blur was attacking Misha. She might not trust the man, but she wasn't going to let him die on her watch. After all, she had to find out exactly who he was.

The dark blur shaped like a man hit and slashed at Misha, who ducked out of the way in time. They weren't using weapons. Instead, both were using immense strength and fighting skills.

They were far faster than she could ever hope to be, but she tried to lash out with her water at them, attempted to use her strength. However, the two were just too fast for her.

She watched as Misha gripped the other man around the neck and squeezed, and then the enemy sliced his claws down Misha's side. Misha shouted, blood spraying all around him, and Caly moved closer, trying to help. She wasn't going to just stand back and watch Misha die. She might not trust him fully, but she didn't want him dead either. And the part of her that was pulled towards him, that wanted him, refused to let her stand back either.

She moved forward, using her water to slam into the unknown man. He didn't budge, but then she used her strength and punched at the man's face. His head shot back, and he hissed at her, fangs dripping.

She blinked. Fangs? What kind of paranormal was he?

He let go of Misha as Misha staggered back, putting his hand over his side, trying to stanch the blood. She kicked, lashed out at the other man, and got one good blow in before he swept his arm out and hit her so hard in the face, she saw stars. Her back hit the rocks behind her, and she blinked, spitting out blood as she tried to focus.

Misha roared and attacked the blurred man again. The other man kicked, still fighting Misha. She shook her head, wincing at the ache, and then stood up, trying to regain her balance.

She wasn't the strongest mer-kin out there. In fact, she was better at using her brain than her fists, but she went at the enemy again. Fighting, kicking. When he sliced his fangs along her arm, she shouted, pulling her hand back as it stung. It burned, but she ignored the wound, trying to help Misha.

Misha clawed at the man again, then the shadow winked and disappeared just as Misha had before.

She looked down at her arm, the blood welling, and she cursed. "What the hell was he?"

Misha staggered towards her, took her hand in his, and placed his mouth over her arm.

She pushed at him. "What the hell are you doing?"

"I need to get the venom out before it kills you. He left a paralytic agent in your veins. Can't you feel the burn?"

As soon as he said it, she felt it, as if molten silver slid through her. Her hands shook. "My goddess, what is it?"

"Poison. It won't turn you into one of us, but it *will* kill you," he said as if being one of his kind was worse than death. She wasn't sure how she felt about that. She couldn't focus, however, because he latched his mouth onto her arm. She could feel the poison sliding back out, and she went to her knees, her body shaking. It was as if Misha were sucking on a snakebite, trying to get all the venom out. He spat out the blood, along with the silver venom and toxicity.

She rested her head on the cave wall, looking down at him as he kept spitting out the death coming for her.

"There, clean blood. You're fine."

And then he leaned against the floor, his hand at his side, and cursed. "Well, that went a little deeper than I planned." Then he slid to the ground, resting his head on the floor.

She moved to him then, wiping his hair from his brow, looking down at the wound. It looked as if someone had taken a butcher knife to his side, four long gashes so deep that she could see his ribcage.

"Oh, my goddess. We have to heal you."

"Bandages won't help," he whispered, his body shaking.

"Is it the venom?"

"No, it's just deep. Lost too much blood. I need... food." There was a pause as he said it, and he looked at her. She frowned.

"Food? What can I give you?"

He shook his head. "I can't take from you."

And then he passed out. She looked down at him, her hands shaking. Fangs. Venom. Biting. The fact that he wouldn't take from her.

He wasn't supposed to exist, a true immortal didn't exist.

But this man, this Misha, had to be a *vampire*.

The one paranormal the elders *swore* didn't exist.

As she looked at him, her body shaking as the tug within her that wanted to save him as her mate desperately tried to retain its hold, she knew she had to help.

"I hope I'm doing this right," she said as she put her cut arm closer to Misha's face. "Drink," she whispered.

She parted his lips for him, letting the blood drip into his open mouth. It seemed to trigger him.

Fangs dug into her arm, and she gasped, the pain intense before it turned to pleasure that almost made her legs shake.

He bit down, sucking, pulling her life force from her. His arms clamped around her, bringing her closer. Her whole body shook as pain and pleasure wrapped around each other as he fed.

Fed. Because he was a vampire.

And, apparently, he was her mate.

CHAPTER 4

Misha felt as if he were in a dream, his cock hard, blood sliding down his throat. It tasted of honey, a sweet elixir that was going to send him right over the edge. He tugged more, loving the shocked moan and gasp of his partner beside him. He licked, sucked, imagined plunging his cock deep into her wet pussy as he bit down on her neck, her arm. Nibbled and took.

Blood was his energy, his life force, his intoxication.

He thrust his hips, pressing against the woman, wanting more as he ground against her as if he were a rutting animal. And he didn't care. All he wanted to do was fuck her, take her blood, and bring them both ecstasy. And then a hand pressed against his shoulder, pushing at him.

"Misha, it's too much. I need you to stop."

Dread slid over him and wrapped around his body like an iron fist. He froze, his fangs still deeply embedded in the woman's arm. He recognized that voice. His eyes shot open, and he growled like a shifter, an animal, his vampire senses electrified.

He slid his fangs out, kissed the wound, and lapped it shut before he looked at Caly, who blinked at him, her body pale, her lips almost white.

"Fuck," he growled. He pulled Caly into his arms as he ran his hands down her body, checking for more injuries. The only wound on her that was of any consequence were the two fang marks on her arm. There were still a few cuts and a bruise on her forehead, but he was the one who had harmed her, who had almost ended her life because he had taken too much. He hadn't done that since he was a babe, learning how to control his hunger and his needs using the humans who had willingly given their blood. There were always humans within their compound, even when they were on the run, families who gave their life force and were given families of their own, as well as payment. They were not their slaves or workers. They were their helpers, their life mates.

And Caly was not one of them. Instead, she was his mate, and he had almost killed her. "Caly."

"Vampire," she breathed, her gaze a bit wide-eyed and distracted.

"Yes, I'm a vampire. An immortal as we sometimes

call ourselves. We don't tend to use the word *vampire* too often, but that doesn't matter, does it?"

She licked her dry, cracked lips, and then cursed again. "You aren't supposed to exist."

"No, we aren't. We almost died out once. The elders made sure of that. They're afraid of those who they call 'dead.'"

"Are zombies next?" she asked, her voice so soft he was worried that she was going to die. In fact, he knew that he needed to give her sustenance, needed to heal her quickly. He was just afraid that if he did so, it would be far too soon for what would come next, and yet, far too late for what she needed.

"No zombies that I know of. However, you never know what other secrets are out there." He paused. "Caly, pet, you gave me far too much. I will be forever in your debt for saving my life, but I need to give you blood."

Her eyes widened, and she pushed at him. She was so weak that she couldn't do much. He wanted to curse himself for what he had done, but there was no going back. Not now.

"It won't turn you. Vampires, just like every other paranormal out there, are born, not made." He paused. "Well, the lightning-struck seven might be a little different, but you are not one of them. You will not turn into a mer-vampire." He paused. "Those do not exist, at least that I know of."

"I can't drink blood."

"It will replenish you. It's the only way. You're dying, Caly," he ground out, his fangs extending and his claws curling. "Because of me. Let me save you."

"At what cost?" she asked. It was as if she could see right through him.

"It's the first part of the mating bond," he whispered. The truth lay heavy between them. "If I do this, there's no going back. But if I don't, you're going to die, Caly. *Because of me.*" He slid his hands through her hair, her body cold to his touch, her gaze unfocused. Her heart-beat was slowing, and he knew she didn't have much time left. But he wouldn't take this choice from her. The first part of the mating bond would cement their fates together far quicker than he had ever imagined. But he wouldn't take her choice from her. He couldn't, not after what she had already been through, and given who he was.

"I don't want to die," she whispered, her voice so faint that he barely heard it.

It wasn't the declaration of love a true mating should have. It wasn't a mating call at all. But it was permission.

And so, he slid his fangs into his own wrist and cut deep. His body was already back to full strength, even past it with the potency of Caly's blood in his veins.

She was dying because she'd tried to save him, and he would never forgive himself. He put his bloody wrist to her mouth, and her eyes closed, her body limp in his arms.

He didn't have much time. He forced blood down her throat before she greedily latched on, sucking. His blood wasn't just pure, it was an elixir of sorts, one that would send her over the edge into bliss if they weren't careful. And it would send them into their mating, the urge too strong for either of them to deny or prolong. But he would wait for as long as it took. To keep his people safe, and to give Caly a choice. He was already taking one decision from her. He wouldn't do it again.

Misha moved so Caly was in his lap, her head resting on his thigh. He willed his cock not to harden any further.

The act of blood sharing between mates was an intimate one, something that nearly always led to sex and even procreation.

For those vampires who were lucky enough to find their mates, they didn't need to drink from a human or another paranormal. They need only drink from their mate—even if they were another vampire. That was how close the bond was. You were each other's life force, life mate, everything. You were each other's life itself.

And as the bond started to solidify between them, slowly at first, winding between their souls, he swallowed hard at the intimacy.

Because he didn't know her. He didn't know who this

person was. But she would be irrevocably changed, bonded with him until the end of their days, be they long or short.

She moaned, arching her back as she drank more, and he licked his lips, knowing she needed a little bit more to be healthy, but he couldn't let her take too much. Not because it would hurt him, but because it would send them both over the edge into an abyss neither of them was truly ready for. At least, he hoped there would be no pain, no confusion—only bliss.

He didn't know, he didn't know anything. His long life of being a warrior for his people, the secret keeper, a leader, all amounted to nothing with this woman in his arms.

He pulled her away gently and licked his wound closed before wiping her lips with his thumb.

Her eyes widened, and she blinked quickly as she swallowed hard.

He slid his hands over her shoulders, checking for any more wounds, ensuring that she was safe.

He had almost killed her, and now he was hers.

"What...what happened?"

"The bond between us has started," he whispered.

"What does that mean?"

"It means whatever we need it to mean." He swallowed hard. "But the mating urge between us? It's not going to die down anytime soon."

He let out a breath and did his best not to adjust himself in his pants. He wanted to be inside her, needed to, and there was no controlling it.

She squirmed in his hold and shook her head. "Why am I feeling like this?

"We can stop, we can walk away from each other right now."

"We both know that's not true. And not just because of who you are. I know what happens to mates when they begin one part of the bond and don't finish it." She sat up and moved away from him, but not far enough that her hand wasn't able to touch his thigh. He looked down at her pale skin against the blackness of his jeans and he swallowed hard.

"Caly," he whispered.

"I can see. I can see you."

He frowned, looking at her.

"What do you mean?"

"You are my future, the one I should trust. You always were. You're the shadow within the darkness that I hid from. I always knew you would be here, I just didn't know what form you would take."

"You're a Seer?" he asked.

"Not exactly, but I have some prophetic abilities. It's why I'm so good at looking at legacies and finding family trees. Because I can see beneath the truth. And I can see you, Misha. I can see what we need to become, even though we're not there yet."

"I won't take what's not freely given," he whispered.

"I can trust in the future because I know we have to be stronger together to fight what's coming at us."

The heat between us isn't going to slow down anytime soon."

"So, you're saying we let it cool down by completing the bond, and then we figure out exactly who we are later?" she asked, looking down at her hands. "That's pretty much the exact opposite of how most matings are supposed to go."

"Work backwards?" he rasped, his predator on edge.

"Yes, we work backwards. We figure out what we need to do."

"Okay, then."

And then he was on her, his mouth on hers as he groaned. She wrapped her arms around his neck, arching into him. They were on the ground of a cave where his enemy could arrive at any minute, and yet, he didn't care. Not with the mating urge riding them so hard.

He slid his hands across her body, over her shoulders, her hips, and then grabbed onto her ass, pulling her closer to him. They were lying on their sides, one of her legs wrapped around his waist as she arched into him. He ground into her, her heat scorching against his jean-clad cock.

"We'll figure out the rest later," he growled.

"Emotions and feelings later. This first."

He didn't have a problem with that. He didn't have many emotions as it was. Only the need to protect. And Caly would be his to protect. But first, he needed to get inside her.

He tugged at her shirt, and then they were both sitting up, pulling at each other's clothes. He had his mouth on her nipple in the next instant, groaning at the sensation of her flesh in his mouth. She shivered, pressing his face closer to her breasts. They filled his palms, far larger than what he could hold, so he pushed them together, sucking and licking, imagining thrusting his cock between them.

She tugged on his jeans, so he stood up with her and shook them to the ground, tugging off his shoes at the same time. She wiggled out of her own jeans, and he ignored the fact that there were bloodstains on both of them.

He was a vampire, after all, this was part of his life.

And then she was naked in front of him, and he went down to his knees and pressed his mouth to her core. She shouted his name, and he groaned against her, spreading her flesh so he could lap at her clit and pierce her with his fingers.

She clamped around him, and he pushed harder, faster, his thumb circling her clit.

"Come for me, pet."

She looked down at him then, her eyes glowing blue as her whole body shimmered. She didn't have scales, she was still in her human form, but she was glorious, the purples and pinks and blues of her tail sliding up her flesh in an iridescent glow before going back to the color of her skin. She was losing control, and he loved it. So he lapped at her, pushed her forward, and then she came, her knees going weak.

He pulled her forward so he was on his back, her straddling him, the wetness of her pussy pressing against the hard, rigid length of his cock.

"Ride me, my mermaid."

"You're going to make me do all the work?"

"Oh, I might, but don't worry, I'll make sure you enjoy it. He reached up and slid his hands over her breasts, plucking at her nipples, twisting ever so slightly to near the edge of pain. She moaned, rocking her hips along his length, and then she lifted herself and sat down right on top of him. They both groaned, her pussy tight, wet, slick, hot. He was balls-deep inside her, and he moved his hands to grip her hips, keeping her steady.

"Goddess," he whispered. "If you don't stay still for just a minute, I'm going to blow right here, and I'm going to feel like a teenager, rather than the five-hundred-year-old vampire that I am."

She raised a brow. "Five hundred, you say? Okay, old man. Show me what you learned."

He grinned then, knowing he was showing fang. But she didn't back away. Well, apparently, seeing the future as she did was a good sign for them. He just wished she would've been able to see him before this so he wouldn't have had to be such an asshole. Or maybe that's what they had needed. He didn't understand fate, only that Caly was his. And he was going to show her exactly what she'd gotten in the bargain. He lifted her off of him and then slammed right back into her.

She shouted, her whole body shaking, and then he moved one hand up to her breast, playing as she rode him.

They moved together, him lifting up, her pressing down, both of them rocking. The sensation filled him, making his entire body shake. He couldn't help but groan, wanting more.

He pulled her down then, needing her mouth, and his fang nicked her lip.

"Fuck, sorry."

"It's okay," she whispered as the taste of her blood settled on his tongue.

"You can bite me if you want. I know you want to." She winked, and he groaned.

"Mates."

He bit down on her lip again, just a little bit, and they both froze for a minute and then shattered. The bond slammed into place between them, so intense that he pulled her to the side, holding her close as they shook from their orgasm and the bond cementing into place.

He had never been mated before, had never truly understood what any of it meant. And, honestly, he couldn't fathom what it meant now.

He could feel her soul, her wants, her desires, her fears. He knew she was just as uncertain about whether they'd made the right decision as he was, but he also knew that they both understood there hadn't been a choice. This. This was how they were going to defeat the darkness.

And he couldn't hold back his own fears.

She slid her hands up and down his body even as his cock still twitched inside her.

"I'm scared, too," she whispered. "But it's okay, we'll save your people. I promise."

He buried his face in her hair, not knowing why he couldn't speak.

He had waited a lifetime for this, more than one, actually, and now that he had her, he was afraid that he was going to lose her.

Because he couldn't always protect those he loved, those who mattered.

And he didn't know if he was strong enough to protect her.

CHAPTER 5

Caly had done many impetuous things in her life, but mating with a man she didn't know, and had only just met? Well, that had likely won her first prize in the what-the-fuck-was-she-thinking category.

However, she couldn't go back now, and she had to trust her gut feelings. They had kept her and her family alive for a long while.

"What do we do now?" she asked.

Misha frowned. "You should see what I'm fighting for."

Her brows rose. "Where are you hidden?" she asked, staring into his eyes. She could feel the bond pulsing between them and knew that there was no going back from this. She didn't love him, how could she so soon? But she knew the potential was there. That's what the bond created. It wasn't automatic for anything, other than the fact that they would be irreparably changed. And she would figure that out. She would find a way to work through her emotions.

But she needed to focus on the here and now first. Had to concentrate on what she could change. And if that meant protecting Misha's people, or at least finding out why they were hidden and who that man was who had attacked them, then that's what she would do. She would figure out the rest of her life, her romance, and her heart later.

"I only left a note for Seth saying that I was leaving for work. I didn't tell him where I was going," she said after a moment before they left.

Misha stared at her. "Do you need to tell him that you're with me?"

She shook her head, looking down at her hands. "No, because he's going to want to kick your ass, and we don't have time for that, do we?"

"I would say he could try, but I would probably let him beat me at this point." He reached out and tucked a piece of hair behind her ear. She froze, the contact new and exciting.

"Seth has a very powerful mate. Two of them, in fact."

"One of the fabled triads, then?"

"I know of a few of them, not so fabled. Dante, the

dragon you were looking for? I'm friends with him, as well. He's also in a triad."

Misha frowned but nodded. "I shouldn't have come into the Conclave like that. I should have found another way. But we were running out of time."

"Why? You keep saying that. But I don't understand."

Misha lowered his hand and then began to pace again. "The Conclave won't let us create our own realm or have a voice, not when we are hidden from existence. Meaning, we've had to stay hidden from the paranormals, as well. We can't congregate, not in large numbers anyway. So, we've had to spread out over time. That causes a chink in the communication lines of our kind. And when that happens, I'm not able to protect all the people that I need to. The weak, the ones who can't protect themselves? They need us to help them, and we can't do it. Not with enough power to keep them protected from our own kind anyway."

"That was another vampire that attacked you, then? I guessed, but I wanted to make sure."

"He attacked us, yes. He's a dark one. One who has killed humans and paranormals alike. He lost his soul in the process."

She took a step back, her eyes wide. "I thought only demons lost their souls," she whispered.

Misha shook his head. "If a demon doesn't take a soul, he loses his own. With vampires, if they take enough life forces, they slowly drain their own soul in the process. The dark one has been coming for my people because he wants to control all of them. He wants the weak to be purged, and then he wants to take the Conclave by force." Misha let out a laugh, but there was no humor in it. "As if he could."

"What can I do?" Caly asked, not knowing what else to say. Because she was tied to this man forever now. There was no going back. Only, according to whatever visions she sometimes had, there never had been any avoiding it.

"I'm going to take you to one of the areas where some of my people are. That way, you can meet them." He ran his hand through his hair. "And then, I'm going to ask you to go with me to the Conclave."

She twisted her hands in front of her but nodded. "We need to know why the elders shunned you." She paused. "Did you deserve it?"

His eyes glowed red, but then he closed them tightly, taking a deep breath. "I'm sorry. Our eyes glow red when the predator is at full force."

"Mine sometimes glow blue, and wolves' glow gold. It's who we are as paranormals. Just because your eyes are a different color, doesn't mean that you're evil."

He snorted. "The whole no pulse and not needing to breathe thing doesn't help. And we're technically dead because of that, at least according to the elders."

Pieces clicked. "That's how you got underwater."

He nodded tightly. "I don't need oxygen." He raised a brow. "Of course, that can come in handy for some sensual things."

She rolled her eyes. "I'm not going to blush. And we're not going to talk about that. We'll deal with exactly what this bond means, and the fact that we might have had the best sex of my life later."

"Best?"

"Later."

"Come with me," he said, holding out his hand. She shook her head.

"First, we need to get a few things straight."

He tilted his head but didn't lower his hand. "Okay."

"I don't know what's going to happen next between us. And that's just fine. But I had a feeling the elders were being hinky about this, just like they were with the shades before you."

"They only do what's best for themselves."

"Perhaps now, but I don't think that was always the case."

"And yet we've never been allowed to be part of the Conclave."

"The Conclave isn't all it's cracked up to be."

"You say that, and yet you have a realm that you're safe in." He lowered his hand and began pacing again.

She might not have one forever, but she didn't

mention that. "Were your people ever part of the Conclave?"

Misha shook his head. "Not in my time. Perhaps before, but the Conclave is relatively new. The elders aren't. But how the governing body works now? It's new."

"The fact that the paranormal world just recently realized that they have a governing body sort of makes that apparent."

"Yes, they were secretive for so long that I didn't even know they existed until recently. How was I supposed to keep us safe if I didn't know who to reach out to for help?"

"Show me your people, and then we'll figure out what to do about the elders. Because it's not right that you don't have a voice. That you don't have a home."

"The elders have never liked the dead."

"You're not too cold to me. I don't think you're dead. I think it's just a stigma, don't you?"

"Perhaps."

"Okay, where are we going?"

"Hold my hand, and I'll take you."

"How?" she asked, looking down at his hand and frowning.

"It's glimmering."

"Really?"

"Yes, I'll take you from one place to another. Not all vampires can do it, and many need to be able to see where they're going. But I and my cousin, Broderick, are two of the few who can do this."

"Broderick?"

"He's a good man. He has a mate, and a child. They'll be where we're going now."

She looked down at his hand and then slid her palm into his. "I'm already jumping into fate as it is. Why not do this, as well?"

He squeezed her hand, and she felt the pulse through the bond. "You won't regret it."

She hoped that was true.

She closed her eyes and felt as if she'd been pulled through a vacuum, her whole body shaking. She landed hard, her knees hitting the ground as Misha tried to hold her up.

"Sorry about that, it's been a while since I took a non-vampire with me."

She stood, wiped her knees, and glared at him. "Next time, a little warning."

"Cousin?" a deep voice asked. Caly's head whipped up, her hands outstretched.

"It's Broderick, you're safe." He kissed her temple, and she glared at him and noticed the widening of Broderick's eyes.

"I sensed the bond between you two. Well, it sure has been an interesting few hours," Broderick said dryly.

"Stop it. Don't tease. Caly's here to see our people. Hopefully, she will be a voice for us with the Conclave."

"I hope that's true," Broderick said, looking directly at her. "Not everyone's going to trust you, though."

She raised her chin. "I'm Caly, Conclave member, and one of the representatives of the mer-realm."

"And my mate," Misha growled.

Broderick's eyes rose at his cousin before looking back at her. "I figured the last part, but it's good to meet you, Caly. So, you're going to fight for our people?"

"I'm here to listen. I don't know what use I'll be. Because, after all, the Conclave asked me to come and find Misha, discover who he was and what he wanted. So, here I am. Doing that, and hopefully, trying to help you, as well."

Before she could say anything else, a small child with a mop of dirty blond hair ran towards Broderick and smiled wide, fangs on display. "Daddy!"

Broderick glared at Caly before turning to kneel and lifting the boy up high.

"Duncan, my son. Would you like to meet your Uncle Misha's mate?"

Misha slid his hand around her hip, and she froze, trying not to look as if she were uncomfortable. Things were moving far too fast for anyone in this situation.

"Hi," Duncan said and hid his face behind his father's shoulder.

"Hello, Duncan. I'm Caly."

"Hi," he whispered again and then giggled.

He was adorable, and when he looked back over and smiled, his fangs were evident, the rim of his irises a deep red.

"It's nice to meet you," she said.

"Why don't you go to your mother?" Broderick said and set his son on the ground. Duncan waved and ran towards a tent where a woman with long, silver hair stood.

The woman glared at her but looked scared. Of course, Caly would be scared too if a stranger came up so close to *her* child. The camp was just that, a camp. Tents with soldiers surrounding them. It looked as if they were in the Dean Forest on the human realm, though she had only seen it in pictures. What would it be like to never have a home, to be constantly on the run, using magic to shield yourself from humans and other paranormals?

It didn't seem fair, and even if the vampires had done something truly horrible long ago, these children didn't deserve to have that stigma associated with them. They didn't deserve to pay this price.

"We've been on the run for my entire life," Broderick said.

"Mine, as well," Misha said. "The time when the vampires were part of the Conclave was long before we were born. Our families raised us on the run, deep within the wards of magic. No one knows we exist. Many of our kind live amongst the humans, wear business suits, and own companies, changing their identities over time. This small band has too many children for that."

"What do you mean?"

A dark look crossed Misha's face. "The dark one has hunted us to the point where we can't even immerse ourselves in the human realm anymore. That's why we're here the way we are. It's why we're camping as if we're living in the 1800s and not in our current century."

"Did you know him, the dark one?" she asked.

"Yes, he was my brother," the woman with the silver hair said as she walked up to Broderick, Duncan in her arms. Broderick glared at his mate and then wrapped his arm around her waist.

"My brother-in-law did things he shouldn't," he growled.

"But we will be safe," the woman said, kissing her son's cheek. "Won't we?"

"I love you, Mommy," Duncan said, and sadness filled the woman's eyes.

Caly wanted to reach out and tell her that it'd be okay. To hold her close. But she didn't know this woman. Didn't know what type of pain they had been through recently. All she knew was that she had to find the power to help them. If not, who else? Maybe Dante. Perhaps going to him would have been helpful. But Dante wasn't here. She was. And she had a job to do.

"I'll help, anyway I can."

She felt warmth through the bond and looked over at Misha as he stared at her, his eyes narrowed. He reached out and ran his thumb over her jaw.

"Thank you, pet."

She wasn't quite sure she liked that term of endearment, but before she could say anything, a shadow crept through the camp, and Broderick shouted.

"Get the children!"

"It's him," Misha snapped. "The dark one. Protect yourself, Caly."

"You're not doing this alone. I can help. There's water around, I can do something."

"Then make sure the children are safe."

An arrow shot into the ground between them, and she widened her eyes.

"Derrick was always good at archery," he said dryly.

Derrick, the dark one, was in front of them then. He slammed his hand out, knocking Caly right in the face. She fell to the ground but rolled, getting right back to her feet. She spat out blood, and Misha's eyes turned red.

"Don't you dare hurt her."

"You found someone?" Derrick laughed. "Then she'll be that much sweeter to taste."

"I don't think so. You're done terrorizing these people." She ran forward and used all of her strength to punch at him. He ducked, but not fast enough to avoid her blow to his nuts.

He winced, and she grinned.

"Good to know even a vampire without a soul hates getting kicked in the dick as much as the next guy."

Misha's eyes widened at her comment, but she didn't have time to laugh. Instead, they attacked, the vampire coming at them with his fangs bared.

He was ready to kill, ready to murder. But she wasn't going to let that happen. Misha was a thing of beauty, his skills unparalleled. It was as if he'd been born for this. She just shook her head, standing back with Broderick's mate as Broderick leapt into the fray, fighting the dark one.

Derrick was strong, but Misha was stronger.

She wasn't about to just let anybody fight for her, though, for anyone, without trying to help.

"Help me with the children," Broderick's mate yelled. "He might have friends."

Caly nodded, tearing her gaze away. She helped round up the kids, eight in all, and moved them towards Broderick's mate and two other women, as well as two men. Other vampires glared at her before going to Broderick's and Misha's aid.

Broderick's mate had been right. Derrick wasn't

alone. At least six more shadows approached, and Caly cursed.

"I'm going to help."

"Are you a warrior?" one of the men asked. She shook her head.

"No, but I still know how to fight."

"Good, then help us."

And then she was back in the fray. She fought side by side with Misha, punching, kicking, and using the water as a blade.

It wasn't something she was good at. She was far better with her mind, but at least she could do this. She hammered the enemy, and she took out one and then another along with Misha. But Derrick was still stronger.

Derrick leapt, his fangs going for her throat, but she punched, knocking him out of the way. And in that moment, Misha took Derrick by the neck and twisted. The dark one fell in a heap on the ground.

Misha's chest heaved, blood splattered both of them, and she shook her head.

"What now?"

"We use a spell to rip them into a million tiny pieces so they can't reform. I told you, we're immortal, pet," he said, winking.

Her chest heaved. She felt like she was two steps behind everything again.

"As one who takes down the histories and learns the

bloodlines of so many within the realms, I have a lot to learn," Caly said, looking at Misha.

He tucked her hair behind her ear and nodded. "And I have a lot to learn about you. So, Caly. You'll help?"

She didn't know if he meant help him learn, help his people, or help in other ways. But she understood there was no going back anymore. This was a new beginning for her, a new chance, and she was going to take it.

So she nodded. When his lips brushed hers, even amongst the carnage and the blood, she sank into the embrace.

Because she had been born into the paranormal world and knew that these things didn't happen more than once. You had to take a chance with fate. And this felt like her first everything: her first kiss, her first kiss in blood. But it wouldn't be her last.

She could learn so much about who these people were, what they needed, and who Misha was. She couldn't wait to start.

CHAPTER 6

Misha squeezed Caly's fingers as she slid her hand into his, and he looked down at her, letting out a breath.

"Are you ready, mate of mine?" Caly asked, and he liked the new words on her tongue.

Misha nodded. "I suppose I should do this the right way."

"Yes, barging in on a Conclave meeting and acting dramatic probably didn't get much done."

Caly glared over at Dante, but Misha just smiled. "You're right. In retrospect, it wasn't the smartest thing to do. However, it did get your attention."

"It did that. Though let's not threaten war and secrets, shall we?" The dragon smiled, showing teeth. Misha bared fang in response, but only in fun.

"Are we done comparing the size of our fangs?" Caly asked. Nadie, the dragon's mate, put her hand over her mouth and laughed.

"Are you laughing at the size of my fangs, darling?" Dante asked his mate, and she just shook her head while their other mate, Jace, snorted.

Jace, the big bear shifter with a touch of sadness in his eyes smiled. "Let's not whip out our fangs anytime soon, okay? We have some things to talk about. And, since I am a Mediator, I will be your representative."

"It would have been nice to know your role existed," Misha said honestly.

"Well, you can't know everything about the paranormal world when you hide from it," Caly said, and he looked over at her.

"That is true. But I'm learning."

He was also learning so much about the woman beside him. He knew that everything he was feeling would make sense someday. He would let his emotions surge through him like they should. But for now, all he could do was just want her by his side, while he stayed by hers.

"So, this is exactly what we're going to do," Jace said, but then he began to talk about the politics and the actual legalities that came into play for creating a new realm.

Dante just rolled his eyes. "You know, sometimes I

miss the old days where I could just burn down a village and eat some sheep."

"And if you add taking a willing virgin at the end of that, I am going to have to kick you." Nadie grumbled playfully as she said it, and Caly laughed with her.

Misha just smiled at the way the triad joked with one another, even though this was a serious situation. He looked down at Caly, who smiled up at him, a curious look in her eyes.

"What are you thinking?" he asked, his voice low. The others would be able to hear them. After all, they were each paranormals in their own right. Still, they were all being respectful in pretending that they were ignoring them.

"I was just thinking that one day we might have that."

"Have what?"

"The easy camaraderie. And the way they just seem comfortable."

"It'll take time." He reached out and tucked more hair behind her ears. "But I'm excited to see what happens."

"Me, too. But first, let's save your people. And while we're there, my job. And, oh, let's not get me kicked out of the mer-realm or anything." She added that last part, and everyone stared at her.

Misha just blinked. "They threatened to kick you out of the realm?" he growled, his fangs dropping.

"That won't be happening," Dante growled as well, his

voice sure.

"You're right, it won't," another voice said. Misha turned to see a man who looked remarkably like Caly walking towards them.

Misha stood up a little straighter and was pleased when Caly didn't remove her hand from his.

"Seth," she said and smiled at him. "Misha? My brother, Seth. Seth? This is my mate, Misha."

Seth looked him up and down, the younger man fierce but warm. "Well, I know she said over the phone that she had mated, and we had things to talk about, but this is interesting."

Misha just nodded, yet he didn't lower his eyes. "I'm sorry for the way things turned out, or how we got here anyway. I'm not sorry for having her as my mate, though."

Caly squeezed his hand again, but he kept his gaze on Seth. After all, he didn't need to get his ass kicked by Caly's brother for how things had turned out. Not that he thought Seth would actually do that. However, he wasn't going to risk it, just in case.

"There are more important things for us to worry about. You don't need to be all big brother right now," Caly said quickly to Seth.

The man pulled his gaze from Misha and looked over at Caly. "You're right. But I will have to grill you. And so will my mates. And my son will probably do the same.

However, Caly will be the one to hurt you if you hurt her. I'm not going to threaten you. She's strong enough to protect herself."

"That's a good answer," Caly said, and Misha nodded.

"Understood. Now, are we ready to begin?" Misha said after a moment.

Misha's cousin came out, his family at his side. "We're ready, the others are here, too."

Dante spoke up. "It's good that you're bringing your young with you. It will show that you trust those around you."

"However," Seth said, surprising Misha, "you won't be going alone. We will be going in as your bodyguards."

Misha's eyes widened as he looked at the large group of diverse paranormals, not recognizing them. "Who are all of you?"

A brownie came forward and grinned, her skin gold, and her smile wide. "We are the lightning-struck seven, and these are our mates. Our children are at home right now, though a few of them are upset that they couldn't come and see their aunts and uncles."

"We're here to be your voice if you cannot. The Conclave will hear you, and the elders will listen. Your children shouldn't be forced to hide from their own kind," Dante said, and Caly squeezed Misha's hand.

"Nobody should be forced."

He looked down at her and lowered his head, kissing

her softly.

"Thank you for this," he whispered, knowing it was she who had put this all together.

"Excuse me," Seth growled. "Maybe you could keep your lips off my sister while we're doing this thing?"

Everybody laughed, but Misha kissed Caly again, and then he turned to the large gold doors that led into the Conclave.

"Ready?"

"Ready."

"WELL, THEN. TO BEING AN OFFICIAL SPECIES OF THE paranormal," Caly said, clinking her glass to Misha's. They were at a bar called Dante's Circle, with the seven lightning-struck, as well as their mates and most of the vampires of his small group.

The Conclave meeting had been relatively quick, the elders unable to stand up to all of the lightning-struck and their mates. Personally, Misha thought the dragon alone could have handled it, however, the show of force from everybody from so many walks of the paranormal realms had meant something.

Misha's body warmed, and he held Caly close, not wanting to let her go. He had just found her, and their story was only beginning.

"We have much to do, a new realm to form, and so

many people to find. We've been hiding for too long."

"We will make this work, cousin," Broderick said, looking down at his mate and child. "I never thought we would have the chance."

"Do you think there are more paranormals out there?" Caly asked.

"More secrets? More than what the Conclave has shown us?" Dante asked. "Perhaps. After all, even I didn't know about the vampires."

Misha grinned. "And it's just burning you, isn't it, dragon? That you didn't know all of the secrets."

Dante let a little tendril of smoke leave his nostril, and Misha raised a brow. That was a neat trick. "It's interesting, to say the least. As you are now a Conclave member, you will learn more secrets than you ever hoped to know."

"I look forward to it. And keeping my people safe."

They would always have to worry about the dark ones, would always need to worry about keeping secrets from the humans, but now, they could make a home.

As he looked down at Caly and felt the bond pulsate between them, he was excited to find his new home with her. Ready to figure out who they could be together, and where they would go.

Because they were fated mates, they were instantly connected, but falling in love and finding their paths was only the beginning.

REAPER'S SONG

CHAPTER 1

They said that death came in many forms.

Grieving came in just as many, and those who were left behind after death took, reaped, slayed. They were the ones who proved what death could be.

Not that he had ever truly understood what that meant.

After all, he was no one of consequence.

Death came as a shrouded figure, as one who slowly sucked your soul through the hole where your heart once was and never let go. Death came for those who waited, and it came out of nowhere.

Death could steal your life, but it could also end your pain. Death could be quick, or could come with a vengeance, slowly, inching away life, moment by moment. Time after time.

Death changed with each passing day. And as he found out, it had a face and a name.

The reapers were death. The ones who took souls and ended lives. They weren't few, they were legion. They were of the past, the present, and the future.

Reapers were of the paranormal, *for* the paranormal.

Reapers had once been paranormals themselves, after all.

He did not remember his name, did not remember his face or his soul. He didn't remember what type of paranormal he once was, or if that was even important.

All that he remembered was sliding into shadow, turning to dust, and waking up with no essence.

The others near him spoke in hushed tones or ignored one another, all waiting for their names, for their purpose. But he didn't know what he was waiting for. Or if he would ever be ready for what came.

"It is time," a disembodied voice said from above. The man with no name frowned and looked up into the dark clouds.

His eyes began to focus, and he started to see shapes. Silhouettes of other men and women surrounding him. Suddenly, he knew he wasn't alone.

He just didn't know who these people were. Let alone who they had been or what their purpose was. He only knew the name Reaper, and that should have been important enough. But was it?

"I am Reaper. The one named Reaper, the one who will always be named such. You are reapers, my progeny."

The man with no name frowned, wondering how he had been chosen. Why was he progeny when he felt as if he had been something more before. Yet maybe he was wrong. He didn't know this life, didn't know these shadows.

"The reapers are the ones who are just, who are death. My progeny takes the forms of who they once were, only in shadow. They are no longer light, no longer dark. They are nothing but smoke and myth."

The man with no name didn't like that. He had been someone once. Hadn't he? Images of fire and pain and a smile that made no sense filled him, and he wondered why those things seemed so important. Why was he so confused?

"My reapers find those who are near death, even if they don't realize they are such. They take their souls and usher them to the next phase."

"What *is* the next phase?" a voice asked from beside him, and the man with no name tilted his head.

"It is not for us to know or say. We are merely the travelers, the shadow-bearers."

"I don't understand," another voice said, and the man with no name agreed.

"We are of shadow, we are reapers." The leader paused. "We now have a voice in the Collective, the

Conclave. But they do not know who we are, nor do they need to know."

The man with no name wondered what the Conclave was and why it was important. And why his head hurt thinking about it. Had the man he was before known of the Conclave? Or understood what any of this could be? He wanted answers, but trying to find them seemed like it would take so much, things he didn't have.

"You are reapers. We do not know what happens after we reap a soul, only that it is taken to the next phase. It is not for us to know more than that. But it *is* for us to find. I am *the* Reaper, you are reapers. There are others like me, with other designations, those who help with your paths and your training. They help decide who will be next, and what cords must be cut. You are the reapers, and you will aid in bringing about the next phase of life, death, and existence."

The man with no name frowned but followed along. It seemed like this was important, but all he could do was wonder where he had been all this time, and *who* he had been. He didn't like not knowing, but from what Reaper said, it was not his choice. He was not supposed to know.

That didn't make it any easier for him to understand, however.

"First, we, the Collective of Shadows, will find your names. You will be given a new identity. Soon, you will learn what it means to reap a soul, and what you must do to protect the sanctity of time, life, and death."

"But didn't I have another name before?" the man with no name asked, his voice hard as if strained from lack of use. In all honesty, it sounded like he had swallowed marbles, and he didn't like it. In fact, it sounded as if it were nothing like what he had once been.

Only Reaper said that shouldn't matter, right? So he wasn't who he once was. Still, he wanted his old name.

Reaper shook his head. "You had a name once, but that man is gone. Dead. You died, just like the others. I reaped you," Reaper said, looking directly at him. "I took your soul, and you were chosen for a new destiny. This is your new path. You will be known as Ashen. What once was, and what will now grow into what is."

Ashen shook his head, not liking this new name. It was reminiscent of smoke, dust, and burned things.

He didn't want to be associated with burned things. Imaginary flame danced along his skin, a memory of burnt flesh and screams. The end filled him, but then the memories were gone just as quickly as they came.

Yet he could still hear the screams. Not his own, but of those who watched.

Had he died in a fire?

Had others cared that he died?

Ashen didn't know. But now, he had a name, a purpose.

And he would become a reaper.

Even if he still wondered who he had been before. Even as he tried to remember who had once cared enough about him to scream in agony.

TIME PASSED, ALTHOUGH ASHEN DIDN'T KNOW EXACTLY how long. It seemed like a blink, and he had an eternity. Perhaps that's what a reaper was. Maybe they lived outside of time.

He didn't know. Apparently, it wasn't his place to ask.

"A reaper does what its leaders tell them." Ashen nodded as if he understood. He didn't.

"You are to take the souls of those on your list and bring them to the next phase. You do not look at the next phase, you do not talk with anyone on the other side of the veil. They will not notice you. They will not speak to you. But you are supposed to take the souls of those you seek."

"Are we killers?" Ashen asked, feeling as if that were a very important question. He had already died, although he didn't know exactly how. Reaper wouldn't tell him.

He didn't want to be the cause of death. Didn't want to cause pain. He didn't want to even be near death.

Apparently, however, he *was* death.

Reaper shook his head. "No, you are not killing them. Time has done that. You do not cause their pain, their strife. You are not the center of their demise, or the bearer of their grief. However, you are the holder of their soul. Death will come for them, and you will be there for their souls."

"Am I not death itself?" Ashen asked, confused.

"You are death, but not *Death*."

Ashen really did not like Reaper's rhymes and riddles. Only he didn't have any say. Or any other reference. He was still learning his way. This new body of his. He knew it had to be a new one because the dreams he had when he was allowed to sleep had so much fire in them. The form he held now might be physical in a sense, but it wasn't what he had been originally born with.

He didn't remember his name, didn't remember who he had been. The longer he stayed in this realm, this shadow realm of sorts, the more he was certain that he had once been a bear shifter.

He could sometimes sense the bear within him, wanting to get out. But he wasn't that shifter anymore. His bear had died along with the man, but he missed him.

"Do reapers ever change into what they once were?" Ashen asked one day as they were training.

"Some do. Once they learn more about their new bodies. Others—most, in fact—aren't able to do that."

Reaper looked at him, frowning as he tilted his head.

"Do you know who you once were?"

Ashen shook his head. "I remember fire, but I do not

remember my name, or who screamed for me. I know I was once a bear. I can feel it prowling inside me, wanting to get out, but I am not strong enough to reach him."

"You've progressed farther than most would at your age."

"Is that a good thing or a bad thing?" Ashen asked, truly wanting to know the answer. He didn't know if he ever wanted to be a true reaper. He didn't like the idea that he was death personified now. However, he didn't think he had a choice.

"You died in fire, as you remember. The others mourned for you, and enough time has passed that while you have not been forgotten, they have progressed to a new stage of their grief. You will not see them again, for you are Ashen, not your former self. With the strength within your veins, I suspect that, one day, you may be able to shift into a bear, once your bear finds purchase in this new reality. That will be some time. Now, because of your strength and your training, the Collective of Shadows is ready to give you your first assignment."

Ashen's brows rose, and he stood up straighter, looking down at the scythe in his hands. He took in the long, billowing black robes around him.

He looked exactly like the Grim Reaper of legend, only he wasn't skeletal. Rather he was a man, a shadow of who he once was. His cheekbones were prominent, the flesh slowly sinking in. He had dark shadows under his eyes, and he didn't have as much muscle as he once had. He was still broad, however. Still strong. At least he could remember that much. But he didn't feel exactly like he had once before. How could he after death?

"The Collective of Shadows?" Ashen asked, coming back to what Reaper had said.

"The Collective metes out the assignments. They know whose thread must be cut, just like the fates themselves."

"The fates are real?" Ashen asked, thinking of the three fates of Greek lore.

"Who is to say what is real and what is not? What is myth and legend, and what is pain? After all, we are living in a world of the supernatural, where even our most imaginative minds can't fathom every type of paranormal out there. Every type of realm that exists."

Ashen noticed that Reaper hadn't actually answered the question. However, he hadn't really been expecting it. Not with a life that now consisted of unanswered questions and riddles.

"What is my first assignment?" Ashen asked.

"You will know soon. The Collective will be here with your first assignment."

"And I...kill this person?" He still wasn't exactly okay with that, even if they said he wasn't the bearer of the death.

"You take their soul as they die. You do not kill. You're not that person."

"Yet I still don't have a choice."

"No, it was written in your destiny long ago that this is who you would be. There's no need for you to be worried. Scared of who you are. This is part of life, and there must always be an ending."

"I thought the paranormals were supposed to live for eons. How do I take them from this life?"

"You take them just like I took you. It is your destiny, just as it's theirs to fade into the next phase of existence." He paused. "You are not killing them, Ashen. Remember that."

He wasn't sure people would agree with the other man. It was hard to do so when he wore the black hood and held the scythe of the fictional Grim Reaper who killed and took souls. However, he didn't have a choice in the matter.

He waited in silence along with Reaper until the Collective showed, ten men and women in robes that hid their faces. Reaper slid his cowl farther down his face so he was cloaked in shadows. So, there were eleven. Eleven that made up the Collective. Those who decided who would die and who wouldn't.

"Ashen," Reaper said, his voice deeper than usual. "You are now of the reapers. Your first assignment will be a woman named Eva. It is her time. This is her place. You are not the cause of her death, but the reaper of her soul. You will send her to the new phase and help her in this new stage of her existence. Go forth and reap and know that you are just."

Ashen rolled his shoulders back. "It will be my honor."

"Good, because this is your test," one of the members growled out. Ashen didn't like this one already, even if he didn't know who he was. "If you fail, your end will come sooner than you would like."

The others muttered in agreement, and Ashen held back a frown.

So, if he didn't do this, they would end him? Take him to the next plane? No, he didn't think so. He had a feeling if he didn't do this, if he didn't take Eva's soul, he would lose everything. And he would be but a blip in existence, not able to go to the next phase.

However, he knew his duty, knew his role. He was a reaper. And he would reap the soul.

They sent him the information on who Eva was, along with a mental image of her.

She was of average height, but nothing else about her was average. Her bronze skin glistened under the sunlight, her dark hair lustrous and shiny. He wanted to run his hands through it. He wondered where that weird thought had come from. She had dark eyes that seemed to see into the unknown, and gorgeous curves that begged for a man's touch.

But not his, he didn't think reapers were allowed that.

She was a banshee, one who screamed of death. He wondered if she would scream for hers.

He nodded and then put the location into his mind before he transported to where she stood. He hung back in the shadows, invisible to the naked eye—something reapers could do—and he waited. Eva held a basket of flowers in her hand, picking wild ones from a large hill in the banshee realm.

Banshees mostly lived within the human realm, though they had a small realm where they could hide amongst their own. However, they needed to scream for death or it hurt them, so they traveled to the other realms often, doing what their souls desired. They screamed for death; though they were not the cause of it.

For if you heard a banshee scream, death was sure to come.

These were Eva's last moments. He watched her, wondering what would happen to the others once they noticed she was gone, her soul ripped from her because of his duties.

"Okay, just a few more flowers and then I'll have enough for the picnic," Eva said to herself, smiling. "Little girls love flowers for their picnics, so I am being the best Auntie Eva ever."

A smile twitched on Ashen's lips, but he stayed where he was. She talked to herself and seemed to be a good aunt. He hated that he was going to have a part in her end.

And then she stiffened, all humor and happiness draining from her eyes as she looked to where he stood in the shadows.

Her mouth opened, and she sang. Not screamed, but sang. The song, however, wasn't one he knew, nor one he wanted to hear again.

It ripped into his ears, his soul—or at least whatever soul he had left. It felt like talons shredding him, the high-pitched song one of beauty, death, horror, and, yes, of life.

She sang, the basket of flowers falling to her feet before she followed it, dropping to her knees as she pulled at her hair and screamed and screamed and screamed.

Was this because of her death, or someone else's?

Ashen took a step forward and emerged from the shadows. He looked at her then and froze.

His heart pulsated, and something tugged inside of him. He knew exactly what it was. Her mouth closed, and she stopped screaming, her eyes widening as she looked at him.

"Mate," she whispered, the same time that he growled.

Mate.

Flashes of a bear, a family, a fire, a dragon in the air as

others screamed. Flashes of someone who had loved him, a brother, a family, a life.

It all bombarded him in a moment. He could hear the echo of the banshee's song again, and he dropped to his knees next to her.

And then there was nothing. Just darkness and death.

CHAPTER 2

Eva knelt on the grass and looked down at the man who was going to kill her.

A reaper.

The paranormals in the other realms might not know who they were, or perhaps they were only the bogeymen of the stories that they told children or ones who were doing bad things. But Eva knew who they were. All the banshees did.

After all, her kind knew when death was coming. So, of course, they knew who death was behind the mask.

However, in all of her time in this realm and on Earth, she had never thought the man who would one day be her mate would also be a reaper.

She swallowed hard, trying to understand exactly what was happening.

He looked…sad. Even unconscious as he was. She didn't know why she had never thought about what a reaper might look like. He was big and built, though he looked as if he could stand to have a few more pounds on his bones. It looked as if he were tired, as if he couldn't sleep.

There were dark circles under his eyes, and his cheeks were sunken in.

She felt sorry for him, wanted to make sure he was okay. Only she didn't have answers for how to do that. It wasn't her place to save a reaper, even if he was her mate.

He wore a long, black cloak, the cowl that had once been covering his face pulled back now as he lay passed out before her.

She wasn't sure if she should move him. She wasn't sure what she should do at all.

His scythe had fallen when he had, and she supposed she was lucky that he hadn't used the thing on her—or accidentally cut himself when he lost consciousness.

The blade looked sharp, that wicked curve familiar and devastating.

She didn't know exactly how reapers worked, mostly because she had never met one before. For it was said that if you were to meet a reaper, that was your end. They lived amid the shadows. Although she knew some lived within all the realms, hiding amongst the realm's people as if they belonged there.

Only she had never seen this man before.

Hesitantly, she reached out and traced her fingers along his strong brow. He didn't move, didn't flinch as she touched him, but she could feel his breath on her skin.

He was alive, merely passed out.

Was the thought of being her mate so overwhelming that he would lose consciousness?

She didn't know if she should find comfort in that thought, or be a little insulted.

After all, she hadn't passed out after discovering that the man who was going to kill her was also her mate.

Wasn't that a bit of irony, considering she spoke of death and he was death itself?

"Eva!"

Eva looked over her shoulder as her sister ran towards her, her long skirts billowing around her ankles.

Her sister Jasmine loved wearing long skirts and dresses, even though Eva was more a fan of jeans or leather pants.

Jasmine was softer and sweeter and a mother to four lovely children. She was the picture of maternal perfection, and though she screamed of death if she was near those who were slated to die, she did it with grace and dignity. Eva was a little jealous.

Eva herself tended to scream, her eyes wide, her cheeks turning red, and her sclera getting bloodshot.

She wasn't a pretty crier, and she was an even worse screamer.

And yet, she had sung for her mate…her reaper.

The other banshees used to make fun of her when she was younger, trying to control her power. But she was finding her place. Or, at least, she had been until she realized that the man that lay in front of her was her end *and* her future.

No, that wasn't correct. He couldn't be her future, not if this was her end.

And that meant there would be no mating for her.

"I'm fine, Jasmine," Eva said, keeping her hands on the man. She should probably let go of him, but she didn't want to. She liked touching him. Her soul reached out to him.

Well, she didn't want it to reach out too far, or he would just take it, and then she would be dead, wouldn't she?

"A reaper?" Jasmine said, her hands at her mouth.

He's just passed out. I didn't kill him. Though I don't know if you can actually kill a reaper. Can you?"

"I heard your song of death, and now a reaper's in front of you. My God, sister, what happened? You didn't scream. You *sang*… How is that possible? That only happens in cases of immense change."

"I don't really know. He just showed up, stepped out of the shadows, and looked at me." She wasn't sure if she should tell Jasmine the rest, but this was her big sister. She knew every one of Eva's secrets—not that she had many. "I fell to my knees and sang because I sensed death. But I don't know whose it was. Mine? Perhaps because he is a reaper, and he came for me."

"We will not let this happen. He does not get to have you."

She shook her head. "You know there's no running from the yell, let alone the song of a banshee. Just like there's no running from the scythe of a reaper."

"There's always a first for everything. Why are you touching him?"

Jasmine tugged at Eva's arms, trying to get her to stand up, but Eva didn't budge. She was afraid for this man, not *of* him. How wondrous.

"That's not all, Jasmine."

"What do you mean, that's not all? He is your death. There's more to it?"

"He's my mate, Jasmine. Just like you are to Desmond. He's mine." She let her fingers trail along his forehead, hoping he would wake up soon. Because if she were going to find a way to protect herself and not die, she really wanted to see his face. And make sure that she didn't accidentally kill him in the process.

"How? What? That doesn't make any sense. Reapers don't get mates. They're already dead."

"Well, apparently, we were wrong about that bit of the

legend. It's not like we actually know what happens to reapers. They don't come out into society and let everybody know what's going on."

"Perhaps not. But, darling, he can't be your mate. He's here to kill you."

"Well, he didn't. Instead, he found out he was my mate, said the word *mate* at the same time I did, and then passed out." Eva frowned. "I don't really know why he passed out."

"Well, let's go get some chains. We'll secure him, and then we'll figure out what to do next."

Eva just blinked at her sister. "The first thing you think of is chains? Do I really want to know what you and Desmond do when alone?"

Jasmine turned pink and shook her head. "Don't even start with the sass. We are going to figure out exactly what's going on."

"No, you are going back to your family to make sure they're safe. What if I'm wrong about death. Maybe he's not here for me?"

Jasmine's eyes widened. "Eva."

"I'll be fine. He's my mate. I guess we'll have to figure out exactly what that means, right?"

"Maybe. But, Eva, let us help."

"No, keep the family safe. I'll figure this out. I'm strong, Jasmine. You know this."

"I do, darling. I'm still allowed to be scared for you,

though. With Mama and Papa gone, we're all we have left."

"No, you have your family." Eva ignored the familiar pang of loss she felt at the thought of her parents.

"Don't you dare tell me that you have this," Jasmine said, flinging her hand out to indicate the reaper. "He's here to kill you, most likely. You don't get to have him."

"I don't know what's happening. You know our lives are all about listening to the fates. You need to follow that. And if I have to fight for my life or for those I love, I will. I'm not going to put you in danger by having you be here when he wakes up."

"*If* he wakes up," Jasmine mumbled.

Eva held back a smile, even though she was a little bit worried herself. "He will. Now, go. Protect the babies. Keep the others away. I'll figure out what to do."

Jasmine looked at her, then leaned down and kissed her on the top of the head like she had when they were little. And then went off to protect her family.

Eva hoped she hadn't been lying. Because, honestly, she really had no idea what she was doing.

She lay there with the reaper close to her on the ground for a little bit longer, knowing if he didn't wake up soon, the other banshees would likely ignore her warning and come to help her. She didn't want anyone else to get hurt. And, honestly, she needed time to think about what was happening. In order to do that, she needed him to wake up. She needed answers.

Thankfully, his eyelashes started to flutter. When his eyes opened, she held back a gasp. His eyes were coal-black with white spirals inside. She had never seen eyes like that. Didn't know if it was all reapers or just him.

He frowned at her, and she swallowed hard again.

"Are you okay?" she asked, clearing her throat since her voice was a little husky. After all, she hadn't expected to meet her mate. Or die. She really hoped the latter wasn't going to happen. The fact that she could joke at all, even in her head, meant that she was using a coping mechanism. And she was just fine with that. She really didn't want to die.

"Who are you?" he asked, still flat on the ground, his unusual eyes staring at her.

"I'm Eva. Are you here to kill me?"

The man blinked, and she wondered if she had been a little too blunt. He was a reaper, and she had screamed for a death. She didn't want it to be hers.

"Eva."

He whispered her name, repeating it as if he wanted to memorize the taste of it on his tongue.

Or perhaps she was looking too much into it.

"Did I pass out?"

She nodded. "Yes, after we both realized we're mates."

He blinked again and then sat up slowly, his gaze still on hers. "Are you always this blunt?"

"Yes. It usually startles people into telling me exactly what I need to know. So, what's your name?"

"I don't know. I had one at one point, but they took it."

She nodded, understanding. Reapers didn't have names at first, at least not the ones they were born with. The other reapers named them, gave them identities so they could collect souls. At least, that's what she had read in some of the banshee tomes. "What name did they give you?"

The reaper's eyes narrowed. "You know a lot for someone who is not of that realm."

"I'm a banshee. I speak of death, I sing it, I scream it. Of course, I know a little bit about the end."

"They call me Ashen."

Ashen. The name fit him, but she knew it didn't fit the man he had once been. Though, after death, it would make sense.

"Hello, Ashen. Like I said, I'm Eva. And, it appears we are mates."

"Now you're just trying to throw me off." Ashen shook his head and then stood up, frowning. "You sang for your death. You didn't scream."

She stood then too, not wanting to feel so small next to him. But no matter what she did, she couldn't really help it, the man was large. "You're not going to kill me. You don't get to."

"I'm told a reaper doesn't kill. They take a soul at the moment of death, but they don't cause pain."

Her eyes widened. "Really? I don't really know exactly what happens with reapers. I only know what's in the books."

"Then you may know more than I do."

She frowned. "Are you new to this, then?"

Ashen scowled, then looked down at the scythe on the ground before leaning down to pick it up. "You are my first. And, apparently, I'm not doing very well."

"I'm sorry. I don't want to die, though."

"I'm not supposed to kill you. So perhaps this mission was to follow you and take your soul."

A shiver slid over her, and she swallowed hard. "Even then, I'm going to fight."

"You don't have to fight me. I don't want to kill you."

"Because we're mates?"

"That's a large part of it," he said, not laughing, his voice deadpan. "I don't want to kill at all. But I don't think I have a choice."

"I don't know what's going to happen, but I'm not going to let you hurt my family."

"I'm not here for your family, I'm here for you."

At his equally blunt words, she stood straighter.

"Okay, then. Only, I'm not going to die today." She knew that was a lie.

"I didn't know a banshee was supposed to scream...or sing...for their own death."

Her power slid out of her as she thought of him. Thought about the bond they may share. A song slid through her body, and her eyes widened.

She didn't sing. Banshees didn't. They screamed. And yet...she remembered an old folktale, one she hadn't remembered until now.

Banshees only sang for their true halves, the ones that would be with them for eternity.

But he was death, and she was apparently destined to die. How could that be?

"Do you remember anything about who you were before this? Did you want to be a reaper?" She wanted to get him on a new topic since she was confused. Thankfully, he let her.

"I don't know if I had a choice about being a reaper."

"Well, I don't want to die. So, maybe if you find out who you *were,* we can figure out how to save me."

"I don't know who I was. Would the man I was before help you? Or would he reap your soul without conscience."

She looked down at her goose-pebbled flesh and swallowed hard once again. "I don't know." A pause. "I have a friend who might be able to help us find out."

He tilted his head, staring at her. "A friend?"

"Is that jealousy I hear? Just because we have the potential to be mates, doesn't mean I'm actually going to mate with you."

"I don't feel jealousy. I feel nothing."

Okay, then. "Would you like to meet my friend? Maybe he'll have some answers."

"I didn't help kill you. Perhaps it's not your time. Maybe it's because you're my mate."

"I'm not going to die today," she repeated. "I suppose we might have to think about exactly what the idea of being mated means. Because I scream for death, and yet my banshee wants to sing for you. And that only happens with mates. Sometimes. Maybe. I don't know."

He stared at her, his unusual eyes unblinking. "Your time may still be coming. I might have to reap your soul no matter what."

"I hope to the gods that whoever told you to come here was wrong."

"They can be wrong?" Aohun asked, his voice almost eager now.

"I hope so. Because there's a reason you're here. A reason I am. I suppose we should find my friend to figure out exactly what that might be."

CHAPTER 3

Ashen was confused once again, but as he'd spent nearly the entirety of his new life in that state, he was used to it. He still couldn't quite believe that he had passed out while meeting Eva. Had other paranormals ever done that when they found their mates? He hoped so, because he was already different enough, he didn't want to add to that.

Even as he looked at her as they stood in the middle of the banshee realm, a hill of flowers and darkness surrounding them, all he really wanted was to lean down and touch her.

The mating urge was such a weird thing. He didn't know exactly what happened with reapers. He didn't even know if reapers were able to *have* mates and the bonds that came with that precious gift. However, he could feel the bear inside him prowling. It wanted, it craved. And he didn't think it was going to hold back much longer.

Because when a bear found its mate, it was immediately ready for the inevitable, ready for its future. It wanted to mate, mark, and show the world that this person—or people in cases of triads—were theirs. The bear didn't want to hold back. And, frankly, Ashen wasn't sure he wanted to either.

Yet, he was going to. This wasn't the time or place for him to mark his mate. And he wasn't sure she would want that anyway.

After all, he had come to kill her, or maybe just to take her soul. To reap it.

Reaper had been very insistent that Ashen know he wasn't killing. He was merely there for death and the taking of souls. Ashen didn't want to reap Eva's soul. And not just because she was his mate. Although that was a very large part of it.

No, he didn't want to do it because it didn't feel right. It felt as if something were wrong. Like whoever had pulled her name out of a hat, or the cauldron, or had tugged her thread on the loom of fate had been wrong. Eva had so much light inside her, so much life. She didn't deserve to die. Not that he was the one to decide who deserved death or not. He didn't have that power, didn't have that righteousness within him, but he didn't want to lose Eva when he had just found her.

And from what he could tell, people relied on her.

He didn't want to ruin that.

"Where are we going?" he asked after staring at her for what was probably an awkwardly long time.

She blinked up at him. That's when he realized that she had been staring at him, too. "To the human realm."

He tilted his head, curious. "Humans are going to help us?"

She shook her head. "No, but I know some paranormals who live there. Ones I know happen to know many more things than I do. You'll like my friend, he's a dragon."

Ashen closed his eyes, a pang radiating in his heart as he imagined a dragon.

Why would that thought hurt? He didn't know if he knew any dragons. He didn't think he did. Did he? Did he know *this* dragon?

Another pang.

"What's that look for?" she asked, reaching out and putting her hand on his chest.

He looked down at the bronze skin of her hand on his black robes and sucked in a breath.

Had anyone truly touched him before? Perhaps in his first life, but in this one? He couldn't remember. Maybe when he had been passed out. He could vaguely remember someone touching his brow. Had it been her? Or had it just been a dream, his imagination conjuring what he wanted?

"What's wrong?" she asked again, and he swallowed hard.

"Nothing. I'm not sure."

"It can't be nothing if you're looking like that."

"I don't know, I just have this weird feeling when I think about that dragon. It's like I should know who you're talking about. As if I might know who he is."

Eva nodded as if that made sense. Did it? "Well, my friend knows a lot of people. Perhaps he knew you in your first life."

"I don't like not knowing. The fact that I don't even know my name or anything about who I was…" He paused. "I remember I was a bear."

Her eyes widened. "A bear?"

"Yes, a grizzly, I think. I can't truly tell with the animal prowling inside me. Reaper told me that it would take time for the shifter that I was to show up again."

"So, you lost both of your halves when you died?"

He nodded. "I don't like that I died at all, but I can't go back and change that."

"You have a second chance at life, though," she said quickly.

"If this *is* life. Am I truly alive? Or am I here just to reap souls."

"That is a very heavy question that perhaps we can't answer. Maybe my friend can. Now, let's get you out of here, just in case the other banshees get any ideas."

He went on alert, glaring over her head. "Would they hurt you?" he asked, his voice low.

She shook her head, a smile playing on her lips. "No, they're not going to hurt me, but they may hurt you. Mostly because they would likely take killing or reaping the soul of one of their own very personally." She paused, and he looked down at her. "I would take it personally too, so I'm going to thank you again for not reaping right away."

"I'm not going to reap your soul. You're my mate." He frowned. "And you're not dead. And, apparently, I can only reap those who are."

"That's good to know." She sighed. "However, we do have a problem."

He froze. "What?"

"I can't transport myself like other banshees." She shrugged. "It's a quirk. I have to take the long way from realm to realm. So, unless you know how to transport more than one person, it's going to take us a while to get to the human realm."

"I don't know how to do that. We'll walk together. Or drive or whatever we need to."

"That's good because we'll want to figure this all out fast before whoever is actually coming to kill me arrives."

"I'm not going to let that happen."

"Good, because I don't want it to happen."

She held out her hand, and he looked down at it, wondering why she was so patient with him, so caring already. "We can do this, Ashen. We're going to find the answers."

"I hope so. Because it's the not knowing that hurts the most." And then he slid his hand over hers and squeezed.

She grinned, and they were off.

The realms weren't situated logically. In fact, many of the realms were haphazardly placed next to each other, pressed against one another, or even on top of one another in some cases. Unless you had a portal, a magical spell, or an inherent gift to transport from one realm to another, you couldn't easily just go from one place to the next. And, unfortunately, the banshee realm was in a far distant part of the universe compared to the human realm. Ashen had a feeling that only the hell realm, and maybe even the reaper realm, was farther away.

If it had just been him, he would've transported. However, Eva couldn't, so they were going to do this the slow way. And that meant traversing through other realms, and hopefully not setting off any wards or getting caught. There were traveling portals that could get you from one side of the realm to the other, and they allowed free passage as long as there was a treaty in place between the realms. But it got complicated and a little scary for some quickly. Add in the fact that Ashen only knew part of that from what he had read during this training and couldn't remember all of the intricacies and politics in each realm, and he realized that he was going to have to rely on Eva for a lot.

"What is the nearest realm to the banshees?" Ashen asked as they made their way to the end of the hilly area where a portal to the next realm would be.

"That would be the leprechaun realm."

He frowned, wondering if he had ever known a leprechaun. He'd had to, right? That familiar pain slid through him, but he ignored it. He hated that he couldn't remember his old life.

"And, after that?" he asked, looking around.

"After that, it'll be the dragon realm, and then a few others. But, thankfully, the road from portal to portal on this end is quite short. If you stay on the portal road, you're not technically trespassing."

"That's always good."

"Well, I would hope so. Because I don't really want to end up in a territorial battle or war right now."

"I don't either."

"Especially because most people don't know that reapers exist. It's going to take all day for us to travel, but we'll make it," she said quickly.

"And then we'll figure out exactly what to do," Ashen said.

They made their way through the portal, the magic clinging to his skin. The bear who lay dormant within him started to shift, slowly waking up and stretching.

He rubbed his chest over his heart, wondering what would happen if the bear indeed came back.

Could a reaper shift? Reaper hadn't been too helpful with that question earlier, but Ashen hoped he could take his other form. He missed his bear, even if he didn't quite remember what it felt like to shift. But it still felt as if he had lost a part of himself.

"We're here, at least in the first realm," Eva said beside him. He looked around, his eyes wide.

"Wow," he said, his voice a whisper.

"Yeah, the leprechauns don't really do anything half-way, do they?"

She wasn't joking. There were literal rainbows criss-crossed over the air, and it looked as if that was what they used as roads. Everything was green, and there were gold pillars everywhere. It looked like a box of that children's cereal had exploded all over the realm. He couldn't quite keep his eyes on any one thing because it almost hurt to look at it.

"This isn't my favorite place, even though I know a couple of leprechauns who are amazing. They don't live here, though."

She said the words quietly, and Ashen held back a

smile. He hadn't even realized that he was going to smile, and his face hurt a little doing so, but he liked it.

Eva was funny. His mate was fun.

Mate.

If he were the person he had been before, he knew, unequivocally knew, that this would be what he wanted. To find his mate, and to find that chance for happiness. But he wasn't that person. And he didn't know what he wanted now. He only knew that he had a feeling that Eva was it.

"Okay, this next portal's quick, so we don't have to stay here too long."

They went from portal to portal, walking hours in between realms.

They passed others, but nobody really bothered them.

He was grateful that nobody really gave him a second look because he didn't want others to know precisely who or what he was. Before they hit the leprechaun realm, he had tucked his cloak into his bag and had hidden his scythe in a magical air pocket beside him so he could walk around freely without having to scare others with a large weapon.

That meant he was wearing dark jeans and a dark, long-sleeved shirt that covered up any scars he had.

His new form hadn't come out whole. He still had what looked like burn scars on parts of his body, as if that had been something so relevant in his first life that they had come back in his second. He didn't mind because it was a reminder of who he had once been, and he wanted to remember that person.

"Your hair is getting blonder," Eva said as they made their way through the fifth realm. They were both getting tired, he knew that, but she hadn't stopped moving. In fact, they just kept going at a steady pace, both of them ready to figure out exactly what was happening. He didn't want Eva to die, and he didn't know if he wanted to remain a reaper who listened blindly to orders.

"What do you mean?" he asked, sliding his hands through his hair. It reached his shoulders and had been white before. Now, he saw that it was turning slightly gold.

"That's interesting."

"You're starting to look more like a Viking god rather than the ghost you resembled before."

He shrugged and slid his hands through his hair again. "I wonder if I look the same as I did before."

"I have a feeling your eyes are completely different."

"Yes, I've never known eyes like mine. Though all of the reapers have various hues."

"I never knew that. Of course, you reapers are very secretive."

"I have a feeling that each paranormal realm does its best to be the most secretive."

"Well, that makes sense. Okay, this is going to be a

longer path after this portal. It's the wizard realm, and while they don't mind if we walk through it, we have to be careful with the magic we invoke."

"I wonder if I knew a wizard before."

"I know one. He's actually pretty high up in the hierarchy. If we had time, I would go visit him and see what he and his mate have to say. However, we're on our way to a dragon."

Ashen nodded, and then they slid through the magic into the new realm. It looked like old London, complete with magical fire in gas lamps. Well, old London in the human realm probably didn't have magic, but what did he know? He hadn't been there. At least, he didn't think he had. He honestly didn't know how old he had been when he died.

"Okay, this is going to take a while. We might need to rest."

She rolled her shoulders back, and he frowned. "Do I need to get you something to eat?"

"I'm not hungry, but if I were, I could get my own food. Just because we are potential mates doesn't mean that you have to take care of me."

"I'm a bear, I'm supposed to take care of you. It's our thing."

He said the words, and her eyes widened. "That is a very bear thing to say."

"But I'm not a bear, am I? I'm a reaper."

"You can still be a bear. You said yourself that it could come back. Do you feel him at all?"

He frowned, nodding. "A little. But he's taking a while to wake up from what feels like a long nap."

"Hibernation?" she asked, her lips twitching.

"You know, I would get mad about that joke, but it's an apt description."

"I can barely believe you are letting me get away with that."

He just rolled his eyes, another smile playing on his lips. He liked Eva. And if they both survived, he had a feeling he was going to like being her mate.

But all of that was a big *if*.

As if his thoughts had conjured the man, a male in a dark robe appeared before them. Ashen let out a growl that was all bear.

"Ashen, reaper, you have failed. And now you will have to pay the price. Your charge was supposed to die, yet you frolic with her from realm to realm, defying your masters and the fates. You know the punishment. You will be no more, and I will have the pleasure of ending your charge's life."

Ashen knew that voice, the one who had sneered at him before. He wanted to rip the face from the man's head.

That was a very bear thing to think. Or perhaps, it was also reaper. He *was* death, after all.

"What the hell?" Eva asked next to him, and he used the power of his reaper to pull the cloak back over him, his scythe appearing in his hand.

Eva looked at him and then at the other reaper. And then she opened her mouth and screamed.

It was nothing like the song she had sung to him at their first meeting. Her death? His death? He may never know. Because deep down in his heart, he knew it had to be this reaper's death. There was no other answer.

The other reaper grimaced, his dark eyes with purple spirals narrowing. "I really hope that is your death because you failed. The Collective of Shadows sends their regards. Now, your soul and hers will be ours."

The reaper's scythe formed in his hand, and then they were fighting. Other people roamed about, cursed, and then got out of the way of the two reapers fighting one another in the open. He hoped no one would know exactly who they were, but this reaper had just outed them at least to the people in the immediate vicinity.

Eva finished screaming, her whole body shaking, but he didn't know if she was a warrior. However, she picked up a large stick from beside her and started coming at the reaper, as well. The reaper was much larger and could fight harder than either of them.

Ashen charged, slicing with his scythe, but he wasn't strong as a reaper.

However, the bear within him was now awake. He

threw back his head and roared, claws ripping through his fingertips. The other reaper's eyes widened, and he took a step back.

And that's when Ashen moved forward, clawing at the reaper. He moved, one strike then another. The reaper screamed, and then there was no more sound or movement.

Eva stood next to him, her hands shaking, a bloody stick in her hand from where she had hit the reaper over and over again, fighting for both of their lives.

"Oh my God, I helped to kill someone," Eva practically shouted, and the wizards around them looked on, concern on their faces. But they didn't move forward. It was as if they were used to fights to the death like this. And maybe they were.

Eva started to shake and dropped the stick, her eyes wide.

Ashen didn't know how to make her stop, didn't know how to pull her head out of the panic she was clearly feeling. She hadn't been the one to kill him, Ashen had done that. But it looked as if she had never been in a fight like this before.

He cursed himself for letting it happen.

So, he did the only thing he could. He lowered his head, pressed his mouth to hers, and kissed her.

She froze, her entire body stiffening at the contact, but he kissed her a little bit harder, brushing his lips along hers, and then he moved back. She blinked, her lips parted.

"Oh."

"Are you okay?" he asked, his bear in his voice. His claws had receded, but he could feel his beast prowling, as well as the reaper inside him.

He was now a duality, and he didn't know exactly what that meant or what to do about it.

"What are we going to do?" she asked, her voice small.

"What the hell is going on here?" another man asked. Ashen whirled, his bear at the forefront, his scythe back in his hand.

The man in front of him looked on, his mouth agape, as he just stared.

"Dear goddess."

CHAPTER 4

Eva looked between Ashen and the other man, one that was familiar, but she didn't immediately remember his name.

"It's you. But…how can that be?"

Other wizards began to fill the area, and Ashen cursed under his breath. "We need to go. Come on, we need to head to the human realm."

"Wait, how is this possible?" the wizard asked, and Eva looked again.

"Do you know who he is?" Eva asked, and Ashen tugged her arm.

"Come on, we have to go."

His whole body was shaking, and she looked into his eyes and knew he had to be in pain. Perhaps he had known this man in his previous life. Or at least had met him before. And this wizard, Levi. That was his name, Levi. He must've known him. Right?

Because the last time that Ashen had been forced to think about his past, or even his future when he had seen her and found out that they were mates, he had passed out from the pain. At least, that's what she had thought.

Was he going to do it again?

"We need to go. I feel like someone's watching us."

She looked around. "The entire wizard force is watching us. And we just,"—she swallowed hard—"killed a man."

"I'll handle this," Levi said, looking directly at her. "Please, don't go." He paused. "Please."

Ashen gripped his head, taking a deep breath. "What's happening?"

"I don't know," she said under her breath. "Do you know him? Levi, right?"

Levi narrowed his eyes at her and then nodded tightly. "Eva? You know Dante. I've met you at the bar before."

"Dante?" Ashen said and then fell back. Levi was there, holding out an arm to steady him, but Ashen shook his head. He clearly needed everyone to stay away.

"I can't think. I need space."

"Get everyone out of here," Levi said, and the other wizards around began to move as if this happened daily.

"What about the dead one?" someone asked.

"Cast a spell to hide him from the others, much like you already did to hide what was going on in this traveling space. But speak nothing of this. You know these aren't our secrets, and that is the law of this traveling area."

The others listened to him, and for that, Eva was grateful.

"Now, come with me," Levi said, and Eva raised her chin.

"You're not going to kill us, are you? Because I'm kind of tired of that."

She had screamed for death. She hadn't even known that a reaper could die since they were already dead, but, apparently, a scythe could take anyone out.

And she had helped to kill him. She had blood on her hands, could still feel it warm on her skin. It hadn't helped her mind that she'd wiped it all on her pants.

It was still there. Waiting.

Levi looked between her and Ashen. "It seems we have lots to talk about. Now, one of my homes is close to here. It would be a safe place for you to think, to gather yourselves before I take you to see Dante."

She looked at Ashen and nodded. "He's a friend."

Ashen ran his hands through his long, blond hair and swallowed hard. "I guess we could use a few of those now."

They followed Levi and the two spoke in hushed

tones, and she was glad for that. It was all a little bit too much, considering that it had been almost a full day since she had met this reaper, this man who had been sent to kill her but had protected her instead. What would it mean for his soul that he had killed a fellow reaper and had gone against the rules of his new life?

He had protected her, just like she had tried to protect him. And now she was afraid that he was going to lose everything because of it.

There was a reason they were fated mates, and yet the idea that they were still so new at this was ever-present in her mind.

"Here we are," Levi said after a near-silent journey. She looked up at the two-story house in the woods and could feel the wards pulsating off of it. Protection. Home. Sanctuary.

She didn't have magic of her own, that's not what kind of paranormal she was. However, she could usually sense it. Ashen's shoulders tensed.

"Will this magic harm my mate?" Ashen asked, and she froze, blinking up at him.

Okay, so they were just going to declare it like that, were they? Good to know.

Levi shook his head. "No, it won't." A pause. "Your mate?"

"Yes," she said, hoping that Levi understood. She knew he wouldn't be able to sense the bond, but there was no going back now. Not with that declaration and the fact that they had killed to protect one another.

Her life was tied up in fate, why should she run from it?

They made their way inside Levi's home, but she didn't relax. The other reapers could show up at any moment, and she had a feeling that once Ashen figured out exactly who he was before, everything would change once again.

It didn't matter that had been, what, only twenty hours of her knowing him. She didn't want him to be hurt any more than he already had been.

He had died before and was already risking everything for a life of his own—and for her.

She protected her family, her nieces and nephews and her sister and brother-in-law. She did her best to keep them safe, even if all she could do was be the watcher amongst the others of her realm. She wasn't a warrior, and she couldn't even flash from one side of the realm to the other.

But she had always been there for her family. And now, she would be here for Ashen. Even if she didn't know what to do next.

"You are Levi?" Ashen asked, his voice hoarse.

"I am." Levi looked at his face, trying to see someone there that wasn't.

"Do you know of reapers?" Eva asked, and Ashen stiffened.

"I'm sorry," she whispered.

"No, he will need to know who the reapers are, especially since one died in his realm."

"Reapers. They're real? They aren't just the bogeymen?" Levi asked.

"They're real," Ashen growled. "So real that I'm one of them. Apparently, when someone dies, another can decide, or rather fate can make the decision for that soul to be reborn into a reaper. I don't remember who I was before. I don't remember anything other than the fact that I was a bear and I died in flames."

Levi let out a rough laugh, one that was strange and full of pain. Eva wanted to reach out and hold him, the same with Ashen, but she didn't. She stood still, knowing that this was important.

"So you take souls?" Levi asked, ignoring the giant elephant in the room. Namely, how Levi knew Ashen. She was grateful that they were taking this slow. She didn't know if Ashen could take too much all at once.

"I'm supposed to. I didn't. The man we killed wanted me to take Eva's, and I wouldn't."

"So he came after you. And you killed him?"

"I didn't know a reaper could die again, but he threatened my soul and Eva's. So I used my scythe, and I took his instead." Ashen growled a bit, and she wanted to move his hair from his face just to make sure he was okay. It was such an odd reaction, but she felt as if she had done it countless times before.

"Are you going to get in trouble for that reaper?" Levi asked.

"He already wanted our souls, so I'm going to go with yes," Ashen answered dryly, and she smiled, surprised he could laugh at a time like this. Or at least joke.

Her stomach hurt. She knew she was pale, her body shiny with sweat. They had been going through so much recently already, and her body just hurt. She wasn't going into shock, but she was close.

"If you are the reincarnation of someone who died, and you look just like him, are you supposed to know who you were once?" Levi asked, his voice soft.

Eva reached out and put her hands on the small of Ashen's back. He leaned towards her, and she was grateful.

"I don't know if I should know too much. Because if I do, when I start to remember things, it hurts. I feel like there're hot pokers in my mind. I passed out the first time I looked at this one," Ashen said, gesturing to her, and she blushed.

"Oh," Levi said softly.

"My name is Ashen. That's the name that they gave me anyway." He paused. "Do you know what my name was before this?"

Levi looked as if he were considering holding back, but he blurted it out anyway. "Torrent. You were Torrent. A bear shifter, and a friend."

Eva reached out as Ashen leaned sharply to the side, sucking in a deep breath.

"I don't think I'm supposed to have these memories. But they're slowly coming. Damn it."

"What do we do?" Eva asked.

"I don't think we're supposed to do anything. I don't think I'm normal."

Levi moved closer. "I won't say anything else. There's going to be some people who want to see you, though, Torrent."

Ashen let out a groan. She didn't think of him as Torrent. He was Ashen to her. And he would be until he decided otherwise.

Levi seemed to understand that because he winced as soon as he said it.

"I'm sorry. Take your time. I'll just…I guess I should handle that dead body back there."

"No need," a voice said from behind them. They all turned, the ward's pulsating all at once.

Ten shrouded figures stood behind them in the small house. She shrank back, looking for a weapon.

Ashen's claws were out again, something that had startled her at first, but now she liked it. It was handy to have a bear shifter when she didn't have a weapon.

Levi was on her other side, his palms outstretched as burning flames spun. He was a wizard and would use his magic to protect his home. She was just grateful that his mate and children weren't here to get caught in the crossfire. If anyone came to attack them, he would burn the place to the ground.

"How did you get past my wards?" Levi asked.

"We are reapers." An answer in itself, apparently. "I have no quarrel with you, wizard. Thank you for protecting our secret from the others. I'm sure you'll ensure that none of the others in this realm speak of this."

"I'm not sure of anything," Levi growled out.

"I see."

"I am Reaper," the main man spoke.

"We figured you were a reaper," Eva said dryly, her hand on Ashen's elbow. She needed to touch him, needed to make sure he knew he wasn't alone.

"No, *Reaper*. My title and my name. It's not very original, I know, but I am millennia-old. It's what happens when you are one of the first."

"Oh."

"You're special," Reaper said to Ashen.

"Really?" Ashen asked, his voice a growl.

"Already able to partially shift. And I know your memories are coming back. That makes me think the man who sent me out for you was wrong."

Eva's eyes widened.

"Torrent died protecting his brother's mate. Protecting *my* mate. It was during the first war of the dragons, the one of the lightning-struck. He wasn't destined to die then?"

Reaper looked between them, and Eva sucked in a breath, unable to do anything.

"I do not know. And as one who has held fate in his hands, who has been to the loom itself, that worries me. There has been a shift, not merely that of the lightning-struck, but of something more. I will have to figure out exactly what that means."

"So, I died for no reason?" Ashen growled out.

"Perhaps. Or maybe the reason was to protect those you loved, to come back to safeguard another."

Ashen looked at Eva, and her hand squeezed his arm even harder.

"She was not meant to die," Reaper began, and she started, looking at him.

"Excuse me?"

"The other reaper, the one you so easily killed—something you're not supposed to do by the way—was the one who found your name in fate. He was the one who gave me your name at first, Ashen, when you were Torrent. He lied. For reasons unknown. Perhaps he wanted to be fate itself, wanted that power. We may never know, but I will find out."

Ashen began to laugh, but there was no humor in it.

"I died for that man's amusement? And I almost killed my mate, an innocent, for nothing. I won't kill her. I won't kill for you at all. I want no part of this."

Reaper nodded. "Understandable. However, you will always be a reaper. You will always have those powers."

"I refuse to reap."

There was a finality in his tone that Eva agreed with. After everything that had just occurred, she didn't blame him.

"We can discuss that in a hundred years or so," Reaper said calmly as if he hadn't just passed a century between them in terms of what Ashen needed to do.

"What does that mean?" Eva asked.

"It means, I apologize for the inconvenience."

"Death, an inconvenience?" she asked incredulously.

"When you've been touched by as much death as I have, sometimes, it's nearly just. I am sorry for what happened, but I am glad that you found your mate. We will give you a century, Ashen, for you to find your path. If you choose to come back to us, we would be grateful. After all, there is a spot open in our Collective, and with the fate of the worlds resting on our shoulders, the loom needs to be read."

And with that, the ten shrouded figures disappeared, leaving the three of them standing there slack-jawed and wide-eyed.

"Well, that doesn't happen every day," Levi said,

tapping his fingers on the wood next to him. "Or maybe it does in my case. Being mated to a lightning-struck seems to change everything."

Eva looked over at Levi, blinked, then turned back to Ashen. "What now?"

Ashen shook his head and then leaned down and brushed his lips over hers. "Now, I suppose, we figure out exactly who I am."

She looked up at him and knew that this was the beginning. The start of everything that she had ever hoped for. She wanted to find out what would happen with him, what would happen with them.

And without the reapers on her tail, she would finally have time to do that.

CHAPTER 5

Ashen looked up at the sign for the old bar that reminded him of an Irish pub and frowned.

"Dante's Circle?"

"It's his bar. Dante. And his circle of friends. Plus, I think he enjoyed the *Divine Comedy*."

Ashen looked down at Eva. "Are you my Virgil?"

"Through Hell and Purgatory, though I could be your Beatrice through Paradiso."

"I will have to reread those books. It's been a few decades since I read it," Ashen said with a frown. "Why can I remember things like that, but can't remember the faces of my family?"

"Maybe because those things aren't as important?"

"Maybe." He swallowed hard, his chest constricting. "Will you still call me Ashen? Until I remember?"

Eva reached up and slid her arms around him. "I'll call you whatever you need me to. And then we can find that path where we find each other."

"Thank you," he whispered and then leaned down, taking her lips with his.

The bear and the reaper inside him wanted to take her right then, to claim her as his mate and then figure out the rest later. But he held himself back. Because Eva needed it, and he wanted to figure out who they were before he put them on another trail of fate.

"Are you ready?" Levi asked, his voice low beside them.

"As ready as I'll ever be," Ashen said as he pulled away from Eva, but kept his hand clasped with hers.

"What did you tell them?"

"I told my mate who I was bringing with me. Because I don't keep secrets from her. And I told Dante because you can't keep secrets from a dragon." He sighed. "He wasn't happy because he's mated to someone close to you, at least the old you. And he wanted to tell him right away. I'm not sure what Dante decided. If we were any later, I know for sure he would have already told him, but I don't know about now."

Ashen sighed, unsure of anything at the moment.

"I also told the others that I had someone they needed to meet, but I didn't warn them. I didn't feel I had the right. They're probably going to hurt me for that choice, but I felt like you deserved that moment."

Ashen swallowed hard. "I'm not the man I once was," he whispered.

"None of us are," Levi said sagely, and Eva squeezed Ashen's hand.

"You don't need to be that man." He looked down at his mate and nodded.

Let's go," Ashen said softly, wondering if he was strong enough for this.

He felt like he had just woken up from a dream, one that brought death and destruction.

He had a hundred years to find out who he was before he had to go back to his duties as a reaper. If he wanted to be a reaper at all.

In the interim, he would figure out exactly what he was with Eva. But he already knew that. The loom of fate had already been woven long ago where that was concerned. She was his mate, and she had sung her song for him. There was no going back. He could already feel the bond beginning to take form between them, her song the catalyst. That was why he had passed out initially.

They would need to cement the bonds, but that would come. When they were ready. First, though, he had to face this task. One he couldn't remember.

They walked inside, and there were groups of paranormals all around, each talking to one another and laughing. There was a gorgon behind the bar, secretly making out with who he assumed was her mate, a jaguar with a scar on his face.

Ashen didn't recognize anyone, but there were a few scents in his nostrils that reminded him of something. Like from a dream.

But more likely, from Torrent's past.

Others gave him strange looks but didn't really pay attention to him. Then there was a gasp, a cry, and someone fell to their knees.

"Torrent?" a deep voice asked, and a large man with blond hair and bright green eyes ran to him "Torrent."

Ashen looked into those eyes and wondered if he should know who the man was. He looked so familiar. And yet, not.

If Torrent looked into the mirror, though, he might recognize those cheekbones and that hair. The wide eyes. Though his eyes were no longer green. Or maybe they had never been.

He didn't know.

He couldn't remember.

"Torrent, how is this possible?" The man looked over his shoulder and growled at his mate. "You knew this, didn't you?"

The dragon, it must be Dante, walked forward and nodded, his hands outstretched, palms up. "Levi found him today. And I told him to bring him here. I didn't know if he was actually going to come, however. That's why I didn't mention it right away. Although, if they hadn't shown up within the next five minutes, I was going to tell you, and we would have hunted him down."

The dragon looked at Ashen then, his black-and-blue hair over his shoulders, a fang peeking out of his smile.

Ashen was really lucky that he'd shown up because he did not want to be on the bad side of a dragon.

"You…you came. It's you," Jace gasped as he turned back to Ashen.

Jace. His name was Jace. Ashen's brother, well… Torrent's brother, was Jace.

Flashes of bear cubs and honey, a family and warmth, all filled him. He staggered, and Eva put her hands on his chest.

"Breathe, Ashen. You can do this. It's okay."

"Why are you calling him Ashen?" Jace asked, his voice deadly. "What's wrong?"

"It's my name," Ashen said honestly. He looked up at Jace, his brother, and let out a long breath. "I'm not the man you knew. I don't remember much. Don't blame the dragon for holding back. I think he wanted you to see me first. For I am a ghost. A memory. A wisp of being."

"You are not, damn it," Eva said from beside him, and he looked over.

"I'm not?"

"No, you are Ashen. You are whoever you need to be.

Whoever you want. And if they have a problem with that, they can go through me."

His banshee raised her chin and looked at the rest of the people in the bar, an angelic warrior, a demon, a brownie, a pixie, a leprechaun, a lion, and even a phoenix. So many of their kind all in one room, working together as one. They were friends.

Were they Torrent's friends?

Perhaps.

Were they Ashen's friends?

No, not yet. He didn't even know himself yet, but he couldn't wait to figure out exactly who the rest were.

"Okay…okay," Jace whispered, holding onto Dante's arms. "How is this possible?"

Ashen let out a breath. "I died. Because of the fates or the reapers, I don't know. Maybe it was an accident. I might not ever know, but I died. And then I woke up again, in this new body." He looked down at himself and frowned. "Or, a body similar to this."

"Your skin is a little tanner than it was before, your hair a little blonder than when I first met you. Your eyes are the same, though."

He looked down at Eva and smiled. "I think I'm finding myself, so I'm changing. Just like the bear inside me."

Jace's eyes went gold. "Your bear? You can shift?"

Ashen closed his eyes. "Maybe? I don't know. I'm a reaper."

"What's a reaper?" someone asked.

"It's a long story," he said, and then he spoke of the reapers and the choices and how he'd met Eva. The others nodded, and he felt like maybe they understood. Couples and triads looked at each other as if they got exactly what he and Eva had already gone through in their short time together. And perhaps that was true. He wasn't quite sure, but he couldn't take too much more at the moment, so he wasn't going to think about it.

Not yet. He couldn't remember everybody's name, and he wasn't even sure he had known everybody when he was alive.

"It's been so long since I've seen you," Jace said, his voice a rasp. "Can I...can I hug you?" Jace asked, his face pink.

"If you'd like," Ashen said, his body stiff.

Eva laughed. "Bears are the most touchy-feely shifters out there," she said, and the other shifters in the room laughed.

"She's got that right," a wolf called out.

"Far cuddlier than dragons," Dante said dryly.

The succubus that stood between them laughed. "You're pretty cuddly, my dragon."

Ashen held out his arms, and then Jace pulled him into a hug that was bone-crushing.

"I thought you died, baby brother. I looked at you, and you smiled, and then the flames touched you."

Ashen closed his eyes and took a deep breath, inhaling the scent of family. "I'm alive. I'm here. Somehow."

"I'll never forgive myself for letting you get hurt," the dragon said, and then Ashen remembered.

"It was a war. It was your mother."

The dragon nodded, his jaw tight. "I am sorry."

Ashen shook his head. "It's not your fault. It might have even been the reapers themselves."

"I'll kill them," Jace muttered.

"We already took care of that," Eva said, her face a little pale. Ashen reached out and gripped her hand, and Jace looked between them.

"Your mate?"

"Yes," Ashen said. "Although, we're not bonded yet."

"Well, let's just tell the whole world that, shall we?" Eva said, and Ashen winced.

"Sorry."

"No worries. However, you're going to have to stop saying everything that pops into your mind."

"He was like that as a little boy, too," Jace said, his eyes wide with wonder. "We have more siblings, and our parents..."

"They're all on their way."

Ashen looked at Dante.

"You have been busy."

"I'm a dragon. It's what I do."

Ashen sat there as he was introduced to everybody once again, even his niece and nephew, a baby dragon, and a baby bear, who looked into his newly unusual eyes and smiled, wanting hugs before shifting and playing on the floor like the babies they were.

When a small child bumped into him, he looked down and picked up the baby bear before kissing it on top of the head as if he had done it a thousand times before giving him back to Jace. He'd never met these children, he knew that. A different kind of pain slid through him over the fact that he'd missed so much.

"No worries. It's almost like you're back to yourself."

Ashen shook his head.

"I'm not. I'll never be."

"None of us are who we were before the wars. But you're here. I have to count that as a blessing."

"Torrent?" a female voice said from behind him, and he turned.

A female bear stood beside a larger male bear, as well as three other bears that looked remarkably like Jace.

Ashen froze and knew exactly who these people were.

The woman took a few steps forward, her legs shaking. "Torrent," she whispered.

And then she reached up and pushed a piece of hair behind his ear as if she had done so countless times before.

"Mom," he whispered.

"Torrent," she whispered, and then she tucked her head under his chin and wept as the others looked on and spoke to him, telling him stories of his time before he became a reaper, tales of who he had been.

He didn't know if he would ever be that man again, but that was okay with him. Because now he had a second chance. He looked at Eva and knew who he wanted to take his second chance with. This was their beginning, their chance, and when the time came, he would take every next step with her.

CHAPTER 6

Four months later

"I want you to come," Ashen whispered into her ear.

"You say that every day, and yet, you've never been inside me. I wonder why that is."

"You wanted to take it slow," he said, nibbling at her chin.

She groaned and wrapped her legs around his waist. They were naked, skin to skin, and she wanted him inside her desperately, just like so many times before. But they had waited to go further…until now.

Mostly because everybody in their life had told them that they didn't have to rush into it. They could take their time. And with so much change and the fact that Ashen was still trying to remember every detail about who Torrent was, they had put their bonding on hold.

Because Eva wanted to know who he was, all facets of him, and she was grateful that he was taking the time to learn more about her, as well.

They lived in the banshee realm, mostly because it was safer for her. It was hard for her to be around so many humans and other paranormals when she could scream for their death at any moment. With a denser population, it was harder on her. She would visit the other realms if she had too much power quaking inside her, but the banshee realm was quieter.

And that was good for Ashen because he could find his new place in a world where others might not understand him and know more about him than he did about himself.

All of that fled her mind as he slowly slid his hand between them, cupping her.

"Are you ready for me?"

"I don't know, you better check," she said, licking her lips.

He looked at her then, his unusual eyes gorgeous and sultry. And then he slid one large finger into her, finding that bundle of nerves that almost sent her right over the edge. Her toes curled, and she gritted her teeth, not wanting to come yet.

"Oh, yes, wet and slick, it's so fucking hot."

"All for you, Ashen."

"I love it when you call me that."

"It's the name of the man I love. The man I found."

He was Torrent to everyone else, something that he appreciated. Yet to her, he would always be Ashen. The man who had refused to kill her, and the one that she had sung to at first sight.

He was her reaper, her Ashen, and she loved that she had a special name for him.

"Bond with me. Make love to me. I don't want to wait anymore."

"I'm going to bond with you. As a bear, too."

She frowned. "I am not getting furry with you for your bear."

He threw back his head and laughed. She relished the sound. He rarely laughed, but when he did, it was *everything.*

"I meant I'm going to bite you on your shoulder and mark you as mine."

She blushed. "Oh, that's fine. Get biting. Get in me right now, Ashen. Don't make me reap your ass." She winked as she said it. He rolled his eyes, and then he positioned himself between her legs and plunged. His eyes were on hers, and she gasped at the intrusion, needing more, wanting more. Except, at the same time, it was all too much.

He leaned down, thankful, and she took his lips. She

kissed him, running her hands down his back as he plunged in and out of her. They made love, sweetly, then hard and fast, *everything*. And when she arched up into him, her breasts pressed against his chest, her fingernails digging into his back, he bit into her shoulder and marked her as his. The sensation sent ecstasy through both of them, and he pummeled into her harder. And then he came, roaring her name. She wrapped her legs around his waist and held on tightly.

Then she followed him into the abyss and knew he was hers forever. The bond that tied them together snapped into place.

She was his, and he was hers, and they were mated.

Finally, a reaper and his banshee.

It was a perfect match on the loom of fate.

He was death, and she could sense it. And, one day, if he went back to his duties, she would help him. She could sense the souls that needed to be reaped beyond those that were decreed from on high.

Things were changing, the world was settling, albeit in a new way. And she had her mate.

The man she would stand by for the rest of her life. The one who had helped her find out exactly who she needed to be.

Her reaper, her song, her forever.

EPILOGUE

Dante leaned back against the bench at his bar and looked across the table. His circle had grown over the years. Not only with the seven lightning-struck and their mates. Nor with only his mates and children.

No, they'd added friends and family over the years. People who had fought their own battles and had asked for help when he was able to give it. And, in some cases, not even then.

His mate, Jace, stood next to his brother, talking with Torrent and his new mate—or perhaps his name was Ashen now. They were off to the side, keeping their distance, but Dante understood what was needed. They were new to this life, much like the other couple near them.

Misha and Caly laughed together, though the vampire

and his family weren't mingling with the others quite yet. Dante understood that was needed since they'd spent centuries running and hiding from others who didn't even know they existed. Dante let out a snort with a trail of smoke. *He* hadn't known of their existence, and that baffled him. He wanted to know *all* the secrets of the realms, and as a dragon, the fact that he didn't vexed him to no end.

Poppy, his bartender, laughed at something her mate Jonah whispered to her, and Dante held back a grin. He had a feeling he'd be needing a new bartender soon, but that was understandable. He tended to lose them these days to mates and finding peace. And if that was the price he had to pay, then so be it.

Dante looked over at the final new couple and let out a sigh. He'd watched the two wolves fight themselves for years and find a way to create a family over time. Liam and Alec danced together near the others, their child sleeping in the large playpen that Dante had built. At least six children were sleeping in there at the moment, with others in arms or crawling and walking around the bar.

Dante's Circle wasn't so much a bar anymore, it was a place for family. A harbor in the darkness. He might take out the taps one day, or at least change it up so there were more comfortable places for people to rest and mingle. Though Dante's Circle would always be in his heart, he knew it was time to move on.

"Dante?"

He looked down at his mate and kissed the top of her head. "Yes?"

"You look sad. What's wrong?"

He shook his head and looked up at his other mate, who still stood near his brother, looking as if he'd seen a ghost. In essence, he had.

"I'm thinking about the changes that must be made."

"What kind of changes?"

"This bar. We have children, and our family is here more often than not. It's time to transition it into a new part of our lives. Rather than a bar for laughter and drinks, it should be a place to meet when we need to. Somewhere for those on the run to take refuge and find safety."

Nadie studied his face, frowning. "You could always build a new place. One for families. We could keep this one a bar if you'd like."

He thought on that, nodding. "Maybe. I'm not sure. But change has come. Things changed forever with that lighting strike, then when I found you and Jace. Again when our children were born. Life has moved on, and we must move with it."

"I'll miss the place if it changes too much," Nadie said, leaning into him. Jace sat next to them in the next moment as if he felt their emotions through the bond. Perhaps he had.

"We'll find balance," Jace added. "We're growing so much, maybe an addition rather than two separate places?"

Dante smiled. "I'd like that. My hoard is growing."

"Forever the dragon," Nadie said, laughing.

"You know it, darling."

The others began to give suggestions for what needed to be done, and Dante nodded, listening. There would be change, that was inevitable. Even a dragon as old as he knew that. Before he'd mated, he'd have made all the decisions on his own. Now, however, he'd let his friends help.

And while they worked on that project, on their new beginnings, he knew there was one more path they would begin down, as well. One that the kit now in Alec's arms had put him on.

There were others.

Those who needed him.

Who needed the seven.

He would answer the call. Just as he had before. And as he looked at his family, his blood, felt the bonds and more thanks to the call he'd answered, he had to wonder who would come next.

And who they would meet along the way.

Together.

THE END

Is the end of Dante's Circle?
Perhaps…

For more information about the Dante's Circle series and Carrie Ann Ryan, please visit her website.

A NOTE FROM CARRIE ANN RYAN

Thank you so much for reading **DANTE'S CIRCLE SERIES.** I do hope if you liked this story, that you would please leave a review!

I hadn't planned on returning to the Dante's Circle world, but a voice just wouldn't go away, and now four more HEAs are out in the world!

Thank you so much for going with me on this journey. As for more in this world? Perhaps one day. I'll never say never...

After all...Dante has a plan....

If you want to make sure you know what's coming next from me, you can sign up for my newsletter at www.CarrieAnnRyan.com; follow me on twitter at @CarrieAnnRyan, or like my Facebook page. I also have a Facebook Fan Club where we have trivia, chats, and other goodies. You guys are the reason I get to do what I do and I thank you.

Make sure you're signed up for my MAILING LIST so you can know when the next releases are available as well as find giveaways and FREE READS.

Happy Reading!

Dante's Circle Series:

Book 1: Dust of My Wings
Book 2: Her Warriors' Three Wishes
Book 3: An Unlucky Moon
Book 3.5: His Choice
Book 4: Tangled Innocence
Book 5: Fierce Enchantment
Book 6: An Immortal's Song
Book 7: Prowled Darkness
Book 8: Dante's Circle Reborn

ABOUT THE AUTHOR

Carrie Ann Ryan is the New York Times and USA Today bestselling author of contemporary, paranormal, and young adult romance. Her works include the Montgomery Ink, Redwood Pack, Fractured Connections, and Elements of Five series, which have sold over 3.0 million books worldwide. She started writing while in graduate school for her advanced degree in chemistry and hasn't stopped since. Carrie Ann has written over seventy-five novels and novellas with more in the works. When she's not losing herself in her emotional and action-packed worlds, she's reading as much as she can while wrangling her clowder of cats who have more followers than she does.

www.CarrieAnnRyan.com

ALSO FROM CARRIE ANN RYAN

The Montgomery Ink: Boulder Series:

Book 1: Wrapped in Ink

Book 2: Sated in Ink

Book 3: Embraced in Ink

Book 4: Seduced in Ink

Book 4.5: Captured in Ink

The Montgomery Ink: Fort Collins Series:

Book 1: Inked Persuasion

The Less Than Series:

Book 1: Breathless With Her

Book 2: Reckless With You

Book 3: Shameless With Him

The Elements of Five Series:

Book 1: From Breath and Ruin

Book 2: From Flame and Ash

Book 3: From Spirit and Binding

Book 4: From Shadow and Silence

The Promise Me Series:

Book 1: Forever Only Once

Book 2: From That Moment

Book 3: Far From Destined

Book 4: From Our First

The Fractured Connections Series:

Book 1: Breaking Without You

Book 2: Shouldn't Have You

Book 3: Falling With You

Book 4: Taken With You

Montgomery Ink: Colorado Springs

Book 1: Fallen Ink

Book 2: Restless Ink

Book 2.5: Ashes to Ink

Book 3: Jagged Ink

Book 3.5: Ink by Numbers

Montgomery Ink:

Book 0.5: Ink Inspired
Book 0.6: Ink Reunited
Book 1: Delicate Ink
Book 1.5: Forever Ink
Book 2: Tempting Boundaries
Book 3: Harder than Words
Book 4: Written in Ink
Book 4.5: Hidden Ink
Book 5: Ink Enduring
Book 6: Ink Exposed
Book 6.5: Adoring Ink
Book 6.6: Love, Honor, & Ink
Book 7: Inked Expressions
Book 7.3: Dropout
Book 7.5: Executive Ink
Book 8: Inked Memories
Book 8.5: Inked Nights
Book 8.7: Second Chance Ink

The Gallagher Brothers Series:

Book 1: Love Restored
Book 2: Passion Restored
Book 3: Hope Restored

The Whiskey and Lies Series:

Book 1: Whiskey Secrets

Book 2: Whiskey Reveals
Book 3: Whiskey Undone

The Talon Pack:

Book 1: Tattered Loyalties
Book 2: An Alpha's Choice
Book 3: Mated in Mist
Book 4: Wolf Betrayed
Book 5: Fractured Silence
Book 6: Destiny Disgraced
Book 7: Eternal Mourning
Book 8: Strength Enduring
Book 9: Forever Broken

Redwood Pack Series:

Book 1: An Alpha's Path
Book 2: A Taste for a Mate
Book 3: Trinity Bound
Book 3.5: A Night Away
Book 4: Enforcer's Redemption
Book 4.5: Blurred Expectations
Book 4.7: Forgiveness
Book 5: Shattered Emotions
Book 6: Hidden Destiny
Book 6.5: A Beta's Haven
Book 7: Fighting Fate
Book 7.5: Loving the Omega

Book 7.7: The Hunted Heart
Book 8: Wicked Wolf

The Branded Pack Series:
(Written with Alexandra Ivy)
Book 1: Stolen and Forgiven
Book 2: Abandoned and Unseen
Book 3: Buried and Shadowed

Dante's Circle Series:
Book 1: Dust of My Wings
Book 2: Her Warriors' Three Wishes
Book 3: An Unlucky Moon
Book 3.5: His Choice
Book 4: Tangled Innocence
Book 5: Fierce Enchantment
Book 6: An Immortal's Song
Book 7: Prowled Darkness
Book 8: Dante's Circle Reborn

Holiday, Montana Series:
Book 1: Charmed Spirits
Book 2: Santa's Executive
Book 3: Finding Abigail
Book 4: Her Lucky Love
Book 5: Dreams of Ivory

The Happy Ever After Series:

Flame and Ink

Ink Ever After

Single Title:

Finally Found You

CPSIA information can be obtained
at www.ICGtesting.com
Printed in the USA
FSHW022105290320
68589FS